SUNSCORCHED

ALSO BY JEN CRANE

Jen Crane
reality from reality

DESCENDED OF DRAGONS SERIES

Rare Form

Origin Exposed

Betrayal Foretold

Descended of Dragons 3-Book Box Set

SUBTERRANEAN SERIES

Sunscorched

Terminal Combustion

SUNSCORCHED

SUBTERRANEAN SERIES, BOOK 1

JEN CRANE

<u>Dedication</u>
To Brock, Eden, Lou and Hannah-
the suns in my orbit.

COPYRIGHT WARNING

Published by Carpe Noctem Publishing LLC
Cover Design by Cary Smith
Sunscorched (Subterranean Series, Book 1)
Copyright © 2018 Jen Crane
All rights reserved.
First electronic publication: October 2018
First print publication: October 2018
Digital ISBN: 9780996575676
Print ISBN: 9780996575683

This is the way the world ends
Not with a bang but a whimper.

T.S. Eliot, *The Hollow Men*

SHADOWS IN THE NIGHT

Home of Ana and Norman Chisholm
Ralston, Missouri
United States of America - Or What's Left of It
Latitude: 37° North

Standing beneath the stars in the warm night air, Nori felt almost normal. Her face and hands were healing and she'd regained most of her strength in the weeks since she'd last been burned. If there'd been people in the streets around her, she could've been any girl, every girl.

But she wasn't just any girl. Stuck inside her parents' house, some days she thought she would claw from her own skin. Though they meant well, her parents smothered her. Sure, her condition made her health a bit fragile, but *she* wasn't fragile. She powered through. She had grit.

Closing her eyes on a soul-deep inhale, Nori rolled her neck. Night was her sanctuary, the only time she could let her guard down and relax without fear of the agony sunlight delivered. Too soon, the obnoxious press of time squeezed her chest and she opened her eyes. A few hours of darkness each night weren't enough. She'd take them, though, and wring every last minute from them.

"Running again tonight?"

"Mm-hmm." Nori twisted her dark hair into a loose bun before turning to her mother.

"It's good to see you up and about again," her mother said.

"It feels good to be up and about again."

"You sure you don't want me or your father to come with you? We worry, you know."

Nori bent to tighten the laces of her sneakers. "I know. But I'm fine. Really. No one's ever out but me, and honestly I need the headspace."

Her mother took a tentative step toward her. "Running in the dark, though... It's dangerous. I've heard talk of revolts breaking out up north."

Nori looked up at her mother's face, lovely despite the strain. "Nothing ever happens here, Mom," she said. "It's Ralston. And I can see perfectly well at night. You know that."

"I know, but I just don't understand it. Why is it only you, and not me or Dad—or anyone else we know? Why are you so badly affected by the sun? And this night vision...I wish we had some answers. Is it really the same?"

Nori straightened, closed her eyes, and gathered her patience. It wasn't the first time they'd discussed her unusual condition, and it probably wouldn't be the last. She didn't blame her mother for worrying, but there was nothing to be done. Nori had learned to live with her...disability. She wished they would, too. "When I go out at night," she said, "it isn't the staticky green of night vision goggles in movies, but...well...an overall saturation of light, you know? Like, a

lightening of shadows and a depth to highlights. It's different."
She shrugged. "But it's okay. Does that make sense?"

"No." Her mother's laugh was laced with years of uncertainty and fear. "It never has made sense. Just be careful. And mind the time, for God's sake. It scares us when you cut it so close."

It scared Nori, too, but if she could only leave the stifling confines of her house for a few dark hours a day, there was no way she was relinquishing a minute of her time.

"I promise," she said to mollify her mother.

Nori closed her eyes as her mother ran feather-light fingers over the faint pink scars of her cheek. "I love you, Nori Chisholm."

She leaned into the tender palm. "I love you, too. Be home in two hours, tops."

OVER THE LAST FEW MONTHS, Nori had mapped a course through the center of Ralston. She'd built her endurance bit by bit, and it was the first time she'd attempt to run the course in its entirety. Standing at the starting line she'd made with a strip of rusted tin, she stretched first her legs, then her back, pulling her arms over her head clasping her fingers together.

"On your mark," she whispered releasing her arms and pushed a leg behind her. "Get set." She fisted her hands, preparing to pump her arms, and bent the other knee. "Go."

Nori shot forward, rounding the first corner of the course in a matter of seconds. The burn of her muscles as she picked up speed was cathartic, and the wind in her face wiped away another dreary day spent inside. As she ran, bits of worry about an uncertain future cracked and fell onto the street. The tension in her neck from near-constant fear, both of the sun and of the widespread devastation of another sunscorch eased and she rolled her shoulders to let it all go.

In the moonlit window of a hardware store, Nori caught her reflection. She straightened her posture and took a better look at the girl staring back. Her dark hair and round blue eyes only emphasized a too pale face. She pressed fingertips to the tender, splotchy skin of her cheeks and looked away. Time. She'd heal with time.

Shaking off the tendrils of self-pity attempting to snake their way in, Nori ran until her lungs seized and her calves screamed. She ran until she thought she couldn't go on, and then ran some more.

Rounding one of the last blocks of her course, Nori caught movement from the corner of her eye. She craned her head for a better look. Nothing. A pained cry echoed down a nearby alley and though her heart was already pounding from the run, it thundered harder as fear-tinged adrenaline poured into her bloodstream.

Nori lifted a foot to run in the opposite direction, to run home. But that sound... It was a cry for help. Her father's voice rang in her head. "Times are tough," he often said. "Nobody makes it alone in a sunscorched world. Community is crucial."

Taking a last deep breath, Nori ran *toward* the cry.

The buildings surrounding the alley obscured the moonlight, but that was no problem for Nori. At first, she saw nothing, heard nothing. Holding her breath and searching the shadows, she took a tentative step into the alley. Silence. Another step. All clear. On the third step, her heel met a piece of old wire, which clanged and cut into the silence. A figure sprang from the darkness, running in quick, jerky movements. Running for his life.

"Hey," Nori called. "Are you o—"

Before she could finish the sentence, someone chased after the fleeing man. The second figure was massive, the kind of body that should've been slowed by the bulky weight of muscle, but wasn't. He chased the first runner like a cheetah after its prey. Nori wasn't sure the prey was a good guy, but she knew the predator wasn't. Darkness crept into her bones at the sight of him and her instincts screamed to get far, far away.

She didn't. She couldn't. The runner was in trouble. If she tucked her tail and ran home to her parents, she would never forgive herself. She would lie awake in that stifling house wondering if he made it, cursing herself for being so gutless.

Nori clenched her teeth, powering through her fear, and ran to the next alley. She stopped before reaching the corner and peeked around the brick facade of the building. No movement. Not even the air stirred.

Then she saw him. The runner squatted, hiding behind a tower of trash. His face was steeled and determined, though his hands betrayed him with the slightest of tremors.

A shift in the shadows caught Nori's eye. The predator approached the pile of rubble, sneaking closer and closer. The runner couldn't see him, and there was no way to get his attention without making her own presence known. She was fast, but could she outrun the agile giant?

Nori backed away from the alley and leaned her head against the brick wall. Her breaths came hard and fast. She tried to slow them, to think. She needed a plan to help the runner. She needed to not get herself killed.

Only one idea came to her and there wasn't time for brainstorming. She closed her eyes and nodded. She could do this. Taking off her backpack and fishing for a book from its depths, Nori offered a silent apology for the literary sin she was about to commit.

She peeked around the corner again and froze. The predator was nearly on top of him. One more step and the runner's hiding place would be completely exposed. Nori brought the thick book behind her head and threw it as hard and far as she could. The heavy *thump* of the bound pages striking a dumpster drew the attention of the predator, who abandoned the trash pile and pursued the noise.

Nori glanced back to the runner. He'd spotted her, and the vicious look in his eyes scared her, too. She didn't wait around to see who was more dangerous. She didn't think. Didn't look back. She ran.

Backtracking her earlier course, Nori ran for her life this time, instead of release. Fear drove her faster and faster, but her feet couldn't keep up with the pace of her legs. She faltered, scraping her knees on the rough concrete. She caught herself before she fell completely down, though, and pushed back up into a run.

Even through the thunder of blood pumping through her veins, Nori heard footfalls behind her. They were uneven but light. And quicker than hers. She turned to see who was chasing her. The runner was limping, but he was fast.

Sweat-soaked hair stuck to his face, which was drawn in pain. He held a hand out toward her and called, "Wait," just before the whites of his eyes shone like tiny beacons and rolled back in his head. He dropped to the street unconscious, incapable of softening his fall. The sound his head made when it hit the concrete sent Nori's stomach lurching. She slowed, concern overriding her good sense, but jogged around the block.

Bent at the waist and hands on her knees, Nori worked to catch her breath. She listened, but nothing moved. Gathering the nerve to peek around the corner, she saw the runner still lay in the middle of the street. He was out cold. Nori threw her head back and groaned. She didn't owe this guy anything else. She'd already endangered herself by sticking around and creating a distraction. He had escaped. Her job was done.

So why couldn't she shake the feeling she should help him again?

"Fine," Nori whispered to the unconscious figure in the street. "But if I get killed helping you—again—I'm coming back to haunt you, grimy or not."

She sprinted toward him, her lip curling in distaste when she neared. He didn't smell bad, but was covered from head to toe in a grayish-black grime. His clothes were probably dirty, too, but he wore all black so she couldn't tell. Working quickly, Nori arranged his arms over his head and used them to drag him out of the street. She stopped twice to wipe her hands because he kept slipping from her fingers.

He was larger than she'd first thought. Probably around six feet. He'd seemed so much smaller than the monster chasing him, and as she struggled to drag him to a nearby building, she wished he *was* smaller. Much of Ralston was barren; abandoned after years of abuse from the elements. The building Nori drug him into had long been empty, its foyer and outer doors unlocked. Perfect for emergency shelter. Nori left the man to prop open one of the doors, and struggled to pull him inside. Just as she bent to remove the door prop, she sensed, more than heard, someone nearby. A slimy darkness skittered across her spine. Quick and quiet as a mouse, she shut the solid foyer door...locking herself in with the stranger.

Nori had faced physical challenges her whole life. By now, she was used to scurrying out of the sun, or lying with her eyes and body covered in cool cloths when she didn't make it to cover in time. Her life had never been typical or easy, and she was okay with that because what she lacked in physical capability, she made up for with instinct and common sense. It was instinct that told her the man at her feet was the lesser of two evils.

2

IT'S ALIVE

A trail of blood disappeared beyond the door of the small foyer. The man Nori rescued lay face-up, the knot near his temple swelling fast. His leg oozed blood, the scarlet pool closing in on the tiny corner of space Nori occupied. When she found the wound—and the gaping tear in his leather riding pants—dread settled in her gut. The bleeding would have to be stopped if he was going to survive, which meant she had to do it.

Nori groaned and scrubbed her eyes, then set to work. She sifted through her backpack for something to tie around his wound, finding both a pocketknife and the thick, sun-blocking canvas she always kept nearby. She ripped a long strip of the fabric and wrapped it several times around the man's injured thigh.

"Probably a good thing you can't feel this," she said to his unconscious form and, catching another look at the knot on his head, grimaced. "You're gonna have a pretty bad headache, too."

After tying the two ends together, Nori sat back to admire

her work. Blood had soaked through most of the bandage, but it wasn't seeping onto the floor anymore, at least.

Mom and Dad are probably freaking out by now, Nori thought. Curled in the corner of the foyer farthest from the man, she sat with arms wrapped around bent knees. The man outside hadn't made a sound. Maybe he hadn't seen her. Maybe he'd left. Or maybe he was waiting just outside the door.

Nori rocked back and forth, forehead pressed to her knees. Finally, she let out a long breath and stretched her legs. She was leaving. She'd saved the stranger. Twice. He was hidden in the foyer, and when he came to, he could find his own way back to safety.

Bracing herself on the wall to stand, she kept as far as possible from the unconscious body between her and the door. Stretching over him to reach the door, she extended one leg, straddling him only a moment until she lifted the other to join it. But as she raised her back foot, the front one was knocked from under her, sending her roughly down onto her butt. She yelped and looked wildly around, scurrying back to the foyer wall. Hands in front of her face, she prepared to defend herself as best she could.

"I'm not going to hurt you," he said. His voice was deep, but not threatening. "Where are we?"

Nori flattened her palms to the wall, pushing herself against it to stand again. She didn't answer.

The steely eyes from the alley focused on her face. He surveyed her hair, her shoes, and her clothes before finding her eyes.

"What did you throw?" he asked.

The question caught her off guard. "Wh-what?"

"What did you throw? To distract him?"

"A book."

"A book?"

Nori nodded as she edged toward the door—and the street.

"What were you doing with a book?" he asked.

"Reading," she said, pinning him with a look that seriously doubted his intelligence.

Dark eyebrows lowered over narrowed eyes. "In the dark?"

Nori bit the inside of her cheek. "Of course not," she said. She'd been running in the dark, not reading, though she often did. But he didn't have to know that. "It was in my backpack from earlier today."

He squinted, as if he didn't quite believe her. "What happened to your face?"

She reflexively touched the pink patches, a fresh new layer where sun-damaged skin had peeled away. The pink was fading, but not entirely healed.

"Sunburn," she said. "Stayed out too long."

"That happen a lot?"

"What business is it of yours?" she snapped. "And you can say 'thanks for saving me' anytime."

His eyes shot down for a moment before he lifted them to meet her gaze. "Thank you." His voice was quieter, sincere. "I know you put your own life at risk. Thank you for saving me."

"Twice," she said. "I saved you twice. Once with the book, and the other by hauling you in here when you were unconscious to bandage your leg. Technically, I guess that's three times."

"All right." His lips twitched. "I owe you one. Or three." As if he hadn't noticed it before, he looked down at his thigh and then back to Nori. "First time to make a tourniquet?"

She lifted her head. "You were bleeding all over the floor. I did the best I could with what I had. What happened to you, anyway? You must've lost a lot of blood to pass out like that."

"I tried to clear a chain-link fence, but my leg caught."

Nori looked at the bandage again, but quickly averted her eyes from the exposed skin of his thigh. She cleared her throat. "Why was he chasing you?"

He shrugged.

"You're not going to tell me?" she asked.

He shook his head, all nonchalance.

"Fine." Nori huffed a breath. "What's your name?"

"Cooper."

"That your first name?" She asked and extended her arm toward the door handle, making sure she could escape if necessary.

"It's what people call me," he said. "What's yours?"

She didn't answer as manners battled with self-preservation in her brain.

"Oh, come on," he goaded. "You can't ask to see mine and not show me yours."

"Nori," she said quick and low. The concession pained her.

"That your first name?" he shot back.

She scowled, and he threw up his hands in defense. "Okay, okay. I'm just messing with you. Anyway, thanks again for the help, Dory."

"It's Nori."

Cooper nodded, an amused smirk tightening his lips. "Thanks, Nori." He rose slowly, hopping on one foot at first, and reached for his backpack in the corner. As he slipped it over a shoulder, he stopped and caught her gaze again. "Why'd you help me—three times? You didn't have to."

"I did have to," she said. The answer came easily. "You were in trouble, and I could help. No brainer."

"Kindness is not so common as you think," he said lifting his chin and narrowing his eyes as if trying to get a better read on her. "How long have you been like this?"

"Like what?"

"You burn easy. And you can see well in the dark, right?"

"I've been this way my whole life." The answer was smooth, and without thought. Nori gasped and balled her fists when she realized what she'd revealed. Her condition wasn't a secret, though it was a mystery. But she didn't like a stranger knowing so much about her. And she hated that he'd gotten her to talk so easily. Her teeth creaked under the pressure of her jaws.

"Anyone else up here like you?" Cooper closed the distance between them and searched her eyes for an answer. "You know anyone else who burns like you do? Who can see better in the dark?"

She shook her head, blinking in incomprehension. "How do you... What do you mean? What do you know about it?"

"You should go," he said and pushed open the door.

"No." Nori pulled the door shut, her heart thundering in her chest. "Tell me how you knew to ask those questions. Do you know someone else like me?"

Cooper let out a long breath, his wary gaze never leaving hers. "It'll be light soon," he finally said. "If you want to make it home in time, you'll already have to run like hell."

He turned to open the door again, but Nori stopped him. "Wait." She fumbled for something to say. "Do you live around here?" She threw on her own backpack, wishing to know something about the man who knew so much about her.

"Right under your nose," he said, and with one last nod,

ran from the foyer, into the dark alley, and out of sight with no noticeable limp.

As Nori watched him go the shadows changed, and her heart seized. The sun was on the rise. "Stupid," she told herself, racing home on shaky legs. "Stupid, stupid, stupid."

HER FATHER'S voice echoed in the distance. It was panicked, urgent. "Nori?" he yelled. "Nori? Answer me!"

Nori's name in her mother's mouth, though, was more like a scream.

She could just see the stretch of orange on the horizon. Beautiful, she thought, not remembering ever having seen a sunrise. It deserved the hype. She was lost in the way the world shimmered under its attention. She slowed, in awe of the maize and terra-cotta hues, of the impossible beauty framing the burned-out and rusted landscape.

When her eyes began to sting, she rubbed them, and the skin of her face felt hot. Too late, she thought as pain seared behind her eyes. It's too late, but it just might've been worth it.

When she stumbled onto Skyler Court, her parents were halfway down the street. Her father ran to her, scooping her up and crushing her against his chest as he ran into the house.

"What were you thinking?" her mother screamed as she slammed the door behind them.

Even through the pain, Nori's eyes widened with shock. Her mother was a nurturer. She was tender. She never raised her voice.

"One more millisecond, and you would've been back in a drug-induced coma," she said. "One more millisecond. What the devil was so important that you risked your own life, Nori? Where have you been?"

"I...I'm sorry, Mom," Nori said as her father deposited her in a chair. "Someone was hurt, and being chased, and then he passed out, and...and I threw a book."

"Wait, wait. Slow down." Nori's father said, smoothing a hand across her back. "It's all right, Ana. She's gonna be all right." He turned to Nori. "Now, what happened? Who passed out? Start from the beginning."

Nori's heart raced like she was locked inside the foyer with Cooper again when she told them what she'd seen and how she'd dragged him to safety. She told them about his oddly-accurate line of questioning, and they joined in her frustration at his lack of answers.

What she didn't tell them, though, was that despite Cooper's outward playfulness, she'd searched his eyes in the foyer of that building and only found sadness. She didn't tell them she'd have stayed there for hours to see them brighten.

"Thank God you're alive," her mother said, peeking through the fingers that hid her delicate face. "Don't ever do anything like that again. Do you hear me?"

The way her eyes and skin was hurting, Nori doubted she'd be able to do much anytime soon.

"I promise," she said on the way to her room. "Next time I'll let him die."

She hung her backpack on the peg inside the door, remembering too late she hadn't gone back to get her book.

3

AND THE DAYS WERE GETTING LONGER

"Sunset was 11:55 tonight."

Nori could hear her father's frantic voice through the walls of her room.

"Daylight came at 3:20 this morning."

She imagined him stalking across the living room, running nervous hands through the hair at the sides of his head.

"Three hours and twenty-five minutes, Ana."

"I know." Her mother's voice was much more solemn.

Her father's clipped steps turned to a full-blown pace. "How will we ever get back to the 25th Parallel with only three hours of dark each day?" Her mother didn't answer, but the question had been rhetorical anyway. "We can't risk taking her that far, even in the van." He paused, and Nori imagined him looking toward her door. "How bad is it?"

"Pretty bad," she said, her voice was desolate. "She's resting now. I'll take her back to the doctor tomorrow."

"It's not worth the risk, and you know it," her father boomed. "They can't do anything for her."

"It's all I know to do, Norm," she said. "I have to do something."

Nori pulled the pillow over her head, but it didn't smother her mother's torment.

"She can't...live...like this," her mother said between sobs. "I can't...watch her...live like this."

Nori's chest squeezed painfully and she turned her head to the wall as her tears flowed. She could endure her own pain. That she could stand. But causing her parents agony was unbearable.

4

A TRAGIC LOSS

Temps holding steady throughout the week with a high today of 127. Lows tonight of 99. Sunrise was 03:19, folks, and sunset is expected at 23:56.

This decrease in dark hours is the most rapid we've seen since the first sunscorch twelve years ago. At this rate, experts suggest nightfall may cease to occur within the month. As we now know, the increase in the tilt of Earth's axis is responsible for these extreme temperature fluctuations. Experts warn to take action now if you haven't already. To move to the temperate regions, to the 25th parallel befor —.

N orman pressed the television's power button with such force it rocked backward, threatening to tumble off the stand. He leaped for the TV, using both hands to right it before growling in frustration.

"Shh," his wife chided from the kitchen. "Nori's still sleeping."

"Still? It's nearly eight."

Ana shrugged and wiped her hands, wet from the sink. "Teenagers," she said. "What you gonna do?"

Norman smiled at the thought of his teenager lazing in the bed. Remembering the reason she was asleep, though, sucked the air from his body. She'd developed a fever during the night, her skin blistered and nearly raw in places. He could scarcely breathe as the extent of his daughter's suffering, and his inability to relieve it, threatened to pull him under. His ears flashed hot and roared unmercifully. Burying his face in both hands, Norman sucked hard breaths through his fingers.

Ana stood in front of him, at first trying to pull his fingers from his face, but giving the effort up to simply hold him. He stiffened in her embrace. He would not be comforted, protected. That was his job, and he'd already failed too many times.

Lowering his hands and pulling away from his wife, he darted for the door. "Be back after work," he said and slammed the door behind him.

"HOW IS SHE?" he asked as soon as he pushed through the door. He'd thought of little else all day.

Sunken and bruised, the dark circles under his wife's eyes were made worse by the loose skin around them. Swaths of hair had fallen from her ponytail and hung limply around her face. "She's sleeping."

"Again?"

"No, not again," she said. "She never woke."

"My God." Norman started toward his daughter's room, wiping sweaty palms on his pants. "Did you check on her? Is she all right?"

Ana's spine straightened. "Of course I checked on her. I've

cared for her all day. She's feverish and fitful. Her body is just one big sunburn."

Norman said nothing as his eyes lost focus on Nori's closed door. He was hollow, hopeless. Was there really nothing he could do to help her?

He must've said the words aloud because Ana nodded and pushed some of the hair off her face. "She could probably use fresh cloths on her head and neck. Nice and cool. That would help."

Norman dragged himself to Nori's room. He knew what he would find there. Drawn with pain, her face was an angry red and had already begun peeling. Her neck was splotchy from the fever, and her body covered with a thin white sheet.

The sight of his only remaining child laid before him burned and miserable flooded him with memories, and he cried out in agony. The first sunscorch had taken the lives of over four billion people, including his two youngest children.

It had been a Saturday, and Bevin's birthday. The kids had been so excited to go out for pancakes they'd giggled and bounced all morning. Nori, five at the time, was excited, too.

As they'd left the café, the little ones wore sugared smiles and syrup-stained shirts. Norman had held Bevin's sticky hand as they waited beneath the metal awning for Nori to come outside. "Hustle, big sister," he had called a second before the sunscorch hit.

No warning. No time to escape or find shelter. One moment, he stood smiling down at the baby-faced birthday girl, and the next, a scalding blast of heat blew over them like a wave of cosmic radiation.

Driven by instinct, Norman had dived for Bevin, for Ana and Liam, scrambling to shield them with his body. Even beneath the metal awning, the heat blistered the clothes from his back. He had screamed in pain, in fear, but the sounds of melting and collapsing, of explosions everywhere, drowned out his loudest wails. He'd moved out of reflex, had protected his children as best he could, but he hadn't done enough.

Although Ana had been holding him under the awning when the sunscorch struck, tiny Liam's body couldn't withstand the blast, and he stopped breathing in her arms. Bevin's short life ended the next morning, the day after her third birthday. Nori, who'd still been inside, recovered with time. But she was never the same.

The days following the scorch had been a miserable blur of despair. Each stab of pain as his back healed was a reminder he hadn't done enough, that he hadn't saved them. For months, he wished for his own death with each throb of his still-beating heart. He couldn't run from the suffocating agony of loss. It haunted him like a throng of specters through the too-quiet house. It tortured him each time a toy or a memory fooled his brain into thinking the children were still alive. Too soon, he'd remember they weren't, and re-live the loss all over again. He'd very nearly gone mad. The smell of syrup still brought him to his knees.

And his sweet Ana. He'd been in no shape to comfort his wife, though she was as anguished as he was. She'd found purpose in tending to Nori's recovery, but she cried at night for months, Norman knew, because her sobs rocked their too-empty bed.

In the end, it was his love for Nori and Ana, and nothing else, that paved the way for his redemption. Well, love and time. An awful lot of time. He could get through most days now without breaking down.

But as Norman watched Nori's face contort in her sleep, the crippling memories of losing Bevin and Liam crashed down around him, and he fell to his knees. With one fist at his aching heart and the other shoved to his mouth, Norman curled into a ball beside his daughter's bed and tried to smother his anguished sobs. He failed to do that, too, and once the dam was breached, he couldn't stop until the reservoir was dry.

Like so many times before, his body gave out before his memory did.

5

A SLOW RECOVERY

Nori woke to her father running smooth hands over the hair at the top of her head.

"Wha…" She cleared her throat and worked not to grimace. "What time is it?"

He raised his head from the side of her bed and stretched his back. "Hey," he breathed. "How you feeling?"

Nori inspected the sores on her arms and felt her cheeks and forehead with a feather-light touch. "I'm all right," she said. "How do I look, though?" She arched her eyebrows and posed playfully. "Gorgeous, right?"

Her father smiled. "You always look beautiful to me."

"Oh, Dad," Nori groaned. "You have to say that."

"Okay, that's true. But even if I didn't, I'd still think so."

Nori rolled her eyes, but smiled at the man whose worry darkened his face with each passing day. "I'm starving," she said. "Let me up."

He backed away from the bed, the beginning stirrings of a sparkle in his eyes. "Ana," he called. "Our girl's up, and hungry as a horse." He grinned at her, though his gaze lingered too long on her face. "I'll go on down and let you get dressed."

Suppressing a groan at the pain searing the backs of her eyes, Nori nodded.

After her father had left, she held the bedpost and stood with a muffled gasp. She didn't want her parents to know how bad it had gotten, but sometimes, when she was alone, she couldn't stop the tears.

At first, she'd felt cheated she couldn't enjoy the warm feel of the sun on her face. That didn't last long. The tiniest sliver of sunlight was like needles to her flesh. Scalding, relentless needles. If it was just her skin, she could deal with that. Maybe. But the sun also caused blinding pain behind her eyes and into the very depths of her skull.

She wouldn't cry in front of her parents. She was alive. She had a life, such as it was, and her tiny brother and sister did not. Sometimes when they looked at her, she knew they were remembering. The light would fade from their eyes, and their movements became stiff and rote. They'd try to hide their misery, too, but she knew.

One breath at a time. One step at a time. One day at a time. It was how they all lived now, and it had become her motto.

Nori closed her eyes against the pain and took timid steps toward the bathroom. How long had it been since her mother had given her a pain pill? She needed another. Hers was a love/hate relationship with the medicine, which blocked the pain, but also made her drowsy, like living inside a dream. She didn't remember a lot and fell asleep watching TV—sometimes even eating.

Staying indoors to avoid the sun wasn't ideal, but sleeping her life away was unacceptable. Too many of those kinds of days gave her the blues. It was a dangerous, slippery slope toward depression.

Nori found the big white pills in the cabinet and halved one. Maybe the reduced dosage would take the edge off the pain and she'd stay alert. She took it with a gulp of water, and with a final, fortifying breath, emerged from her room.

"Did I sleep all day?" she asked, pasting a grin on her lips.

Her parents smiled back, their relief an almost tangible thing.

"Nearly three, sweetie." Her mother tilted the cast iron pan over a plate at the table. "I made you dinner."

Nori's mouth watered at the sauté. "Smells great, Mom," she said and dug into a dish of heat-tolerant grains, tomatillos, and seaweed. "You know," she said around a bite. "I'll never understand why you named me after food."

Her father threw his head back and laughed, and a grin pulled at the sides of her own mouth.

Nori's mother, though, was not amused. "Oh, not this again." She blew out a breath and slid the pan into the sink. "Nori Chisholm, we did not name you after seaweed. We named you after your father. Nor-man. No-ri." She over-enunciated each word. "We didn't even eat that much seaweed until the last few years." Nori and her father both snickered, and Ana pointed a finger at them. "It's got a lot of protein, you know, which you need since there's no meat. And it's easy to get now that they farm it in the Gulf." She stopped, smoothed her apron. "You know what? You two are in charge of dinner tomorrow."

Nori held her stomach as the burst of laughter she and her father had tried to contain finally broke free.

"Wait a minute," she said when she recovered. "Did you say I slept three days?"

"Mm-hmm." Her mother nodded. "No wonder you were starving."

"Three days. No kidding. Well, I feel great." At her parents' dubious looks, she shrugged. "I do."

Her father patted the hand not occupied with scooping up food. "Good. That's good. You up for playing cards? How about a little Rummy?"

"I was really thinking of going out, Dad," she said around a mouthful and hurried to head off his protest. "It's dark out. There's no sun, no harm. I need to get out of this house before I go crazy."

He looked to her mother for the final decision, who closed her eyes, relenting. "All right," he said. "Let me get my shoes."

"No." Nori's objection was more forceful than she'd intended, and she said more softly, "No. Thank you. I just... I would rather go alone."

Muscles feathered along his jaw, but he nodded. "An hour. And no more. You know the sun's rising earlier every dang day."

"I promise." Nori pressed a kiss to his cheek and he smiled, but his eyes still held concern.

"Why do you go to that old park, anyway?" he asked. "It's so sad. A relic of what used to be."

Nori shrugged. "I dunno. But maybe that's why—to imagine what life was like before the scorches."

"There used to be grass, you know. Lawns, we called them. Not the weeds you've seen popping up here and there. Thick, lush blankets of grass. You could walk—even lie down on it." Nori shot her father a skeptical look. "It's true," he said. "But this you won't believe: people used to put water on grass to keep it alive."

"Oh, Dad!" Nori rolled her eyes and turned for the door.

"I swear," he laughed. "There were whole systems set up to spray water onto lawns so they'd stay green. They irrigated grass you couldn't eat—for looks!"

She snorted and turned the doorknob.

"Don't forget your bug-out bag!" her mother called. Nori groaned at the reminder, and her mother's fists flew to her hips. "Just because there hasn't been a sunscorch in years doesn't mean there won't be one. You take that bag, or you're not going."

"But it's so heavy it weighs me down. Anyway, if there's a scorch, water and protein bars aren't gonna save me."

"No, but if you get stuck somewhere they might keep you alive until we can find you. And you never know when you'll need matches."

"Or a knife," her father added with a wolfish grin.

"Fine." Nori held her hands up. "I'll take the bug-out bag."

Closing her eyes, Nori breathed in the night air. Some of the weight of worry, of stress, and of pain left her body in exhale. The medicine had helped. Doing something to take her mind off the pain helped, too.

Slowly walking the perimeter of the abandoned park near her house, Nori stopped at the boarded entrance. Rusty metal contorted to form macabre sculptures from the old play-ground equipment. She couldn't imagine children ever playing at such a desolate and dangerous place. She tried to envision the park as it had been twelve years before, with laughing children and swaths of green grass. Irrigating lawns, her father had said. Nori shook her head. She couldn't imagine such a time, or such a waste. The city barely had enough water to irrigate its produce farms now.

Nori groaned and slowly took a seat on a metal bench outside the gate with a perfect view down Frontage Street.

The city's buildings formed shadows onto dark pavement. There wasn't a soul about, the people of Ralston taking advantage of the precious few dark hours to sleep. She felt a pang of regret that she didn't have more friends. It would be nice to have company on her outings.

Clearing the emotion from her throat took two or three attempts. Maybe tomorrow she would feel better. Maybe then she would explore the store windows and find a new book.

She might even catch a glimpse of an alley cat. It had been a long time since she'd seen an animal. Between the far-reaching devastation and the depletion of food stores, few animals survived before the vegetable farms were up and producing again. Her father told stories of seasons, of temperate days and abundant food. His tales of eating meat from animals she'd only seen in books seemed like fairy tales. They might as well be.

Though she'd always been homeschooled, her mother had taught her why the world faced such extreme weather. Earth's polar ice sheets were destroyed during the first sunscorch twelve years before. The resulting change in water levels across the planet's surface caused a greater tilt of its axis. Like a weighted ball, Earth fell heavily to one side before bouncing back up and balancing out—only at a forty-degree tilt, instead of twenty-three.

The result was longer, hotter days on half the globe, and dark, tundra-like conditions on the other half. The North Pole leaned toward the sun, blistering land, animals, and people in Canada and Russia, and the northern halves of China and the United States. Millions of people in the northern hemisphere, where most of the world's population existed, were killed in the first scorch. At the other end of the Earth, the South Pole experienced a complete cold snap, destroying everything there, too.

Of course, even with its new axial tilt, the planet still revolved around the sun, so the areas with extreme heat only faced it half the year before suffering debilitating cold.

There were only 25 degrees on either side of the equator considered temperate, livable: the 25th Parallel. Those who survived were early adapters, people who accepted the necessity of migration. Nori's mother had described the post-sunscorch Earth as a volatile, treacherous mess, but it was all she'd ever known. They'd never made the trip because of her. Because of the uncertainty and her inability to suffer the sun.

There were others who'd stood their ground. Those too stubborn to leave their homes and migrate. They'd formed a reluctant community of survivors.

Pulling a thick book from her backpack, Nori was reminded of another—the one she'd thrown that night in the alley. Looking up at the night sky, glittering stars were visible even through the constant overhead haze. There was time, and she was feeling up to it. She should get that book back. It was one of her favorites, after all. Slipping on her backpack, Nori went in search of it.

Okay, if she was being honest, it wasn't the book she wondered about most. As they had over the last couple of days, her thoughts turned again to the man. Cooper. Who was he, really? Why was he out that night, and who was chasing him? Where was he now? And what had happened in his life to pollute his eyes with such a bottomless pit of sadness.

Oh, God, she thought. What if I run into him again? Her stomach seized at the prospect, but she walked a little fraction faster. He was probably a couple of years older than she was — twenty max. She'd seen a hint of stubble along his jaws, but the smooth skin around his eyes was the only part of his face not smudged and dirty. What did he look like under all that grime?

Nearing the corner she'd ducked around to throw the book, her steps slowed. Dread pushed her heart into her throat. She slowed her breathing to better hear, and scanned the alley. Nothing. No one. The pile of trash Cooper hid behind was still there. She vividly recalled the determined set of his face as he crouched behind it. What would he have done if she hadn't created a diversion? Fight? He didn't seem the type to go down silently.

She caught sight of her book half-beneath the dumpster. The cover was bent back, the top few pages blowing in a slight breeze. Nori bent on hands and knees, grunting as some of her still-tender skin stretched.

Her heart raced as she picked it up and flipped through the pages. Had he come back? Did he leave a note? Her shoulders slumped as it came back clean. Ah, well. It was a nice daydream.

At her father's voice in the distance, Nori's head snapped up. Sighing, she shut the book and stood. The side trip had cost her. She'd have to move quickly to make it home in time. Though she didn't feel up to hurrying, it was preferable both to the agony of more burns and to the isolation of another long recovery. As she rounded the last corner, she caught sight of her father, whose body sagged with relief. His eyes closed for the shortest moment before he smiled.

"There she is," he said. "There's my night owl."

"Hey, Dad." Nori squeezed his clammy hand. "Ready for that card game?"

6

IMPENDING DOOM

The grating, high-pitched alert Nori instantly associated with disaster blared through the old box-set television in the basement. Her parents gathered behind her and together they waited.

Scientific experts from across the globe have gathered at the Climate Research Center today to make a special announcement. As we reported last month, these professional forecasters suggest nightfall may cease within the month. Let's go live now to an exclusive announcement.

"Since the first sunscorch almost twelve years ago," a woman with long, curly hair said in a voice almost too low to be heard, "we have worked to develop and refine a system to detect sunscorches before they happen." Her eyes bounced nervously around the room before she continued. "I'm pleased to tell you we have perfected such a system." The woman swallowed and glanced at a man scowling on the sidelines. "We at the Climate Research Center are confident in the ability to predict the next time this eco-devastation threatens our world."

Nori and her parents' reactions mirrored those on TV. An excited murmur ran through the crowd, and scattered applause broke out. "Please," the woman giving the press conference said, her eyes wild. "Let me finish." She surveyed the room again and cleared her throat. "Un—unfortunately, we can now predict that the next sunscorch will occur in a matter of days. One week at a maximum."

Nori's stomach plummeted and hollowed out, and her mother gasped. Her father moved in behind them and laid a hand on their shoulders, which Nori reached up to clasp.

Back on television, the enthusiastic murmur soured. The medley of voices became even louder, the tone fearful and anxious. Hands flew into the air, but others didn't wait, peppering the woman with questions. "How certain are you?" and "Do you know how extreme the scorch will be?" Reporters abandoned their chairs and crowded close to her. "Should we go to ground now?" someone called out.

She opened her mouth to speak, eyes filled with the wide panic of a hunted rabbit. She opened her mouth, and it stayed that way. She stood at the podium, mouth agape, as her gaze flicked from one side of the room to the other.

With an irritated grunt, the man who'd been standing off to the side crowded the woman at the microphone. She closed her eyes, as if relieved, and removed her papers from the podium with trembling hands.

"Thank you, Amy," he said, but didn't look back at his colleague. "Dr. Hansen and her team have worked tirelessly to get this system up and running, and it's going to save lives. But only if the public uses the news to prepare for the impending danger, to protect their families. Though it's been twelve years since the last sunscorch, it's vitally important to take precautionary measures now. Stay indoors until the threat is over. Due to the risk of being caught in a car during the scorch, it is not advised to travel at this time."

The man grunted and directed sleep-deprived and reddened eyes into the camera. "I'll repeat that," he said. "It is not advised to travel to the 25th Parallel—or anywhere—at this time. Act now to move your family to designated shelters, basements, or bunkers. And if you don't," he shook his head, "may God preserve your immortal soul." He stared meaningfully into the camera one last time and left the stage.

The scientist, Hansen, who'd stood rigidly off to the side, tripped toward the microphone as reporters repeated their questions with a desperate sense of urgency.

Neither Nori nor her parents spoke. The television was still on, but after the bomb the scientist dropped, she tuned out, her mind racing.

Her father's hands dropped to his sides, and he tapped fingers restlessly against his thighs.

"No." He paced from the television to the table across the room. "No. I won't let this happen." A worn chair creaked beneath his weight as he sat, and again when he shot up.

"Daddy." Nori followed him and ran her arms around his wide shoulders. "It's going to be all right. We'll be careful. I already know how to protect myself. We'll all stay in the basement. It can even be fun. We can pretend we're snowed in at a cabin in the mountains. We'll buy supplies for s'mores." She looked at her mother, who still held her own cheeks with shaky hands. "Right, Mom?"

Her mother raised her face and sniffed, putting on a smile that didn't fit. "Yes. It'll be fun."

"You know damn well what this means, Ana." Norm's

voice boomed through the small space, causing both Nori and her mother to jerk. "Nori was too young to remember, but you know. You were there."

Her mother's voice was so thin Nori barely heard it. "I know."

"What?" Nori looked to them both. "What does it mean?"

Her father's pent-up breath came out shaky, strained.

"Tell me, Dad."

She could almost see the thoughts scrambling inside his head. He'd protected her from the truth for so very long. He gave her a long, sober look, and then he gave it to her straight.

"With your sensitivity, there's no way you can make it through another sunscorch, Nori. Not even if we dug you a bunker."

"Don't be silly," she scoffed. "I survive in this house every day. And we've prepared the basement. Worse-case scenario, we hibernate for a few days and watch old movies until the player runs out of batteries."

He shook his head as if she hadn't spoken. "A sunscorch is different than your sensitivity to the sun, Nori. Deadly different. It took your sibl—it took people in a matter of seconds. Staying in this house—even in our basement—is not an option for you. Scorches are so pervasive they can burn right through roofs."

"But we've taken extra precautions with the basement, Norm," Ana said. "We've worked to make it safe for her."

He scrubbed a hand across his mouth. "It'll protect us, but I can't guarantee it'll protect her. And I can't," he sucked in an uneven breath, "I can't take that chance. We have to find another way."

Her mother nodded soberly. "What about the Mayflowers? Brooke would let us stay with them until it's over."

"Their house is even more susceptible than ours. Don't you remember? Last time, it seared right through the basement door."

"That was twelve years ago. They've replaced it with something stronger." Her father opened his mouth to argue, and she held up her hands. "But I get the point. Surely, we know someone else with a subterranean room. We just have to think." Her mother's eyes lost focus as she considered other options.

"Subterranean," her father repeated, his voice faint. "*Subterranean*. That's it."

"What's it?" Nori and her mother asked at the same time.

He turned to Nori and his blue eyes, so much like her own, were heavy with remorse. "I should've planned for this," he said. "I should've already prepared a safer place for you than a basement." His face was pale and desolate, and then his eyes shot wide with panic. "I won't let this happen. Not again." He turned on a heel, snatching his hat from the pegs near the door.

"Daddy? Where are you going?" Nori asked softly, afraid to spook him further.

"To see a man about takeout," he said cryptically, and left Nori and her mother staring after him.

7

A WAY OUT

The soft ding of the grocery store's door alert sounded when Norman pushed inside. A fit, dark-haired man looked up from the counter, which was covered with boxes of energy bars, lighters, sunglasses, and emergency SPF ponchos.

"Hey, Norm," he said.

"Nate."

"You here to visit, or shop, or both?" The store owner's smile was easy, friendly.

Norman looked at the long line of people waiting to check out, arms heavy with canned goods and bottles of water. "I, uh, I wanted to talk to you about something."

"Sure. The news today's brought in a rush. Come around here to the side, and we can talk while I ring up these customers." Nate turned from him to a mother with a baby in one arm and a big can of powdered formula in the other. "That'll be $55.50."

Norm fidgeted with a box of liquid protein pouches and

said in a low voice, "I'd rather talk in private, Nate. Can we go in your office?"

"This about my books? Let me check out these customers so I can afford to keep this place open…and pay you for accounting services." Nate smiled at the woman as he made her change.

She tucked the money into her pocket and left the store through a door held open by an entering customer.

"No, it's about something else." Norman's gaze shot nervously to the back room. "Do you have a minute?"

"You can see I don't. Everybody's stocking up on necessities before the scorch hits. Deanna's in the back now restocking the shelves. Can't it wait?"

"No." He took a step closer to his friend. "It can't."

At his sharp tone, the grocer huffed out a breath. "What is it, Norm? Just tell me."

"It's about takeout."

Nate's gaze shot to Norman's, searching for meaning, for what he knew. Whatever Nate saw, he took seriously. "All right," he said and cupped his hands to yell through a swinging door. "Deanna! Come take the front for a minute."

The grocer's eyes were calculating as he led Norman to an office in the back. The second the door closed, he turned on him. "What do you mean, 'takeout'?"

"You know exactly what I mean," Norman said with more confidence than he felt.

"I know what takeout is, sure." Nate nodded, but wouldn't meet Norman's eyes. "But what do you know about it?"

"I know it's been a substantial source of income for you for the last five years, at least. I know there's a whole lot of inventory unaccounted for in your storefront sales. A whole lot. And I know from receipts that some of that inventory is products a grocery store like yours has no business keeping in stock, nor have I ever seen it here. Barrels of water, pallets of non-perishables. Survival-type things. You got some of that in the store, sure, but not the amount you've been buying."

"Well, so?" Nate said. "Just because you're my accountant doesn't mean you have to know every detail of my business dealings. Some things are my business alone."

"I understand that." Norman's voice was strained as he ran a hand through his hair. "And I'm not here to point fingers."

"Then why are you here?" Nate tapped the pads of his fingers on the top of the desk.

"We've been friends for, what, fifteen years? You know what my family has been through—what the last sunscorch did to Nori." Norman's voice cracked as he said, "What it did to the babies." He ran a fist high over both cheeks and cleared his throat. "Nori can't make it through another one. Her health...she can't stand the sun as it is now. She was bedridden for days from a few seconds at dawn. I thought the infection would take her, if the burns didn't, but she fought through it. She sleeps most days. She's depressed."

Nate sighed and closed his eyes. "I'm sorry, Norm. I didn't know she'd gotten so bad."

He nodded, pausing before he spoke again. "Every day there's less dark. Less time my baby can feel normal, that she doesn't hurt. She doesn't complain much, but I know the sunlight kills her no matter how we shield her from it. And with the sunscorch coming..."

"What do you want me to do, Norm?" Nate stood from the desk chair to put a hand on his friend's shoulder. "What can I do?"

"Let us come with you," he pleaded and his eyes burned with unshed tears.

Nate squinted. "Come with me where?"

"Wherever you're going. I know you're planning for something, that you're stockpiling all these supplies somewhere. You've moved enough inventory to live for years. Let us come. I've got a little money saved up, and it's yours. Just let us come, too."

Nate shook his head at his friend, and his eyes held such pity. "You've got it all wrong. I don't— I mean, I have a few things set back for me and Deanna and the kids, but it's not what you think. Our plan is to stay home. We can't stay here at the store—it'll be looted first. We're going to board the windows and doors and stay in our basement."

Norman lost his battle with self-control. "Don't lie to me! I know you've got food, and lantern fuel, and water, and God knows what else stored somewhere for just such a time. Are you going to turn me away? Are you going to turn Nori away? She won't survive, Nate. She won't survive unless I get her underground."

Nate closed his eyes and his shoulders sagged. "It's not what you think, Norm."

"Well, what is it? If you know something, help me. Help me save the only child I have left."

8

GOING UNDERGROUND

Norman stood near the rusty chain link fence with his family at his side. Darkness had fallen forty minutes before, which meant the man they were set to meet was thirty minutes late.

"What exactly did Nate say?" Ana's shaky voice betrayed her fear. "Who is it we're meeting? Does he have a place for us to stay?"

Norman didn't answer, but that didn't stop his wife's nervous rambling.

"How will we find food? I only had room to bring protein bars. Where exactly are we going?" She looked up when she finally realized her questions had gone unanswered. "Norm?"

His nerves were shot, and her barrage of questions didn't help. "I know next to nothing, just like you. Nate arranged everything with his contact, the man he orders all the extra supplies for. Supposedly, he runs some sort of underground network of old doomsday preppers. Nate said he'd take us on for a few days for the right price."

"This whole thing makes me nervous," Ana said and fidgeted with her shoulder bag. "Does Nate trust him?"

"It's not like we have a lot of options," he said. "I'm doing the best I can to get us all through the next week. And the best plan I can come up with is getting Nori as far underground as possible before the scorch hits."

"Yes, I know." Ana said as she surveyed the old piles of debris around them. "I know you are."

Nori, who'd been unusually quiet, whipped her head toward a noise at the edge of a collapsed building nearby. "What was that?"

Norman stepped forward, putting himself between the noise and his wife and daughter. "Hello? Who's there?"

A figure emerged from the shadows, oozing from the night itself. Had he been there the whole time?

"You Chisholm?" The man's voice was like rocks rubbing together.

Norm stepped forward, his movements tense and jerky with nerves. They had a lot to lose. "Norman Chisholm. Are you Barker?"

The man nodded. Though he moved toward them, Norman couldn't distinguish much more about him. His clothes and hair were dark. His skin was dirty, tarnished almost, with a dark gray dirt.

"I'm doin' this as a favor to Nate," the man croaked. "Well, less a favor than a necessity to keep my supply movin'. I'm not happy about it, so let's get this over with." He eyed first Norman, and then his wife and daughter. "Where's the money? Which one of you's goin'?"

"Which one?" Norman cocked his head. "The three of us. All of us."

"That wasn't the deal. I'm takin' one. A girl, he said."

"No," Norman said at the same time Ana whined, "Norman?"

"No," Norman repeated. "It's all or none. We all have to go."

The filthy man—Barker—opened his mouth to reveal pink lips under the smudges. Pink lips, gums, and no teeth. "Suit you'self," he spat. "No skin off my back. Didn't want stow-aways no way." He turned without another word and bled into the night.

"Wait!" Norman scurried forward. "Please," he said. "Wait."

Though the man didn't re-emerge, his gravelly voice slithered through the darkness. "Change your mind?"

"I've got this money. Plenty of money." Norman thrust wads of cash in his direction. "Take the three of us. Please."

"No can do." The man slid into sight again and produced a cigar from his shirt pocket. He lit it, pulling air into his mouth through toothless gums. "Only one passenger 'board this train. Take it or leave it."

"But my daughter...she has to go, and she's not old enough to go alone. Please. Let one of us go with her."

The man threw a smoking match to the ground and pressed it into the soil with thick boots. "What part of 'one' don't you under-stand? Now, I'm startin' to lose my patience. You people decide who's goin' in the next three minutes, or I'm goin' back alone."

Ana whimpered, but Nori stood still and quiet.

"Just—just give us a moment." Norman pulled his wife and daughter aside. "It's just until after the sunscorch."

Ana wheeled toward him, disbelief distorting her fine features. "Surely you're not considering sending her alone. Tell me you're not thinking that, Norman."

"There's no other way!" His words were angry, loud. "I've been over every scenario I know, Ana, and this is all we have. Tell me a better plan, and I'll follow it. Tell me anything else that might save our daughter."

She held his gaze, angry tears threatening to spill onto her cheeks.

Norman's jaws clenched painfully. "There's no other way. This is life or death, and you know it. We know it all too well."

"But we don't know anything about this guy or where he'd take her," Ana said. "He could be a thief or a psychopath, for all we know. Both, by the looks of him."

"Nate vouched for him," Norman replied. "He's done business with him for years. He knows how to find him, how to contact him. It'll be fine." His voice was softer, resigned when he said, "It's our only shot, Ana."

"He's right, Mom." Nori had been so silent he'd forgotten she was there. "There's no other way. And it's just for a week or so. Just until the scorch passes. I'll be fine," she said. "I mean, it's risky, but it beats burning to death in a fiery apocalypse."

Norman flinched at the images Nori's words evoked, and the color drained from her face. Her eyes shot wildly between his and her mother's, the regret clear.

"You folks in or out?" Barker fell into a coughing fit, ultimately spitting something foul onto the ground. "Ain't got all night."

"In," Nori called, hitching her backpack over a shoulder. She set her feet wide as she faced him and her mother. "I'm going," she said. "I have to. Is this," she waved her hand at Barker, "whole thing ideal? No. But it's necessary. It's what

I've got to do to survive. I'm smart, Mom. I'm tough. I've got food and supplies. And it's just for a little while."

Ana nodded, wiping beneath her eyes. "No, I know. I just..." She looked away, unable to finish the thought.

Norman squeezed his wife's hand and led her toward Barker as Nori marched stoically beside them.

"My daughter is in the most danger," he said. "She'll be the one to go, but under one condition. You must care for her like she's your own. And you must meet us back here, at this location, at nightfall one week after the sunscorch. The fires will have died down by then, and any lingering risk of exposure will be gone."

Barker pulled the cigar from his lips and pointed it at Norman. "You seem to be operatin' under a misunderstanding. I ain't takin' no one to raise. What I'm offerin' is gettin' her underground. She wants to meet you at the Surface, that's fine with me."

"But where will she go? How will she find shelter?" Ana's voice was pitched high with emotion.

"I'll give 'er the lay of the land," Barker said. "Tell her what's what. She's a big girl. She'll either make it," he put the cigar back between his gums and mumbled past it, "or she won't."

"No, no, no," Ana chanted as the old man cackled. "I don't like this. I don't like it one bit."

Norm looked at his daughter, at the old man, and back at his wife. Then, looking down at his hands, he whispered, "You have to go."

"I know." She stood on tiptoes to kiss his cheek. "Thank you for trusting me, Dad."

Ana wrapped her arms around Nori and held on. "I'm so sorry," she said. "Sorry this is the only way, that you have to do it alone, that it's even necessary in the first place." She drew a deep breath and stood back from Nori, still clenching her hands. "I know you'll be so careful, so brave."

"I will, Mom. And hey," she paused. "I've got one advantage. I can see." Nori's tight smile was forced. "I'll meet you two right back here a week after the scorch."

Norman nodded, unable to speak. If he opened his mouth again, he might scream for her to come back, and that wouldn't keep her alive.

"Let's do this," Nori said to the old man and raised a hand to them in farewell.

Norman clutched his wife's shoulder with one hand and waved goodbye with the other, his arm extended long after she'd disappeared into the night.

9

BARKER'S BETRAYAL

"W here are you taking me?" Nori asked a few minutes after she'd parted with her parents. She trudged behind the old man, thankful she'd worn hiking boots even though they made her feet sweat.

"Subterranean," he said without looking back at her.

"How will I find my way back?"

"Beats me."

"Well, can you help me draw a map or something?" she asked. "What if I get lost?"

Barker did turn then, and the cold-blooded look in his eyes made Nori back up a step. "Listen, kid. What happens to you after we get underground doesn't concern me. I made a deal with Nate, and I'll keep my end of it. I promised to get you underground, and I will. Now, give me that money and put this on or we're not goin' any farther."

Nori balked. "A blindfold? What for?"

"Protection. You think I'm gonna show you the way in here so you can bring back all your pasty friends? You people really are stupid." His lip curled in disgust. "Put it on."

Nori tied the filthy rag around her head and tried not to think about where it had been. Like him, it was covered in gray soot and smelled of sweat.

"The money?" Barker grunted.

Nori fished out half of what her father had given her before they separated, and left the other half in the pocket of her jeans.

"Where's the rest?" he growled.

"That's my portion," she said. "Even through the blindfold, she could sense his extreme displeasure.

"The price I gave was for you alone. This ain't enough. Either fork over all of it, or stay aboveground and melt."

Nori had no choice and she jerked the remaining bills from her pocket. Barker grabbed her wrist and pulled the cash from her fingers, grunting his approval.

"This way," he said.

"I can't see where I'm going," she complained. "I'm afraid I'll fall."

"Best stay close, then. And pick up your feet. I'll tell you when there's a step."

Nori ground her teeth and crept forward, hands stretched out in front of her. She was thankful her father had thought to put at least some of the money in her shoe.

"Are we getting close?" Nori pushed herself upright with a groan after the third fall. The last one had left the palm of one hand bloody, she was sure of it. She wiped her hands on the sides of her jeans and moved blindly forward.

"A mite farther. Then we go down."

Nori didn't speak, but followed the old man, her hands outstretched to protect against another fall. Her heart ached for her parents already. They were probably worrying themselves sick on the way home without her, her mother a wreck and her father trying to control his own emotions and consoling her. Tears fell from Nori's eyes, but were soaked up by the dirty cotton tied around her head, as if they'd never fallen at all.

"Now we go down," Barker finally said.

As their angle changed, Nori shifted her weight, pulling her shoulders back and reaching out with her toes at times to explore before taking full steps. Barker wasn't leading her down steps, but over the rough terrain of a rocky slope. Had they gone down the side of a mountain? No—there wasn't a mountain nearby. How could they be going so far down? Where were they?

With her eyes covered, Nori's remaining senses worked overtime. The wind had stopped, and something smelled faintly moldy, like the stale air in a basement. Had he taken her to a bunker somewhere? Did they know she was coming? What if they were hostile? What if they wouldn't let her stay? Lost in thought, Nori nearly jumped from her skin at a loud metal clanging. The slow creak that followed made her think a metal door had been opened, but she couldn't be sure.

"Through here," Barker said, pushing down on her shoulder. "Duck your head."

She followed his orders, hunching her shoulders and head, inching toward the sound she'd heard. As she crept forward, the air pressure changed. The space around her became quieter, but also magnified. Some kind of tunnel or passageway? The air smelled different, too. Stale. Not bad, necessarily, just damp.

"All right," Barker said. "No chance you'll find the way in now." He pulled on the blindfold, taking with it several dark hairs still attached to Nori's head.

She rubbed the tender spots and then her eyes. The tunnel

was pitch black. Not a single lantern or light showed the way. And yet, she could see. At home, it was hard to achieve total darkness. Even at nightfall, some light remained. But this, this was darkness. She smiled in spite of her dicey situation, in spite of her perilous future. She could see. And it didn't hurt.

Barker slipped a headlamp onto his forehead and switched it on, taking off without a word. Focused away from her, the beam of light reduced her vision a bit, but not enough to matter. Nori adjusted her backpack and trudged after him.

At first, she thought the constant low roar was nothing, just the background noise of being underground. But then a thought struck her.

"Is that— Do I hear water?"

Barker stopped mid-step, his body rigid. He didn't turn to face her; he didn't answer. After a few seconds, he simply stalked forward again.

Nori knew better than to ask twice. His reaction suggested she was right anyway. She filed that, and the round shape of the metal door they'd come through, away for future use. They might be the only clues she'd have to get back to her parents.

As she followed Barker deeper and deeper into the tunnel —and underground—the temperature changed. It was much cooler in the depths of the passage. It had been so long since she was anything but hot. Air conditioners could only do so much when temperatures rose into the 130s, even on solar power. The air was moist, too, not the blistering arid heat she was used to. She was energized, lighter. Despite her uncertain future, her lips pulled into a smile. She liked the underground...so far, anyway.

Nori sped up to walk alongside Barker. When she reached him, he turned and snarled, and his headlamp shined into her eyes. Nori turned her head reflexively, blinking to regain her sight.

"Damnation," Barker whispered almost reverently. "The hell have you gotten me into, girl?"

"What?" Nori said. "What are you talking about?"

"Those eyes. That's what I'm talking about. Shining like new nickels." Barker shook his head and paused to spit. "You shoulda told me. This wasn't parta the deal."

"Told you what?" Nori asked. "Oh, you mean my eyes? How they reflect in the light?" She shrugged. "Didn't think it mattered. Just one more of my eccentricities."

She smiled, but Barker was not amused. He let out a long breath and shook his head, then set back into his hurried pace.

Nori fell back and resumed her mindless trudging, observing the details of the tunnel. The floor was permanently damp, its gray gravel worn flat with footfalls. The sides of the tunnel were the dense gray of wet earth, and when she ran her fingers along the wall it was rough, even sharp in places.

When Barker stopped abruptly, she did the same. He faced her, the lines of his hard face dark, worn, and well-travelled, like the ground beneath them. Cold gray eyes peered at her, his thin lips curled in distaste.

"This is where you get off, kid."

Nori shook her head and squinted at the wiry old man. She exuded confidence, but the beginning stirrings of panic were sneaking past her tough facade. "What?"

"I'm going this way." He jerked his head to the left. "You'll want to go that way." He motioned toward the right. "That means our arrangement is fulfilled, and we're separatin'."

"No." Nori's reply was more decisive than she felt.

"I said I'd take you Subterranean, and I have. This is the

crossroads," he said. "We're partin' ways. Go on, now." When Nori stared at him dumbfounded, he said it again, as if running off an unwanted pet. "Go on, now. Go on."

"You're supposed to help me," Nori said, her shock at the abandonment morphing into indignation. "You're agreed to get me through the next sunscorch."

"I did no such thing."

"But Nate...my father...you're supposed to help me." Nori's voice broke on the last words, and she turned her head to hide the tears that fell unwelcome down her cheeks.

As Nori wiped her face with her sleeves, humiliation smothered her like soured air. She was not a crier. She'd never wallowed in pity or panicked in distress, and she'd sure never been a damsel. When life handed her a raw deal, she rolled it into sushi.

Being forced to leave her home and loving parents to live underground with strangers for God knew how long was bad enough. But for the one person she'd known for a few silent hours to abandon her in the darkness and send her directionless down an empty tunnel... No. No, that was too much for one girl to bear, tough or not.

Nori sniffed and cleared her throat then turned to Barker. "You're really going to abandon me here? I don't have the first clue where these passageways lead, or who I might meet along the way. What do you expect me to do?"

Barker had produced another cigar from his shirt pocket and held it between slick gums. "Well, I tell ya what I expect you'll do. I expect you'll learn a valuable lesson." He pulled the cigar from his mouth so his next words were clear. "Don't trust nobody. Don't depend on nobody for nothin'. And for God's sake, don't ever let another human bein' see you cry."

"Oh, screw you, you vile old fart." He'd hit her right where it hurt—her pride.

Barker wheezed a laugh and re-inserted his cigar. "That's a start."

"Where are you going, anyway?"

"This way." He motioned with his head. He showed his gums, but it wasn't a smile.

"No kidding," Nori mumbled. "What if I follow you?"

"I wouldn't advise that. This ain't the way for you. This way holds... Well, let's just say this direction leads to more endings than it does beginnings."

"What's that supposed to mean?" Nori's voice was sharp. "How do I know you're telling me the truth?"

He closed in on her, his face so close that the acrid stink of his liquored breath made her gag. Before Nori knew what had hit her, he jerked the backpack from her and held it out of her reach.

"Give me that back." Her voice was high, desperate. "Give it back! Please. Everything I have is in there."

Barker's look of disgust filled her with shame, but also fury. How could he be so heartless?

"You'd better get tough if you want to live down here, girl, and fast." He threw the backpack at her feet. "Now get out of here before I take everything you've got, including your clothes. I could sell those boots for a fortune."

"You wouldn't," she seethed.

"I sure as hell would," he said. "Follow me, if you think I won't." He held Nori's gaze until she cast her eyes to the floor.

"One more thing," he said, "in case you're ignorant of this, too. You let anyone down here see those eyes, and you're good as dead." His lips stretched and Nori knew what came next.

Those disgusting, toothless gums. "Or you'll wish you were dead," he said and turned, trudging down the dark passage.

Nori stood at the crossroads of the subterranean shaft with her hands balled into fists as Barker left her behind. She had a few more choice words for him, which she muttered with the full knowledge that they bounced and echoed down the tunnel toward him. He'd heard her, she could tell from the cackles he let out before he fell into another coughing fit. Served him right. She hoped he choked on the filthy cigar and fell gums-first into the mud.

Should she follow him, despite his warning, or go the way he'd directed her? Where was he going, anyway? Where was he sending her? And what did he know about her eyes?

With one last look at Barker's retreating back, Nori huffed out a breath and attempted to get herself together. She bent to grab a loose, jagged rock, took a running jump up the side of the tunnel, and carved a wide arc in the earthen wall. She hoped she'd recognize her own trail of breadcrumbs when the time came to follow it home.

10

TREK THROUGH A TUNNEL

The rumbling growl of Nori's empty stomach echoed through the small space. Over the last several hours, she'd trudged through the tunnel, cautiously at first, keeping both her eyes and ears on high alert. It was quiet underground. Disturbingly so. She hadn't seen anything but blackness and rock for miles. At times, chills skittered up her back at the sound of creepy-crawlies scurrying behind her. She'd whipped around, arms in in front of her face, ready to fend off whatever pursued her. But even with her remarkable night vision, she never caught sight of anything.

"Probably true what they say," she mumbled, just to hear something solid. "Only cockroaches could survive the scorches."

The tunnel was maddeningly monotonous, expanding in some places and narrowing in others, but just a long, dark tunnel all the same. She closed her eyes in relief when the landscape finally changed. At first glance, she thought the tunneled passage would fork, but instead found a large alcove carved into the rock. A dead end. Rusted cans littered the ground, as did charred pieces of wood from long-extinguished fires.

She shivered and rubbed her arms, which had sprouted semi-permanent goosebumps. A fire sounded heavenly. The air underground was cold and damp, and she wished she'd brought a heavier coat. Though it was her favorite, the olive-colored utility jacket didn't fend off the constant chill. There were matches in her backpack she remembered, perking for a moment before sagging again. Using them to start a fire seemed a terribly naïve thing to do. She might as well announce her presence with a bullhorn. Or, maybe it didn't matter at all. She'd walked for hours and hadn't seen another soul.

Closing her eyes against the barrage of questions that had hammered her mind every step of the way, Nori finally allowed herself to honestly consider her options. Where would she stay the night? Should she backtrack and wait out the week where she'd entered the tunnel with Barker? Was that a smarter plan than following a tunnel with no idea where she'd end up? Maybe if she really conserved her food she could make it the entire week on what she had. But if she couldn't, where would she get more? Would she ever feel warm again? Could she stay sane while waiting alone over a week in the damp and cold until she could see her parents?

The weight of helplessness sat heavy on her chest, making it hard to breathe. She slid to the ground in the alcove and buried her head in her knees. Nori stayed there, arms wrapped around her legs, her whole body squeezed into a ball, until the feeling of hopelessness passed. It took a while.

Finally, she raised her head and pulled her backpack around, fumbling for one of the energy bars her mother had so carefully packed. Mom. Nori hoped she was managing all right. She probably wasn't, but her father could help her through it.

At least her parents didn't know Barker, that jackass, had abandoned her. Every time Nori thought of him, she ground her teeth. God, she hated him. If she ever ran into him again, she was going to show him "tough." As she sat in the frigid alcove, her jeans and hands covered in gray silt, and her eyelashes still damp from the last round of tears, she decided she would get tough. She would *be* tough.

Working to unclench her fists, Nori gave a long-gone Barker the finger. Then she threw on her backpack with tenacious flair and stalked farther into the tunnel toward the great unknown.

Several miles down the passage, Nori's head shot up, eyes wild at the sound of a voice. A man's voice. No, *men*. Her heart thundered as she searched the small space around her. She couldn't see past a curve in the passage ahead. Were they friend or foe? No way to know. She did know what lay behind her, though. The alcove.

Running on the pads of her feet in the direction she'd come, she tried not to breathe too loudly, to stay as silent as possible. The alcove's shadow was just ahead. Nori closed her eyes, praying for ten more seconds. When she finally reached it, she slipped into the space, staying low to the ground and not daring to make a sound.

The men approached, their footfalls clipped and intentional. They were in a hurry. Nori couldn't make out the words of their muffled voices, but the tone was stern. One was clearly giving instructions to the other.

Though her palms lay flat on the rocky path, they shook. She pressed them into the stones until the sharp edges threatened to break her skin. She focused on the pain and put her ear to the ground, making herself as small as possible. The tunnel floor didn't smell like she'd expected it to. It smelled of minerals. Metallic, almost. Foreign.

Heavy footsteps slowed as they reached the alcove then stopped at its entrance.

"This the place?" The voice was guttural.

"Yeah."

"We're early."

"Yeah."

"I'ma take a piss."

No, no, no, Nori silently begged. She closed her eyes and prayed to anyone who'd listen that the man wouldn't pee in her corner.

He didn't. She made a silent sigh of relief at the splattering sound against the wall opposite her.

Inch by inch, Nori turned her head to sneak a look at the man's back. He was huge. Dressed in threadbare military fatigues, he laid a gun against the wall as he conducted his business. A big gun. She squeezed her eyes shut and prayed a fervent prayer she was uphill from Mr. Drizzle.

Who were they? Who were they meeting? Why did they carry guns? God, how long would she have to lie on the cold, wet ground?

"Here he comes," the second man called.

She heard it, too. Someone approached from the opposite direction. Anger rippled through her as she imagined Barker's return.

Though she couldn't see outside the alcove, she could hear, and she listened. Someone else spoke—not Barker's voice. Whoever these men were, they weren't brilliant conversation-alists. They communicated in short sentences when one-word answers wouldn't do. Emotionless, straight to business.

Almost military-like. A trade or transaction was made, but she had no idea of the details. As soon as their business was complete, the three men left.

Pressing her forehead to the rocky floor, Nori squeezed her eyes shut. She had no idea if there was another alcove ahead, a place where she could seek shelter again, if necessary. What should she do?

The new, tougher Nori resolved to wait for a count of one-thousand then keep going.

NORI WOKE to a sting like a knife to her cheekbone. She jerked from the pain, and the back of her head struck something hard. Groaning, she blinked and tried to move her arms, but the right one wouldn't budge. Soon, everything came into focus, and her brain computed her circumstances. She'd fallen asleep in the alcove. Her cheek was pressed against a particularly vicious rock and her arm trapped beneath her body. She lay on her side against the wall, the back of her head bleeding into it. She closed her eyes, thankful no one had found her unconscious and vulnerable.

With a hand to her aching back, Nori stood and stretched. She rolled her neck and tried to form a plan. There was no way to know how long she'd slept. Then she shrugged. Even if she'd known what time it was, it made no difference.

Nori rubbed her eyes and let out a frustrated groan. Her hands were filthy. She wiped her face with the front of her pale orange shirt and scrubbed her hands on her jeans. No wonder Barker had been so grungy. It was impossible to stay clean in such conditions. Could she make it a week without a shower in this filth? The thought caused saliva to pool at the back of her throat, and she took a deep breath before it formed into a full-on gag.

One thing she couldn't live without for a week was water. She had only enough for two days. Three, maybe, if she made it last. With that in mind, she sipped from the stainless-steel canteen in her backpack. Her stomach growled in protest. She needed food, but she had to be smart. Best conserve supplies until she knew where to find more.

Drawing her leg up, Nori patted the sock where the little money she had left remained hidden. She might need it in the days to come. With the few, but very important, goals of seeking food and water and staying alive, she stood and donned her backpack, resuming the trek through the tunnel.

11

WE MEET AGAIN

Nori angled her head to the side as she tried to determine the source of a low hum. The sound increased, its pitch both higher and louder. It was getting closer. Was there more than one hum? If she hadn't been underground, she would've almost thought—

"Oh God," she breathed and jerked to a stop. Turning, she looked frantically, futilely for an escape. She'd walked for two hours at least. Much too far from the alcove to reach it.

The motorcycles were coming fast, the sound of their high-pitched motors reverberating through the tunnel. They would be on her in a matter of seconds. Her heart clamored toward her throat as she realized her only chance was to sprint ahead and hope for a place to hide.

There wasn't one. With nowhere to go, Nori slowed to a stop and pressed her back against the cold wall. Her ears rang and her heart beat wildly in her chest as four motorcycles sped into view. They looked like dirt bikes, or those old military-style motorcycles—small and made for speed and quick turns.

She lowered her head, keeping her eyes on the tunnel floor. The bike in front stopped just inches from her, sliding to the side and spraying her with gravelly silt. Instinctively, she covered her face with an arm and held her breath. The silence was deafening when, almost in unison, the bikers switched off their wild machines. She risked a look over her arm, and wished she hadn't.

"What do we have here?" the man in front sneered, throwing a long, leather-covered leg over his bike to dismount. She couldn't see the other men's faces, but they all wore riding boots. The man in front looked her up and down, gaze snagging first on her face then her shirt. "What's a matter, sister?" he asked. "You lost?" When he looked past her, his eyes widened. "Surely you're not alone?"

A man in the back let out a hyena-like laugh that put Nori's nerves on high alert. It didn't take a genius to know they weren't Boy Scouts out to help lost girls. No, these were the type of men who preyed on them. She took a step back, scraping her shoulder on the rocky wall.

A second man snaked toward her. He flanked the first man, effectively pinning her to the wall. If she ran right, the first biker could grab her. If left, the second.

"Don't worry, hon," the second man soothed, as if he were speaking to a frightened animal. "We've no mind to hurt ya."

Hyena boy laughed again and crept forward. There was something not quite right about him. His inset eyes were too close together, what her mother had always called "beady." He said something horrifically vulgar, and the others laughed. Nori's gut twisted. Surely, she hadn't heard right.

She was in trouble. Four foul-mouthed men in filthy riding leathers against a single girl. They weren't on their way to church on those bikes.

"I-I'm just meeting some friends down the road," she croaked, her heart making a frantic attempt to exit through her chest. "My guy friends," she added and swallowed hard.

"Oh, I don't think you have friends anywhere close to here." The first biker, who appeared to be the leader, pushed loose, greasy hair behind his ear.

"Yeah," Beady Eyes barked. "We look stupid to you?"

Nori held her tongue.

"Shut up, Jenks," the leader growled. "Where you headed, anyway, sweet thing?"

Nori's breath left her in a rush. "That way" was probably not an acceptable answer. She didn't dare tell them she was lost and alone, that she didn't know where she was going or a soul in the entire underground world except the wiry old fart who'd ripped her off.

"My friends will be here any minute." Nori forced the words through her lips, commanding them to sound bold. They came out too loud and desperate.

"No. Now," the second man, the greasy one, said. "We're past that. You ain't got no friends nearby." He slithered in close to her and ran a finger down her sleeve. His nails were long and packed with that same black grime. It took every ounce of strength Nori possessed not to scream. She turned her head from him and squeezed her eyes shut as he said, "But you could make some. We'll be your friends."

Nori whimpered and inched away from him, which put her closer to the leader. By the looks of him, he had no interest in playing savior today. There were four, though. What was the other one doing? Was he sneaking around one side? Would he stand up to these three? Would no one help her? Nori searched for him, but couldn't see past the ones who had her cornered.

"Your eyes are pretty," the dumb one—Jenks—said. "Blue. Like I remember the sky."

"Oh, write her a sonnet, why don't ya?" the slithery one taunted.

"Shut up, Wallace." Jenks's mouth twisted into a petulant scowl.

"We ain't got time for romance, boys," the leader said, leaning his head to the side as he ogled her.

Nori fought to remain upright as her knees buckled beneath her. She spread her arms out, clasping at the sides of the tunnel. She couldn't speak. And there was nowhere to run.

"You know what we oughta do?" the man she hadn't yet seen said to his comrades. "We should sell her to Big Hank."

The slithery one, Wallace, tossed a scowl over his shoulder. "She ain't a fighter. Look at her."

"Yeah," Jenks chimed in. "She's tender."

"I'm a lot tougher than you think, a-hole." That drew a round of snickers from the men. Nori cringed, and a terrified whine leaked out.

"Big Hank's always buying. We could sell her for a fortune," the faceless one went on, "but we'd probably get less if she's damaged."

Something about the voice was familiar. Recognition tugged at the corner of her mind. The only person she knew in this new world Barker. Well, unless— Nori's eyes flew wide when she realized who'd spoken. She opened her mouth to call his name, to plead with him to help her, but his face came into view behind the first three men. He shook his head ever-so-slightly and closed his eyes.

Nori snapped her mouth closed, at least until she could understand what was happening. What was he trying to

63

communicate? Why was he acting like he didn't know her? Why in the world had he suggested they sell her?

She glanced from Cooper to the leader, whose face was drawn in concentration as he weighed his options.

Cooper looked just as she remembered him, though he seemed much more at home in the subterranean space than he had above-ground. His dark hair fell in messy clumps around his face. Not curly, exactly, but close. His eyes were as sharp as she recalled. At that moment, those intelligent eyes pinned her down, told her not to make a move. She didn't.

Wallace, though, couldn't keep his eyes—or his hands— off her. He closed in again and reached to touch her hair, looking at her as if they were the only two people in the world. As if there weren't three other men crowded around him in a dark tunnel. As if Nori wasn't trembling with a nauseous blend of fear and loathing. When he ran the back of his hand across her cheek, she could stay silent no longer.

"Get your filthy hands off me," she seethed and jerked from his touch.

Jenks howled a laugh. "Maybe she is a fighter, Sarge."

"S'all right," Wallace purred with menace. "I like 'em feisty."

"No." Cooper's deep command echoed through the tunnel, his tone drawing every eye in his direction.

"What's that?" Wallace turned his head, as if he hadn't quite heard right. "You telling me what to do, boy?"

Cooper straightened, preparing for a fight. "Leave the girl alone. Or can't you find a willing participant?"

Wallace jerked, his face contorting into a sour sneer.

Nori closed her eyes, breathing through her nose as relief washed over her. The shaming had worked—for the moment, at least. Wallace's full attention shifted to Cooper, whose widened stance and fisted hands screamed *bring it on*. Cooper rolled his shoulders and stretched his slender neck. When he opened those steely eyes again, his face had morphed from easygoing and detached to world-hardened and violent. Nori gaped at the transformation.

Wallace had been posturing, too. He tossed his leather jacket aside and spread his arms dramatically in invitation.

"Cut the crap, you two," the leader—Sarge—barked. "Cooper's right. Let's take her to Hank."

Cooper's eyes narrowed infinitesimally. He was relieved, she realized. Relieved she was being sold to someone named Big Hank.

12

WELCOME TO TROGTOWN

"**Y**ou can't do this." Nori said, jerking away as Cooper tightened zip ties on her wrists. "Please," she shook her head, her chest tight with panic as she searched his stoic face. "Don't do this."

Cooper slipped a finger between her skin and the tie and gave her a look that spoke volumes. I won't hurt you, it said. Follow my lead and stay alive.

Nori's gut clenched. Trust Cooper, whom she didn't know at all? No way. Not that she was overflowing with options. She wracked her brain for another way, any way, but didn't come up with one. There was no choice but to have faith in the man she'd saved in the alley that night. With a shaky breath, Nori closed her eyes in acknowledgement. She understood; she'd go along with his plan.

"I'll stoke 'er." Wallace's words jarred Nori back to reality, his hungry leer sending cold shivers down her spine.

"I don't think so," Sarge said sharply. "Cooper, this was your idea. She's your burden now."

Cooper scowled, but nodded as he threw a leg over his bike. "Get on." His voice was rough, harsh. He jerked his head toward the back of the bike then stared straight ahead without another word.

Nori had never touched a motorcycle in her entire life, much less ridden one. She approached it slowly, cautiously. Unsure what to do, she looked at Cooper, who offered no assistance. Not even a glance. She pressed her bound hands hesitantly to the leather at Cooper's shoulder, balancing herself as she mounted the bike. Astride the seat, she didn't know what to do with her hands, and placed them first on Cooper's shoulder then back down in her lap.

When he stood to kickstart the motorcycle, Nori lost her balance and grasped at the bottom of his leather coat, bracing her legs on the ground with a yelp. She didn't dare risk a look at the other men.

"Put your arms around me," Cooper yelled over the sound of four anxious engines.

Nori leaned around his wide shoulder, catching his gaze and offering her bound hands as a reminder.

"You'll have to put them over my head," he said, narrowing his body by pressing his shoulders inward and fists together at his forehead. He looked like he could be praying, and Nori offered a silent prayer of her own as she slipped her arms over his shoulders and down to his waist.

Cooper nodded, more to himself than Nori, who jerked at the force of sudden acceleration. Though there was no way she could fall backward, she pressed herself tight against his back, her eyes and jaw squeezed shut as they accelerated through the tunnel.

"Hate riding sweep," Cooper spat after a while.

"What?" Nori opened one eye and peeked around him, regretting the move immediately as mud flew into her face.

"Riding last sucks," he said, his voice muffled through the narrow opening of his mouth. "The mud."

Nori nodded against his back, unwilling to leave her shield again.

Cooper slowed and hung back from the group after a while, mumbling a curse at the spray of silt and gravel from Wallace's back tire.

"What the hell are you doing down here?" he yelled over the engine, twisting in his seat to look at her.

Nori assumed they weren't in danger of being overheard, though she could still glimpse the others up ahead. "Sunscorch coming," she yelled. "Won't survive another."

"How did you get here?"

Nori shrugged, boiling her story down to words that would carry over the engine. "Dad knew a guy."

"They sent you alone?" Cooper swung around to look at her again, his expression disbelieving and...angry?

"No." Nori shook her head. "Well, yes. Long story. Betrayed." It wasn't a great explanation, but it would have to do under the circumstances.

"Got any friends down here?"

Nori's mouth twisted at the thought of Barker. She shook her head.

"First lesson," Cooper said. "Don't trust anybody."

"Duly noted," she mumbled.

"What?"

"Nothing," she said. "Cooper?"

"Yeah?"

"You're not really gonna sell me, right?"

He stiffened, his stomach clenching beneath her hands. "I don't have a choice."

Nori jerked from him, but her bound hands kept her close. Too close. She couldn't go anywhere, even if she wanted to jump from the speeding motorcycle. She wrestled with the ties at her wrists, but it was hopeless. A knife was the only thing that could get her out of them.

"Stop it," Cooper ordered, his voice rough. He'd shifted from easygoing to vicious. "It's the best I can do. Hank's fair, at least. And not violent toward women that I know of." He nodded toward the men in front of them. "You want to stay with these animals?"

"Oh, and you're not an animal?" Nori demanded. "You're one of them."

"I'm nothing like them." Muscles worked in Cooper's jaw. "I saved you, didn't I?"

Did he? Being sold sounded nothing like salvation. Were her only choices this Hank, or Sarge and the others? No. Cooper would help her like she'd helped him that night in the alley. He had to. He wasn't bad. She knew it. She knew it in her bones.

Nori stood on the foot pegs to speak close to his ear. She could hardly plead with him if she had to yell. "I just need…" Her lip trembled, so she bit it, steeling herself against the pain. "I just need a place to hide for a week or so," she said. "To wait out the sunscorch. I'll go back to my parents. I'll leave this filthy place."

Cooper pulled away from her, and that familiar feeling of hopelessness resurfaced. "Too late now," he said, eyes focused straight ahead. "Can't escape those three. Hank's your best bet to stay alive."

"Can't we outrun them? Just turn this bike around and

hide me somewhere?" She wasn't above begging. "Please."
When he didn't respond, she said again, her voice cracking.
"Please, Cooper."

"I'm sorry. I'll try to make it right somehow," was all
he said.

Nori let the tears that had been threatening to fall rush
over her cheeks, and pressed her forehead to Cooper's back.
They rode for miles and miles, but she didn't look up again.

Not until the bike slowed.

They came to a sliding stop, spraying gravel and mud in
Wallace's direction. Wallace jerked up and shot Cooper a look
that promised their fight was far from over.

"Arms up," Cooper muttered, and Nori obliged as best she
could. He wiggled out of her embrace, stepping from the
motorcycle and clasping her arm as she dismounted. His grip
was meant to appear as though he kept her from escaping, but
he was really helping her off the bike. She couldn't understand him. One minute, he was saving her from molesting
bandits, and the next, he was selling her. One minute, he
barked callous orders, refusing to save her, and the next, he
chivalrously helped her from the bike.

Nori risked a look at her captors. Wallace and Jenks were
noticeably irritated, their eyes lingering on her as Cooper
directed her from the tunnel and up a set of primitive stairs.
Sarge had stalked ahead, but not before ordering Wallace and
Jenks to stay behind with the bikes.

When she reached the top of the stairs, Nori's legs
stopped working. Moments before, the dungeon-like darkness of the endless tunnel was the only thing she'd seen in
hours, maybe more than a day. And now...what stood in front
of her was like nothing she'd ever laid eyes on, or even
imagined.

"It's a city," Nori breathed, craning her head to see more of the vast expanse.

"It's a city," Cooper repeated drily. "Come on. There's Sarge just up ahead."

Nori's wrists chafed from the zip ties, the abrasions worsening each time she slowed to take in people milling about the alley-like streets and the unkempt stores that lined them.

"You're hurting me," she said through clenched teeth.

Cooper looked down at her raw wrists and his eyes softened. "Well," he groused, his words incongruent with his expression. "Keep up."

"How much farther?" Nori wished her question hadn't sounded so much like whining.

"Just through there." He nodded toward a dark street between two buildings carved from the sides of the cavern. How deep must those buildings go, she wondered. How had these people chiseled entire structures from stone? How long had it taken to build an underground city this size? And most confounding: how had she and the people aboveground never known of its existence?

As Cooper urged her toward the buildings, Nori's heart raced. This was her chance. She could break free of him and escape down one of the alleys. The cavernous city extended farther than she could see. She was fast, an excellent sprinter. Surely there was someplace she could hide. Even if she had to lie low for a few days, it was better than being sold for God knew what purpose.

Nori swallowed hard, chanting, *I can do this. I can do this.*

With a final huff of breath, she pulled back hard with her bound hands, causing Cooper to turn and face her. "What's u—"

Nori kicked him in the stomach. Cooper grunted and bent

reflexively, wheezing to catch his breath. With no time to lose, Nori kneed his face as hard as she could. She cried out at the pain of connecting with his forehead, but it worked. In his shock, Cooper released her hands. She bolted.

Risking a look behind her, Nori saw Cooper had recovered fast. As she ran for the nearest alley, she marveled at both his sprinting ability and his familiarity with the more colorful aspects of the English language.

She put her head down and kicked her body into a higher gear, thankful she'd taken up running so long ago. Sprinting toward the darkest place she could find, she hoped her excellent night vision would give her an advantage. She made it to the alley in record time, and stuck out a hand to grasp the corner of the stone wall as she rounded it.

Cold stone beneath her fingertips was reassuring, and she took a stabilizing breath milliseconds before something attempted to separate her head from her body. Her neck throbbed with a thick, blunt pain. Her vision faded. Her butt hit the ground.

Nori grabbed at her brutalized throat, blinking in confusion. She tried to piece together what had happened, but couldn't spare a thought for chronology. Every fiber of her being was concentrated on one action: breathing. She wheezed, she coughed, she gasped for breath, but none came.

Her esophagus wasn't working. It hurt. Not a stinging or burning, but a deep, debilitating pain. Like someone had punched her in the throat. Nori swung her head to search the alley, but saw only stars. Closing her eyes against the pain and confusion, she tried to calm down. But, fun fact: a body simply refuses to relax when it can't get oxygen. She curled into a ball and struggled to catch her breath.

When she could finally inhale, when her vision finally

cleared, Nori looked up to find Sarge's satisfied and conde-
scending sneer above her.

Cooper rounded the corner so hard in pursuit he nearly
fell on top of her. He swung his arms to stop quickly and
remain upright. He looked down at her, chest heaving, and
she flinched at the furious set of his face.

"Clotheslined 'er." Sarge raised a lip to reveal short gray
teeth. It was meant to be a smile Nori thought dimly as he
stalked toward her. He turned to Cooper. "How embarrasin'.
Little thing like this gettin' the best of ya."

"It won't happen again." Cooper grabbed Nori's bound
hands and jerked her up so hard her teeth snapped together.
Her wrists were bruised and raw, despite the breathing room
he'd given her.

"Ow," Nori yelped, whirling to kick at his knees. He
dodged her awkward attempt easily and swept his leg behind
hers. She grunted as her butt connected with the hard ground.
Again.

"What are you thinking?" Cooper vibrated with fury as he
loomed over her. He wasn't just pretending for the group
this time.

"I was thinking to escape before you sold me into
slavery." Her voice was loud, and sounded much more
confident than she felt sitting in filth and humiliation on
the street. "What did you expect me to do? Just go along
with it? Oh, yeah, sure. You wanna sell me to Big
Hank? Sounds awesome." Nori scoffed and leveled her
gaze at Cooper. "I'm not really a 'go along with it'
kinda girl."

"Yeah, I noticed," Cooper mumbled darkly.

"Let's move," Sarge commanded, leading them from
the alley.

"That was really stupid," Cooper said moments later when Sarge couldn't hear them.

"It's better than whatever you've got in mind."

"No," he said hotly. "It's not. You wouldn't last one night on these streets, much less a whole week. You don't have any idea what life is like down here. These people are here because they're hard, Nori. They're fighters. Generations of ex-military and doomsday preppers, most of them. And in case you haven't noticed, there aren't a lot of women."

"So?"

"So?" Cooper repeated the word so loudly Sarge turned at the commotion. "So," he said lower, "people get lonely. Cute girl like you is manna from heaven. You'd be a ray of sunshine in this dark world for somebody."

"Well, I'd never agree to that," she said, and raised her chin haughtily.

"No one would stop to ask you, you little fool."

Nori jerked at his sharp tone and stared up at him, trying to understand as he dragged her along.

"What you need is protection," he said. "And Big Hank is the best I can come up with. Nobody will mess with you if they know you're his."

Nori's gaze left Cooper's face as they approached the buildings carved into the sides of the monstrous cavern. The structures were flanked by thick brown columns of ancient natural stalactites and stalagmites, and a few that appeared constructed. Thousands of straw-like mineral deposits loomed from the cavernous ceiling. The floor had been leveled and the ceiling illuminated. Big, square lights were affixed to the ceiling. How had she not noticed before? The lights gave off a distinct buzzing that bounced and echoed around her. She tried to ignore it, as the others appeared to do, but the constant, low-level buzz was maddening, like a gnat living just inside her ear.

She stopped moving again, but Cooper didn't jerk her hands this time. "You coming?"

Nori nodded absently, still in awe of her surroundings. "Stinks down here," she said.

Cooper shrugged. "Welcome to Trogtown."

13

A DEAL IS STRUCK

"Cooper. My man." A meaty hand clapped Nori's captor on the back with such force he stumbled forward.

"Hank." Cooper nodded and grinned—a real grin that reached his eyes. "How's business?"

Hank's wide mouth snapped shut and puckered into a frown. His eyes held, of all things, sadness. "We lost Kade's handler a few days ago. Up and jumped into the gorge while everyone slept." The big man closed his eyes, the blink lasting a moment too long.

"They find him?" Cooper asked.

"No." Hank shook his head. "Sent a search party downstream, but there was no sign of him. Couldn't have survived that drop, though."

"Light deprivation's gettin' more and more of 'em all the time," Sarge said and spat on the ground near Nori's feet. "Only the strong survive. Fundamental truth right there."

Cooper raised his eyebrows and quickly turned back to Hank. "That gonna affect odds next weekend?"

"Prob'ly, once word gets out. Kade's pretty torn up about it." Hank caught Nori's gaze and she watched his face as curiosity replaced regret. He cleared his throat and looked to Sarge and Cooper. "What can I do for you boys today?"

Sarge stepped forward, grabbing Nori by the bicep and motioning up and down her body with a flourish. "Got a Grade-A, prime selection for your discriminatin' survey."

Nori jerked from Sarge's grasp, her spine straight but her stomach nauseous. "Ugh. Get off of me!" As she ground out the last sentence, she leaned back and kicked Sarge right between the legs. She knew she'd scored a goal as the light in his eyes died like a candle drowning in wax.

A wicked smile pulled at the corners of her mouth, and she reveled in a brief, perfect moment of victory before her head snapped back. Blinking and dizzy, Nori touched her mouth with trembling fingers and pulled them back bloody. She looked up at Sarge in disbelief.

"You hit me," she said numbly, pain throbbing across her swelling lip. She turned to Cooper. "He hit me."

Cooper didn't react. He stood unflinching, barely breathing, though she caught a barely-perceptible twitch in one eye.

Sarge spat filthy names at Nori that she'd never heard before, but had a relatively good idea of their meaning. Rage like she'd never known built inside her, and when he threatened more than a backhanding, Nori launched herself at him. She could never beat him in a fight, and she knew it. But at that moment, she didn't care. One good shot at his face would be worth another bloodied lip.

Before she reached him, though, Big Hank grabbed her around the middle, spinning her around and putting himself between her and Sarge. "Yes, sir," he said, holding her back with one hand and scrubbing at the scruff on his jaw with the other. "Fiery little thing. This one'll do fine."

"How much?" Sarge snarled. "If it ain't top dollar, I'd rather just get my money out of her hide."

Hank turned and shook his head at Nori, his nostrils flaring with irritation. "You've cost me more money, girl," he said, his voice low. "Best be prepared to earn that back."

Nori opened her mouth to tell Big Hank where he could shove it, too, but caught sight of Cooper, who shook his head furiously and mouthed, "Shut. Up."

She turned her head to the side and heaved a breath, working hard to control herself. She wanted to scream, to kick them all in the balls like she had Sarge, but she didn't say another word.

"I'll give you thirty-five," Hank said, releasing Nori to cross thick arms over his chest.

"Shoot." Sarge laughed without humor. "I wouldn't part with'er for less than eighty-five."

"Keep her," Hank said, and stepped away. "She's nothing but trouble. Not worth more than forty."

"Sixty-five." Sarge extended a bony hand in Hank's direction.

He didn't take it. "Fifty-five."

Sarge eyed Nori, his distaste sending one side of his lip toward his nose. "All right," he sneered. "Fifty-five."

Cooper closed his eyes and released a pent-up breath. "What, ah, what are you gonna do with her?"

"Pair her with Kade, I guess," Hank said. "A little spunk's a good thing with a bear like him."

Nori didn't like the sound of that one bit.

"I'll let you two work out the details," Cooper called and put a hand on Nori's back, inching her from Sarge's grasp.

"Take her to the Pit," Hank called. "Good a place to start as any."

When the two were out of range, Cooper spun Nori around to face him. He was once again the hard-nosed authoritarian Nori had glimpsed before, and she backed away from him, her back hitting the wall behind her.

"That was so stupid." He was seething mad, hands clenched at his sides. "Are you trying to get yourself killed? Do you want to make it out of here alive, or not? I told you Hank was your best shot at protection."

"Protection? What's this 'pairing' with 'Kade the bear?'" Nori snapped. "What kind of protection is that? I'd rather fend for myself in the tunnel."

"No." Cooper grabbed her arm, but when she winced, relaxed just a little. "No, you wouldn't. Trust me."

"Well, there's the fundamental problem," she said. "I don't trust you. Why should I? Why should I go along with this whole plan? What makes you think selling me is an acceptable alternative to anything?"

"Whether you trust me or not, I saved you." His voice was low, serious. "Just like you saved me. Now we're even."

Cooper had gotten so close to Nori their noses nearly touched. She hadn't noticed before, but the center of his irises was a different color. She'd thought his eyes were an earthy green, but this close, the area just outside his pupil was a brilliant gold, like a ray of sun peeking past an eclipse.

"What were you doing in that alley, anyway?"

Nori's question caught him off guard, and he nearly answered her. "I was— None of your business. Just concentrate on making this work. Keep your head down and your mouth shut. Can you do that?"

She didn't answer, but did let him lead her the rest of the way.

Nori jerked in surprise when they passed through a set of double doors. "It's a fighting pit," she said.

"It's a fighting pit," Cooper repeated gravely. "Come on. I'll have to catch up to Sarge in a minute."

"But," Nori stammered, "what do they do here?"

Cooper cocked his head to the side. "Fight?"

"For money?"

He nodded.

"Whose money?"

"Gamblers', Hank's, the other owners'."

"But. You can't own people," Nori argued. "Slavery is illegal."

"Oh, honey," Cooper's voice dripped sarcasm. "Tell that to your new owner."

Nori stared at his face, blinking as seconds inched by.

Cooper squirmed under her scrutiny. "It's not like *slavery* slavery. More like indentured servitude." Nori's shocked gaze never left his face. "Okay," he said. "So we acquired something we knew Hank would find valuable. We sold it to him for a price. When you work off that money, and whatever Hank deems a fair return, he'll let you go."

"Indentured—acquired—fair return," Nori repeated, her brain-to-mouth synapses overheating and misfiring in her fury. "Are you people crazy?"

"No," Cooper said. "Just hard. It's tough down here. You're gonna have to adapt—and fast—if you want to make it past that sunscorch."

When Cooper peered down at her the sorrow in his gaze pissed Nori off. The look in his eyes said he found her so young, so naïve.

She straightened and clamped her jaw shut. She was not soft. Not naïve. She couldn't remember a single day she had lived without pain or discomfort, but she didn't complain if she could help it. It would've been so easy over the years to lie down and quit, to allow herself to fall into the misery that called to her unceasingly. It would've been so nice to wallow in pity and curse the world that had cursed her.

But she never had. She'd found a smile amid the misery for her parents. She'd muscled through the torment for herself; to work toward some kind of future, lonely and insignificant as it may be.

Tough? Yeah, she had more tough in her pinkie toe than someone like Cooper would ever see. He only saw the surface, a scarred and lonely girl out of her depths, and equated her kindness with naïvity. No. Her hands clenched to fists. She would make it past the sunscorch and get back aboveground to her parents, no matter what.

Unable to speak, Nori nodded and swallowed past the lump in her throat. She could do anything for a week. Even this.

"Listen," Cooper whispered, suddenly serious. "I have to get back to Sarge and the others. Hank's rough around the edges, but he has a good heart. Keep your head down, do what he says, and you can make it down here until you find a way back home."

"Find a way… " Nori trailed off as reality set in. "I don't know how to get back home. You brought me what, twenty miles to this place on your bike? There were so many turns. I don't —"

"More like fifty," Cooper said. "But your way home is not my problem. I paid my debt. I kept you out of Wallace's hands and brought you to a safe place. What you do next is on you."

81

"But…" Nori's eyes filled with tears as the weight of the world came to rest on her shoulders. "I can't do it alone, Cooper."

"I'm sorry." He closed his eyes before he whirled and left, heavy black boots stomping her heart as he stormed away.

14

BIG HANK

"Yep." Big Hank yanked at the back of his faded jeans with both hands. The waistline wasn't wide enough to fit over his considerable gut, but was too big for his narrow hips. The result was a constant flux, and Hank's perpetual yet fruitless attempts at tugging them up. "That Sam Cooper's one in a million."

"Sam?"

"Aw, now. Don't cry, darlin'. No sense in gettin' mixed up with one like him. He doesn't stay still for long."

"What?" Nori said, looking up at the big man in confusion. "I don't— I'm not—"

Hank's shoulders were wide as a door frame. The sleeves of his t-shirt had been cut off, so she had a clear view of arms as big around as her waist. His cheeks were ruddy, like his temperature always ran at overheated, and his short, graying hair may once have been black. But Hank's eyes were the thing Nori lingered on the longest. Despite the man's imposing stature and what she'd seen of his gruff nature, his eyes were kind.

"I'll make sure you're all right. Don't worry." He leaned toward her, towering over her. "You're going to have to work, though. No free rides around here."

"I'm not staying long," she said, lifting her chin.

"Is that so?" While his eyes danced with amusement, there were faint traces of something else behind them. Something darker.

"Mm. Hmm." She couldn't force actual words out, hard as she tried.

"We'll see," was all he said.

"Wh-what will I do?" Nori stammered. "While I'm here?"

"You got any particular skills you'd like me to take into account?"

She scoured her brain for an answer. What could she do that would be useful down here? She doubted they had much need of someone who excelled in the application of sunscreen. What use did she have in this gritty, dark world?

"I can draw," she said with a shrug. At Hanks snarl, she hastily added, "and I'm fast." She pointed to her muscular thighs. "Strong legs."

He shook his head, his mouth retaining some of the snarl. "You'll do, I guess. Just so happens I'm in need of a handler. No skills required you can't learn. Come on. I'll show you to your room."

Nori nodded and followed him past the blood-stained fighting ring and into the shadowed halls beyond.

While the buildings and streets of Trogtown had been constructed from an enormous natural chamber, the area Hank led her toward was nothing more than a primitive tunnel carved into the earth. At the entrance of the dark hallway, a trickle of water slid down the wall, forming a slick layer of brown-green algae.

Just inside the hallway, Hank motioned to a door on the right. "This is where you can find me." He led her farther into the narrow hall and dug in his pocket to find a metal ring heavy with keys. "And this is where you'll stay." He took a single key from the ring and handed it to her. "Get settled in then go lookin' for Kade. His room's around the corner on the left, but I imagine he'll be in the weight room. I'll tell him to expect ya."

"Thank you." The words were a question more than a statement as she looked from the man to the door, her gaze sliding in the direction she'd come, to the way out.

Big Hank's eyes shot from kind to keen in a heartbeat. "You, ah, you think about boltin', you should know me and my friends are excellent hunters. This is a business, you understand. I'll not have defectors." With a final nod, Hank turned and left, mumbling something about a gorge being the sole exception.

Pocketing the key, Nori pushed open the metal door. The ominous creak when she swung it wide was a suitable soundtrack for what was inside. A thin mattress sank into a platform carved from the stone wall. The floor was that same gritty graphite color she found everywhere she turned. The floor, the walls, the ceiling. Cavern grunge was the backdrop of her new—temporary—life.

A worn rug lay on the floor by the bed, its dingy saffron and ochre the only colors breaking up the monotony of gray. Even the dark wool blanket tucked neatly beneath the mattress slowly faded into the walls. Nori ran a palm across the fabric and hissed. It was as rough as it looked. She plopped onto the bed, regretting the move immediately as her tender derriere hit the stone shelf just under the mattress. Nori searched the room for signs of life, but found none.

Either no one had occupied it in ages, or they'd been short-timers, too.

So, the room was bleak and cold and filthy, she thought. So, the only souls she knew in the subterranean hell had both abandoned her. So, she had no idea what Hank would do with her or who the ominous Kade was. She could survive anything for a week or so.

With a hand behind her head, she lay back on a stiff pillow and stared at the stone ceiling. Still for the first time in hours, or days, Nori's thoughts ran to her parents. How was her mother taking the separation? Surely her dad knew she was safe. He understood her, had always seen her strength. Her parents would be all right. Her dad would hold her mom together, and she'd offer him strength, too. They had each other, and that was good.

THE BOOM of a fist on metal sent Nori straight up in bed. In the haze of sleep, she couldn't put a finger on where she was. She blinked and took in her surroundings—the dingy room, the stiff wool blanket, the sore neck, and the sharp taste of blood on her busted lip. Awful memories fell into place like pieces of a grizzly puzzle. Parents gone. Alone. Narrow escape in the tunnel. Sleazeball bikers. Cooper. Big Hank, and the fighting pits, and Kade.

Kade. She was supposed to have found him, but fell asleep on the stone slab that was her new bed.

"Wh-who is it?" she asked.

"I am not in the mood today. Don't test me. Be out here ready to go in three minutes." The deep timbre of the man's voice sent chills up her spine and her heart rate into overdrive.

"Okay," Nori squeaked, though she suspected he'd already stormed away.

There was a small, broken mirror above a narrow chest. She risked a quick look at herself and jerked at the reflection. Her face and neck, even her hair, were covered in gray grime. She wiped her face with the tail of her shirt and hastily pulled her hair back with an elastic stashed in her pocket.

GUTTURAL GRUNTS and the clang of weights hitting the floor echoed through the narrow hall, which reeked of mildew and stale sweat. Nori followed the sounds to the fighting pit she'd passed on her way in with Cooper. Weights and training equipment were strewn around the ring.

When she emerged from the hall, she flinched as all eyes tore in her direction. Hardened, cruel eyes, most of them. After a few smirks and shrugged shoulders, the onlookers turned back to their tasks of annihilating punching bags and kicking sparring partners' gloved hands.

Nori snapped her jaws shut and stood tall, not wanting them to think her a gape-mouthed fool. With no idea where to find Kade, or what he even looked like, she eased into the room, touching weights and pretending to have some purpose. She hoped he wasn't the barrel-chested mouth-breather in the corner who adjusted himself as he looked her up and down.

"You my help?"

The proximity of the voice sent Nori skittering back toward the hallway. All she could see was a man's thick chest rising and falling as he bench-pressed a stack of weights.

"You scared me," she said.

With a groan, the man replaced the bar and sat up, his dark eyes already squinting to size her up. "Name's Kade," he said and stood.

Nori had thought Hank was big, but this guy... He thrust a fist in her direction, and she wasn't sure what to do with it. Finally, she slid her own hand inside his, her eyes widening at the difference between the two.

"Holy wow," she said as conscious thought struggled to catch up to her mouth. "You're enormous."

Kade shrugged, obviously less than impressed with her assessment.

"Ah, sorry." She stood straighter. "I'm Nori."

His eyes slid from her face to the nearby weight bench. "Want to spot me?"

She barked a laugh and he raised his eyebrows. He was serious. Okay, straight to work then. Nori cleared her throat and moved between the bench and rack of weights against the wall. As he lay back on the bench, she tested the bar in front of her. It was stacked with thick black weights at both ends. There was no way she could spot him, no way she could even lift the bar. She quickly added the numbers printed on each weight. Yep, heavier than she was.

"You can't be serious," she said.

Kade didn't look in her direction. He placed his hands under the bar, pressed up, retrieving it from its resting position, and began a series of reps that left Nori's mouth open and mind blown.

"You realize," she said after he'd slowly lowered and then thrust the bar up several times, "I can't lift that thing if it falls onto your neck. Best case scenario, I scream for help and someone arrives just after you've asphyxiated."

"Yeah." It was more a grunt than an actual word.

"Then why insist I spot you?"

Kade braced his arms, suspending the weight over his impossibly thick chest. "Best make yourself useful if you wanna stick around here. Or look like you're busy, anyway."

"Or?"

"If you can't cut it as my handler," he said, "there's always the Pit."

"What do you mean? You," Nori motioned at the muscle throughout the Pit, "you guys are the fighters."

"I'm the main attraction." He smirked. "Undercard bouts are a big draw, too, though. And the more blood the better."

"Oh, fighting is not my thing," she argued. "Look at me. I couldn't give a hemophiliac a bloody nose."

"I meant *your* blood. Freaks love to watch a slaughter. The weaker the lamb, the better."

Nori's stomach lurched at the thought of being forced into a ring to fight not for sport but for her life. She took in the people around her—wiry, vicious types with crooked noses and broken teeth. Then she spotted Hank leaning against a doorway, his eyes intent on her.

"Fifty-seven," she said after a thick swallow. "Fifty-eight, fifty-nine."

The creases at the edges of Kade's chestnut eyes grew deep as he smiled. "You're gonna do just fine."

"So, what exactly am I expected to do as your 'handler'?" Nori asked as Kade stood from the bench and spread his legs.

With practiced ease, he balanced on his front foot and rested the toes of his back foot on the weight bench. He began a set of one-legged squats that made Nori tired. His quads strained and thickened, but he focused straight ahead.

"You'll be in charge of scheduling and nutrition, opponent

research, things like that. In time, you'll help with focus and consistency. Maybe even strategy."

"But, I don't know the first thing about training or fighting. Why would he assign me to you?" Nori scowled. "I heard your last handler...left. Why?"

Like a storm front blowing in, Kade's eyes clouded, and he looked away. "That's enough for today." Without another word, he strode toward the locker room, his back and shoulders stiff, his movements forced.

Nori stared after him. Should she follow? Apologize?

"Plenty to do around here." Hank said around the toothpick in his mouth. He'd materialized from nowhere. "You're in charge of laundry, so best head down and get started." He pointed toward the hallway. "You'll find it. And when you're done with that, you're to clean the locker room."

"So handler means maid, too?"

Hank's eyes sharpened, pinning Nori with a look that said she'd better tread lightly. "If you want to eat, want a place to sleep, it does." He threw the soggy toothpick on the floor. "I can always send ya back to Sarge. He wasn't too keen to get rid of you in the first place, seemed to me."

He took a step closer, a challenge. "You want to go back to Sarge?" Nori raised her chin, but didn't answer. "That's what I thought. You wanna stay here, you wanna eat? Earn your keep."

One breath at a time. One step at a time. One day at a time. She could do this. She could do anything for a week or so.

15

THE PIT

Nori had been certain she would never smell anything worse than the filthy bodies and sweat-saturated weight room and fighting pit. She'd been wrong. The laundry room was stacked halfway to the ceiling with used towels and filthy workout gear. She gagged, her eyes watering at the foul stench, and pulled her shirt over her nose. Breathing through her mouth, she located the washing machine. Another gag. She needed hazmat gloves to touch some of the stuff. Unfortunately, there weren't gloves of any sort in sight.

With two fingers, she picked up stiff t-shirts and towels, tossing them into the mouth of the washer before they stayed in contact with her skin too long—as if she hadn't already contracted some kind of foul man-fungus just by looking at them. She kicked the washer door shut and added three-times the recommended amount of detergent, and a dash of bleach for good measure.

With one last shiver of disgust, Nori wiped her hands on her jeans and went in a reluctant search for the locker rooms.

There was only one. She supposed it was unisex, not that it mattered. She hadn't seen another woman.

"Hello," she called out. The word echoed through the unforgiving space, but no one answered.

The cinder block walls supported a few rusty hooks with worn wooden benches propped beneath them. She hefted a basket of used towels she found outside the showers, preparing to haul the load to the laundry. But then she spotted another towel on the shower room floor. With an irritated huff, she snatched the towel from the floor and threw it into the hamper.

Movement in the corner of her eye drew her attention, and she realized with horror that someone was in the shower. She straightened and prepared to hightail it from the room before she was noticed, but she heard the unmistakable intake of a tortured breath. A sob.

Quietly as she could, she toed toward the sound, overactive empathy replacing good sense. In that moment, nudity wasn't a concern. She wasn't scandalized or ashamed. Someone was hurting. Shouldn't she help? Wasn't it her duty? As Nori raised her hand to knock on the shower door, her thoughts flew to her own times of weakness, to those stolen moments alone when she stopped pretending for her parents.

Sometimes, when the pain or the pressure became too much, she would back into the wall in her room and slide to the floor, knees balled to her chest. She'd let the tears flow, releasing the unwelcome weight of self-pity. She allowed the tension of a perpetual attempt at perfection to leave her body, and after a good, long cry, she could breathe again. Her tears, and the release of her emotions, bathed her soul. She would emerge cleansed, restored.

Maybe this person needed a good cry, too. Nori shoved her half-raised hand into the pocket of her jacket. She turned away, but not before realizing it was Kade who held his head in his hands behind the frosted glass door.

Nori's soul-sick heart recognized another. It wasn't sadness he felt. It was loss.

DINNER WAS a soupy concoction of sweet potatoes, lentils, and kale served in a metal bowl. Not half bad, though she hadn't had a hot meal in a while. Well, hot may've been a stretch. It was warmish.

"Olio again?" Muscles flexed almost grotesquely beneath the shirt of a guy taking the seat across from her.

Most of the staff and fighters had already eaten before Nori finished her chores, so the small cafeteria was quiet.

"I think it's good." Nori shrugged and took another bite, struggling not to stare at the man's bruised and angry eye. It was deep purple, and swollen completely shut.

"That's because you just got here," he said. "Trust me, this time next week, you'll already be sick of it. But it's sustenance, I guess. Last place I lived, we survived on okra and protein pellets, I swear to God." His sandy hair was cropped close to his head, military style. Initially, Nori would've guessed he was about her age, but his scarred and haunted face hinted at a hard life impossible in such a few short years.

"Oh, I won't be here this time next week," Nori said, lifting her hands.

The newcomer raised his eyebrows, his mouth twisting into a doubtful smirk. "Is that right?"

"Yes. I'm just waiting out—" Nori closed her mouth. Probably better to keep her business to herself. "I'm just here temporarily."

"I'm Diesel."

"Nori," she said and stuck out her hand. "You one of the fighters?"

"Naw," he said, the smirk resurfacing. "I'm *the* fighter."

"That's not what your face says." Diesel's one good eye narrowed, and Nori flashed him a smile. "Why do they call you Diesel, anyway?"

With a puffed chest that would've made a rooster wither in shame, Diesel said smoothly, "Cause I'm efficient and reliable."

Nori worked not to laugh. He obviously took himself—and this fighting thing—very seriously. "Okra and protein pellets, huh? I heard people used to eat corn and watermelon. That you could pick apples and peaches from trees. There were so many they fell to the ground and rotted."

Diesel swallowed a spoonful of soup. "I call B.S."

"I swear." She grinned at him. "My dad said they ate meat at every meal, too."

"Now I know you're full of shit," he said and Nori shrugged good-naturedly. "Your dad still alive?" She nodded. "Your people aren't from Trogtown, are they?"

Nori looked up at him and searched the one good eye, which gleamed under the room's constantly flickering overheads. "No. I-I was raised aboveground."

Diesel's mouth fell open.

She wasn't sure why she'd told him. Maybe it was because his harrowed face was full of such hopelessness, such torture. There was a light deep inside him, but it was desperately close to blinking out. Her stomach soured. Could her admission cause her trouble? She was new to everything about this subterranean world. Did they hate outsiders, people from aboveground like her? Would they use it as some sort of leverage?

"I'm just kidding," she said in a rush. "I was born...north of here."

"Oh, I don't think you were kidding." Diesel shook his head, his good eye trained on hers. "Not at all."

"I was," she protested.

"Yeah?"

"Mm hmm," she said and picked at the sleeve of her shirt.

"Where were you before you came here?" Diesel thrummed long, slender fingers on the top of the table.

She hadn't heard the name of a single place besides Trogtown. Hadn't known there were other places like it. Her ignorance could get her in a lot of trouble.

"I came here," she said with feigned toughness, "to eat dinner in peace, and you made yourself at home at my table. You want to keep up this line of questioning, this interrogation, you can just find somewhere else to sit."

She took a long draw from the cup of water she'd gotten with dinner. When it hit her tongue, it took every ounce of self-control she possessed not to spit it at Diesel's feet. It tasted stale, chemical. If she hadn't known she'd been purchased, and that she was valuable, she would've sworn someone was trying to poison her. Nori closed her eyes and forced the liquid down.

When she opened her eyes again, Diesel was staring at her.

"What?"

He shook his head. "Nothin'."

"Since you've got so many questions," she said, "how about some answers. Where were you born?"

Diesel folded his arms across his chest and leaned back. "Eaton."

"Eaton," Nori repeated. "Oh."

"Know where that is?"

Her nostrils flared in irritation. He had her. If she said yes, he'd undoubtedly ask her to prove it. If she said no, she'd give herself away.

She changed the subject instead. "Hey, you know what might be wrong with Kade? Or is he always this moody?"

Diesel unfolded his arms and leaned toward her conspiratorially. "You didn't hear?"

"Not everything."

"His handler jumped into the gorge the other day just before dawn. Climbed over the rail and threw himself in."

"Oh." Nori put a hand to her mouth. "My God."

"Yeah?" Diesel barked a laugh, but it held no humor. "Where's he been?"

"Who? God?"

He pursed his lips and nodded, but Nori went on.

"Did they— Did they find his body?"

"Huh-uh. Washed down the stream, they say. But nobody could've survived that fall."

"Jesus," Nori breathed.

"Haven't seen hide nor hair of him, either. Not in this hellhole."

"You're awfully cynical."

"Oh, and what does someone like me—or you, for that matter—have to believe in? I was born near here. I don't even remember my parents. Hank's isn't my first gig, but it's by far the best, and you know why?"

Nori shook her head and didn't say another thing, afraid to send him over the edge he was so obviously balancing.

"Because I'm a fighter. I've fought my whole life. And I'm finally big enough to do some damage. I'm not fighting for my innocence or safety anymore. I'm not fighting to survive. I'm fighting to earn my freedom, and I'll win it, too, just you watch."

Nori sat silent, stunned by the serious turn of their conversation, by the passion, the desperation behind his words.

"You know why they call me Diesel?" he asked after a while.

"Be-because you're efficient and reliable?"

"No." His mouth twisted sardonically. "Because I'm quick to ignite with a slow and deadly burn."

Nori didn't doubt that for a moment.

Diesel didn't leave the table, but he didn't speak again. Though his gaze was focused straight ahead, his thoughts had gone somewhere else entirely.

16

A HAMMOCK, A FRIEND

Nori mumbled an awkward goodnight some minutes later and left the table, though Diesel didn't.

There'd been no sign of Kade since the shower incident. Probably best. She wasn't sure what she would've said. Maybe nothing. Or maybe she would've vomited an admission of overhearing his emotional breakdown. Yeah, definitely best she hadn't seen him.

From a pile of clean laundry, Nori snagged a set of the smallest workout clothes available. The worn gray sweatpants had a drawstring, at least, and she could tie the front of the gigantic t-shirt. A storeroom held a few necessities like toothbrushes and soap, and she snagged those, too, before using the shower herself.

It was hard to be happy about her cold room and thin mattress, but at least she might get a full night's sleep. And there was a deadbolt on the door. Just as she climbed into bed, wincing from the lingering aches of her encounters with Sarge, there was a knock at her door.

"Yes?"

"It's Kade. I thought—"

Nori was up and opening the door before he finished. He smiled nervously and held up a stack of pillows and linens. "I remember my first night," he said. "Thought I could teach you a couple tricks."

Stunned by his gesture, she backed from the doorway and held the door wide.

"You don't want to sleep there," he said, tossing the folded stack onto the bed. "Kills your back."

"It sucks, sure," Nori said. "But it's better than the floor."

"Not the floor. Just wait."

Kade twisted two huge silver hooks into the earthen walls, growling and pressing through his back and shoulders at times.

"Sheet," he called, and she handed him the top one. "Now, tie a knot in your end of the sheet then tie this rope around the knot."

She did as instructed, and when they finished, a hammock hung in the back corner of her small room. Nori looked from Kade to the hammock with a goofy, eager grin.

"Well, you gonna try it out or not?" he asked, hands on his hips.

The hard bed made a good stool to reach the new hammock, and Nori pulled open the linens and fell back into their cocooning warmth.

"I love it," she said, popping her head over the side. "Thank you."

Kade looked at the floor and mumbled, "No problem." He handed the pillow and blanket to a still-grinning Nori. "Better lock this door after I leave," he said, backing out of the room. "See you tomorrow."

"Bye. And thanks again." Nori hopped from the hammock

and deadbolted the door before climbing back into her new perch. Stuffing the pillow into one end and pulling a much softer blanket up to her chin, she thought maybe, just maybe, she might make a friend.

"HEY, NORA, WAIT UP." Diesel jogged through the hall to catch up to her as she headed for the locker room and morning necessities.

"It's Nori."

"Yeah. Nori. What happened last night? One minute we were talking, and then you just left."

"Ah, no," she said. "One minute we were talking, and then you zoned out. I said bye, but you didn't hear me."

Diesel focused his good eye on the floor. The other one, the shiner, was a lighter purple, almost violet with green around the edges. Pretty. He chewed at his lip for a moment before he said, "I do that. Sorry."

"No big." Nori shrugged, and as they approached the locker room, he showed no signs of stopping. She really hoped he didn't follow her into the toilets.

"Catch you later then," he said, and trotted toward the Pit.

"So," Nori asked Kade when she found him in the weight area. "Whatcha got going on today? Need me to spot that bench again?"

Kade smiled, but it didn't reach his eyes. His shoulders were slumped and he took a deep breath and closed his eyes. A fight for control was obvious in the tight set of his mouth.

"He was your friend, too, wasn't he?" Nori took a step closer, but didn't touch the big man.

"Yes," he croaked then cleared his throat. "More than just my handler."

"I'm so sorry." There was nothing else she could say, really. Nothing could curb the pain of such a fresh, raw loss. When she was down, nothing made her feel better except—

"You know what," she said. "How about some cardio today? Let's go for a run."

Kade looked up at her, his eyes narrowing. "Oh, I don't think Hank would like that. He wouldn't want you leaving. Not yet."

"Well, I don't see Hank around anywhere. Do you?"

A sly grin eased across Kade's pained face, and he shook his head.

"You know," Kade said as he ran, "I'll have to chase you if you take off, right?"

Nori nodded, but didn't face him. "What makes you stay?" she asked. "You obviously don't need Hank's protection. Don't you want to get out of here?"

"And go where?"

She shrugged because she honestly didn't know. "Doesn't it bother you to know someone else considers themselves your owner?"

"I've worked off my debt. Hank doesn't own me anymore."

"What? Really?"

Kade nodded.

"Then why do you stay?"

"Hank's honest. I make a good living fighting. Besides," his voice cracked, "Grant was here."

Nori nodded, but didn't say anything else. The two ran together in companionable silence, the sounds of their competing breaths and footfalls their only communication.

Outside the Pit, Nori took in the details of Trogtown she'd been too overwhelmed to notice when she arrived. The man-made columns tucked beside the stalactites, she thought, were some sort of pipelines.

"What are those?" she asked Kade.

"Exhausts, for the air and geothermal systems."

"No kidding. Geothermal, like, from Earth's core?"

"It's a very efficient system," he said, nodding. "They use geothermal energy to create electricity." He pointed toward the extensive overhead lighting. "And the leftover superheated steam for heating. It would be freezing down here without it." Nori recalled her time in the tunnel, where the temperature had steadily dropped as she descended. "The rest of the water we filter and use for greenhouses and such."

"I had no idea," Nori said, fascinated by the high-tech way these people lived. "Have you always lived underground?"

"Of course." He shot her an incredulous look. "Hasn't everyone?"

Nori nodded and shrugged noncommittally, hating herself a little for the untruth. "Such a shame about the surface."

"Mmm. I would've liked to see the wild west. Uninhabitable now, of course."

"The surface of Earth," Nori said in a tone that could've been both a question and a confirmation of Kade's statements.

"Yep."

Nori shook her head and bit her tongue. She didn't know enough about this new world yet. She wouldn't rock the boat until she could navigate her own course.

She had a million questions, and Kade seemed like a pretty smart guy. But as they ran past a ramshackle hardware store filled with men, the question that weighed most heavily on her mind was, "Where are all the women?"

"Hmm?"

"I'm new here, you know, and where I come from there are more women."

"Really? I don't know. Everywhere I've lived was about like this. Mostly men. Some women."

"Are there any in Trogtown?"

Kade laughed. "Women? Sure, a few. Not many. Not young, and not often pretty." He gave her a meaningful glance.

She blushed a bit at the compliment. "Oh. Ah, I haven't seen any."

"Don't be ridiculous. Look, there's one. That's Peg."

Nori followed Kade's gaze toward someone throwing a bag of trash into a dumpster. The person wore dark pants, a shapeless, dirty gray sweatshirt, and military-style boots. When she turned from the dumpster toward them, Nori noticed a bulge across her chest, where breasts would be. Okay, so she'd seen her first Trogtown woman. Made sense. Life was hard in the subterranean world. She supposed neither effort nor expenses could be spared for the trappings of femininity. To survive here, women had to be tough, and there was no way around the filth. Clothes had to be practical, and Nori had already learned the hard way that hair was a nightmare in the damp underground.

Peg saw them running and lifted her head in acknowledgment. They nodded back.

"Have many girls lived at the Pit?" she asked.

"What, our pit?"

Nori nodded.

"No. It's no place for women."

At her sardonic look, he said, "Well, besides you. Obviously."

"Obviously. So, Hank's never had a girl there before me?"

Kade shook his head.

"Why do you think that is?" she asked.

"Cause it's no place for a woman."

As she and Kade jogged breathlessly back into the Pit, Nori caught sight of Hank. Whether his deflating chest was from releasing a furious breath or one of relief she couldn't be sure. Maybe both.

"Don't forget your chores," Hank growled as she passed.

"Oh, like that's even possible," she grumbled and headed for the waiting mountain of laundry.

Nori entered the locker room with a stack of clean towels. "Hello," she called once, twice, three times. No one answered. She called directly into the showers, just to be extra sure. Lesson learned. After depositing the towels on the wooden shelf, Nori turned toward the door. Diesel stood in the doorway.

"Oh! I didn't hear you come in." Nori moved to leave, but he blocked the exit.

"You need any help?" he asked.

"Nope. Just finished up."

"Good. We have a little time to talk. Get to know each other." Diesel's gaze was intent on hers, as if he were attempting mind control. "I've never seen eyes as blue as yours," he said. "So pretty."

Nori's stomach seized. If this was Diesel's attempt at seduction, she wasn't interested.

"Thanks," she said and tried to slip behind him and through the door.

He grabbed her arm, and she sucked in a frightened breath. Her heart slammed against her chest as Diesel stalked toward her, and she backed up to the wall, raising her arm to loosen it from his grip.

"I've really got to go," she said, trying to seem calm when inside she was anything but. "Kade will come looking if I'm late."

At the mention of Kade, Diesel's good eye regained its focus. He looked at her for far too long before backing away to let her pass.

"See you at dinner," he called after her, but she was already halfway down the hall.

Nori found Kade back on the weight room floor. He was deadlifting this time, chest out and knees bent as he hefted the weighted bar up to his middle.

"Hey," she said, her voice shaky.

"What's wrong?" Kade replaced the weight bar and scanned the room before turning his attention back to her.

"Nothing." She aimed for nonchalance, but failed.

Kade stepped closer. "Something happened. You're shaking."

Nori finally looked up at him. "You think…you think you could teach me to fight?" At his questioning look, she quickly added, "Not *fight* fight. Just some self-defense moves."

Without another word, Kade looked slowly around the Pit, stretching his massive muscles as he met the eyes of the other fighters. "Somebody messing with you?"

"No. No. It's just... Well, I don't know the first thing about it if I ever needed to defend myself."

"Yeah," he said, his scowl proving he didn't entirely believe her. "I could show you a few things."

"Good." Nori closed her eyes and focused on a future in which she wasn't always a victim. Toughen up, and fast, Cooper and Barker had both said. She was trying.

17

SELF DEFENSE & SPARRING

"Okay, so." Kade faced Nori on the weight room floor. "The first thing you need to remember is to inflict as much damage as you can, as fast as you can. You may only have a few seconds, so make 'em count."

"How?" Nori spread her legs, prepared for her first lesson in self-defense.

"Your best bet is the knee. It's vulnerable from any angle, whether your attacker is in front of you or behind. And you can kick it without risking him grabbing your foot."

"Okay." She nodded, committing the information to memory. "What else?"

"If he's close in front of you, you could poke his eyes with your fingers or knuckles, you could scratch his face with your nails, or you could hit him in the nose with this part of your hand. Like this." Kade closed in on her, pushing the heel of his hand upward toward her nose. "Those are just some basic moves. The important thing for someone your size is to throw your weight behind whatever you do."

"What do you mean?"

"Well, you're not very strong." At Nori's injured look, he amended, "I mean, you don't have a lot of muscle mass. Or height."

"Okay, I get it. I'm a tiny weakling."

Kade gave her a side-eye, but went on. "Look, when you hit someone, when you kick them, use the force of your body to get the most effect. If you just stood and punched a guy, he'd probably laugh at you. But if you step into it, and throw the entire force of your body into a forearm to the throat or whatever, you'll incapacitate him long enough to run away."

"Can we practice?" she asked.

"We'll work on it a little bit every day, until you're confident. And you know what else?"

"What?"

"I really think you should start weight training with me."

"Seriously? You know I can barely lift the bar."

"Okay, so we start light. Everybody starts somewhere."

He was serious. "All right," she said. "I've got to get tougher fast. Stronger wouldn't hurt, either."

"Good girl," he said, and for once she *felt* good. "Hey, Nori?"

"Yeah?"

"Thanks for today."

He was thanking her for the distraction, but he'd distracted her, too. She shrugged and looked away, but couldn't help the smile that tugged at her mouth.

"You wanna eat?" Nori asked.

Kade's mood had taken a turn for the worse once they finished their workout. Exercise produced endorphins, after all, which made you feel good for a while. And like any chemical alteration, what goes up must come down. Kade was coming down hard. He was headed for the locker room, probably so he could let his guard down.

He shook his head. "You go ahead."

It was late again, but Nori had a sneaking suspicion Diesel would wait for her. "Nah. I'm tired. Think I'll just grab something and take it to my room."

Kade's head hung between his shoulders as he shuffled away, and Nori felt helpless. She hated seeing him so miserable, but sometimes there was nothing to ease loss except the passage of time.

As NORI MADE her way past Hank's office toward the Pit the next morning, he hollered from his desk, "Hey. Girl. See if you can round up Kade, will ya?" He mumbled something else about lazy kids and generational decay, but she didn't catch all of it.

Two fighters she'd seen but not yet met passed her in the narrow hall. "Hey," she asked them. "You guys seen Kade this morning?"

They shook their heads, but didn't stop.

He wasn't in the locker room or the showers. Wasn't in the Pit.

Nori checked his room, knocking gently at first then harder when there was no answer.

"Go away," Kade said from inside.

Her voice softened. "Are you okay?" She hadn't known him long, but it didn't seem like him to hide out in his room.

A pause, then, "No."

"Are you ill?"

"No."

"Are you—are you training today?"

"No," he said more forcefully. "Go away."

"Kade. You can't hole up in there all day."

"I sure as hell can. I'm taking the day off."

"But, Hank says we've got a fight this Saturday and you need to be ready."

"I'll be ready," he said through the door. "I'm always ready."

"But…" Nori's argument sputtered and lost its steam. "Okay," she finally said.

The rest of the day passed without incident. There were people milling about the Pit, readying for the upcoming fights. She thought to practice with weights while Kade wasn't there to stand over her. Completely inexperienced with all of it, she inspected and lifted the free weights, working her way to the various machines and discovering how to adjust them to fit her. It gave her confidence, and she was actually looking forward to training.

Later, Nori found herself outside the fighting ring watching two men spar. She'd never seen such a disgusting display of violence in her life. She couldn't take her eyes off it.

The two men she'd met in the hall earlier circled each other, shuffling their feet to stay balanced and agile. When the redhead—Bron, she thought his name was—swung, the other guy, Peyton, pivoted just in time to dodge the blow. They traded a few more misses, and a few punches, before someone called the match, and they headed toward the water station together.

"Think you'll ever get in there?" The voice was too close behind her, and she jumped.

"Please stop sneaking up on me like that."

Diesel waved away her concerns. She was really beginning to dislike him. "Would you?"

"Would I what?" she repeated irritably.

"Get in the ring? Spar."

She secretly did want to, but no way was she sharing that with Diesel. Instead, she shook her head and peered around the room for an excuse to escape him.

"I missed you at dinner." Diesel's penetrating gaze locked on her face, sending icy tendrils down her back.

Nori shivered, then cleared her throat while she thought of something to say. "Ah. I'd, ah, better get back to the laundry before Hank catches me." She'd already turned to bolt before finishing the sentence.

"Next time, I'll make you dinner," he called after her, but she pretended not to hear.

It was close to meal time, so Nori took food to Kade, knocking on the door to let him know it was there.

"Leave it outside," he said from behind the door.

She left it right beside the lunch she'd brought earlier. The one that sat untouched.

"Goodnight." She put her hand on the door, sending little mental waves of support toward him. "Hope it's better in the morning."

"INHALE, RELEASE," Kade told her as she hefted the weight. "Exhale, flex. Right. That's it."

When Nori thought about it, the ironic change in their roles was hilarious. She'd been brought on partly to help Kade with his weight training, yet here he was, teaching her the intricacies of lifting dumbbells. They'd searched the store room for weights light enough for her, and as if that wasn't humiliating enough, her muscles tired pitifully fast and she couldn't get through a single set.

Kade had shown up for training as if the day before never happened. He made no mention of spending the day locked in his room like a 300-pound Rapunzel, and neither did she.

"Hank says you're sparring Diesel today." When Kade didn't respond, she said, "Careful not to give him a shiner like the last guy. Still needs one operational eye."

"Who do you think gave him the last one?" Kade asked.

"No." Nori's mouth twitched with the effort of not smiling.

"Oh, yeah. He runs his smart mouth the whole time he fights. I admit I lost my cool."

"So you popped him in the eye?"

"He was too busy talking smack to defend himself."

She couldn't help the grin that took over her face. "Wish I'd seen that."

"He talks trash today, I'll give you a replay."

Nori snorted a laugh, and Kade followed suit. Their laughter drew looks from the few fighters still using the weights, which made it that much harder to stop.

———

"COME ON, Kade, shut his smart mouth!" Nori pounded the floor of the ring with the palm of her hand.

Diesel was putting up a better fight than she'd thought he would. He wasn't as tall as Kade, which meant his reach was shorter, too. They wouldn't fight in the same weight classes on Saturday, but sparring was a different story. They were both good fighters. What Diesel lacked in stature, he made up for in speed and agility. He didn't land many hits on Kade, but he dodged two or three punches that would've sent him to the floor.

Nori couldn't hear everything Diesel said as he danced around her friend, but his snide mouth was moving. Kade said it was par for the course that some fighters goaded their opponents to throw them off their game. Diesel seemed particularly skilled in the tactic.

Backing into the ropes not far from the corner she occupied, Diesel spouted insults even as he took a punch to the gut. Kade's face, though, showed no reaction, as if he heard nothing Diesel said. Nori suspected he was playing with the smaller man, that he could end the fight any time he wanted to. He was probably getting at least some pleasure from popping Diesel in the mouth every time he got a chance. Or, maybe he was just holding out until he could dot Diesel's other eye.

After that last gut punch, though, Diesel's features changed. His eyes shone with a determined glint, and the malicious sneer Nori had seen before resurfaced. The fighters came close to her corner again, and she could catch bits and pieces of Diesel's vicious monologue.

"...boyfriend...gorge...rather than...fag."

Nori gasped, her heart pounding with dread and fury. She'd heard enough to piece together Diesel's intent. She looked up at Kade's face, which had morphed into a mask of rage. And pain.

His growl was so fierce Nori backed away from the ring. He swung at Diesel with the full force of his body, landing a hook that sent the shorter man straight to the mat. Out cold.

Without a word or a look in her direction, Kade ducked through the ropes and stomped toward the tunneled hallway.

"Goddangit, Kade!" Hank, who'd been silently observing

the fight, jumped into the ring and checked Diesel's pulse. "Stupid, son. That was just stupid," he said to Diesel's unconscious form. "Are you trying to get yourself killed?"

Nori's voice was reed-thin when she asked, "Is he— Is he okay?"

"Not dead, but he won't be fightin' Saturday. Cost me a fight." Hank went on to curse Kade's temper and Diesel's smart mouth with words that would've made a sailor blush with shame.

Nori went in search of Kade, but didn't find him in the locker room or showers. She left him to the privacy of his room after letting him know Diesel would be all right.

18

ALONE IN TOWN

"Girl!" Hank's deep voice rumbled through the hall and found Nori in the laundry.

She slammed the door to the dryer on her way to his office. Maybe office was too strong a word. There was a desk. And a chair. There were stacks of papers in the underworld's most disheveled filing system. Boxing gloves and other equipment in need of repair littered every spare surface of the room.

Nori stood just inside the door, afraid to touch anything, afraid to move in case she caused an avalanche of junk.

"There you are," Hank said around his toothpick. "I need you," he looked up and into her gaze, obviously doubting the intelligence of his plan, "to go to the square and find Doc Moore."

Nori started at his request, at the fact he was trusting her to leave the Pit by herself.

"Diesel's talking nonsense, and I think he's got a concussion. I need to get him checked out by the doc to make sure he doesn't die on me."

"Okay," Nori said, and swallowed.

Hank mumbled something else about the money Kade was costing him, and looked up with a frown. "You goin' or not?"

"Yes. Yes, sir." Nori hotfooted it from the office and left the safety and confinement of the Pit in search of Doc Moore, though she didn't have the first idea who he was or where to find him.

About two minutes outside the Pit, Nori began to question Hank's rationale in choosing her for the errand. Everyone she passed stared at her, and not because she was new in town. She didn't look the part, didn't fit in. Not at all. The citizens of Trogtown apparently had an agreement with grime. It could stick around on their clothes, their skin, in their hair. In turn, they would make more of it by throwing their food and trash on the ground. No wonder the whole town stank. The spitting was a nice touch, she thought. Very attractive.

With a disgusted shiver that started at the back of her neck and went all the way down to her toes, Nori marched onward, head held high. Maybe if she looked determined, no one would bother her.

That hope was short-lived.

"'ey." A man in his forties in old military fatigues waved his arm at her as she passed. "Come 'ere for a minute." Nori picked up her pace. "I haven't seen you. You up from the farm?" She ignored him and kept walking, facing straight ahead. "Rude ones, them farmers," he mumbled after her. "Think they're better'n e'rbody."

Nori recognized a face at the end of the narrow street. Peg. She approached the sturdy woman, finally letting her guard down a little. "Hi. I'm Nori. I saw you the other day when we were running." At the woman's blank look, she added, "I was with Kade."

No response.

"Anyway," Nori went on, "I'm looking for Doc Moore. You know where I can find him?"

Peg's gaze slipped to a window on the second story of a nearby building.

"He's there? Upstairs?"

Peg nodded just once.

"Thanks for your help," Nori gushed. When the woman didn't respond, Nori gave an awkward wave and left.

The base of the building held a general store. The door was propped open, revealing stacks of batteries, lanterns, food packs, canteens--a hundred little survival essentials.

"Can I help you?" someone said.

Nori realized with a start she'd been staring. "Er. Sorry. Looking for Doc Moore."

The man raised his chin toward a set of stairs at the back of the store. "Second floor, second right."

Nori filed the supplies away for future reference, like the maps and notes she'd stashed in her room. In case the day came when she had to escape Trogtown. Waiting out the sunscorch at Hank's Pit wasn't too bad. She had food and a safe place to sleep. She'd made a friend, and was learning new skills. Like an underground survival camp, really. And she hadn't felt this good—this healthy—maybe ever. Maybe she and her parents could live at least part time underground instead of migrating to the 25th Parallel. It had become impossible anyway.

As Nori trudged up the stairs to Doc Moore, she wondered why some people had never followed safety recommendations and migrated to the 25th Parallel. Loyalty to their homes and homelands? Inability to let go? Maybe something much simpler: to keep away from the crowds. Despite billions dying in the first sunscorch, what was left of the world's population migrating to such a thin strip of the globe caused serious overcrowding.

As she stood with her hand raised, ready to knock on Doc Moore's door, Nori shook her head at the insane turn her life had taken.

"Enter," a thin voice called from inside.

"Ah, hello," she said and pushed open the door. "Hank sent me. Diesel's been knocked out cold and he's worried. Asked if you'd come check him out."

The old man had to be in his eighties. What little hair he had was white and baby-fine. He looked up at her from behind his desk, and his spectacles, his wrinkled brow forming creases on top of creases. "And who might you be?"

"Nori. Hi. I'm new." She smiled and stepped inside. She'd always loved older people, though she didn't know many. Most weren't healthy enough to survive the harsh conditions, but she considered the few she'd known to be precious, fleeting resources.

If he was as old as she thought, that meant...that meant he may have lived on the surface before the first scorch hit. She had no way of knowing how long the subterranean world had existed, how long Trogtown had been a town. Had these people been down here for generations, preparing for the apocalypse?

"New is an understatement, I'd say." The old man slowly stood from his chair and reached for a worn brown fedora lying on his desk.

She couldn't help it. She giggled at the sight of a man wearing a brimmed hat in the underground world.

Doc Moore's head whipped faster in her direction than she'd have thought possible. He caught her eyes dancing. "Old habits die hard," he said with a wink.

19

JANIE AND THE LAKE

"**B**oy'll be fine," Doc Moore said and clapped Hank on the back. "Rest. No fighting for at least two weeks to let the concussion heal. I'd say he should steer clear of ever fighting again, considering the head injuries he's suffered, but you people never listen."

"Thanks, Doc." Hank ignored the dig.

The old man's face softened. "How's Janie today?"

Hank's gaze shot to Nori, his mouth pressing into a thin line. She took the hint and backed silently from the room.

"Who's Janie?"

Nori was forced to talk to some of the other fighters since Kade and Diesel were both out of commission. She obviously couldn't ask Hank.

"Hank's wife," Bron grunted as he spun a jump rope so fast he made a full-body halo.

"I didn't know Hank had a wife," she blurted then said, quieter, "When did Hank get a wife?"

"Always had one, I guess."

"I mean, how come I haven't seen her around here?"

"Hates the violence."

Nori watched his face to confirm he wasn't kidding, and shook her head at the irony. A tender-hearted woman married to the town's pit boss.

"Has she been sick?"

A line of sweat ran from Bron's smooth temple to the top of his copper beard. "She's got the deficiency."

"Oh." Then, "What's that?"

Bron stopped jumping, the rope limp but the handle still firmly in his grip. He cocked his head at Nori, studying her as he would've a mushroom sprouting unexpectedly from the damp earth.

"Maybe it's called something different where I'm from," she added hastily.

He squinted so hard his blue eyes were barely visible when he said, "Not enough vitamin D. Depressed. Doesn't get around well cause her bones are brittle."

"Right." Nori nodded. "Well. Doesn't she take vitamins or supplements or something?"

"Hank can afford them, sure. But her body can't process 'em right, is what I heard."

"How sad." Nori knew too well the mental anguish that came with physical restrictions.

Bron nodded and took up his rope again, and she left to finish her chores.

"KADE," Nori yelled as she banged on the cold metal door. "Kade, get out here."

Not a single sound escaped the room. Probably holding his breath.

"You can't stay locked in your room all day," she said then amended, "again."

"I can, too." His deep voice was faint but firm. "Go away."

"Well, you're not holing up in there today."

"Oh no?" There was a challenge to his voice. It was better than desolation.

"No." Nori put hands on her hips even though he couldn't see her. "You're taking me somewhere."

"Where's that?"

"Bron says there's a lake not too far outside town. I want to see it."

Silence. Then, "Hank'll never let you go."

"Already cleared it with him."

There was faint rustling inside the room, like he was throwing on clothes, and then the door flew open. "How the hell did you work that deal?"

"He gave me some kind of test yesterday." She shrugged. "Guess I passed."

She didn't mention the real reason she suspected Hank had agreed to her plan: to get Kade out of his room—and out of his head.

"Plus, he knows I'll be with you, and you'd haul me back if I tried to run away."

"That I would," he said, brushing past her as she crowded his doorway.

"HERE." Kade thrust a flashlight in Nori's direction as they descended the same steps she'd taken into Trogtown just four days before. "I got us both a light. The overheads stop just past the steps."

She didn't need the light, but pressed the button anyway, illuminating a narrow swath of the tunnel. Though artificial light didn't hurt or burn her the way natural sunlight did, it affected her night vision. In Trogtwon and the Pit, the low-wattage overheads created a sort of permanent twilight. Never too bright, and not completely dark until the town-wide lights out at nine. When the artificial overheads were on, she was on a level with everyone else. She'd have to be careful Kade didn't catch her eyes with his flashlight.

When Kade took a right at the steps a thrill of excitement bubbled inside her. They were leaving town in the opposite direction she'd come. Maybe she'd learn another way back to Ralston.

Though she was trying to make the best of it, being held against her will in a world she didn't know left her humiliated and angry. Life underground wasn't as bad as she'd thought it would be. But at night, when it was quiet and she was alone, fear nearly strangled her. Was she really safe with Hank and Kade? How long could she live like this? How—and when— would she escape to find her parents.

The day was coming when she would have to risk Hank's wrath and escape. She'd been straining to overhear the conversations of people coming in and out of the Pit, listening for any word of the sunscorch. Surely she would hear about it even underground. Right? But what if word never came? Her chest tightened with dread. What if most people, like Kade, thought the surface was uninhabitable, that the world only existed on their subterranean level?

Didn't matter. Nori sniffed and straightened. The people predicting the impending sunscorch were experts. If they said a scorch would occur within the week, it undoubtedly would. Another week for the after effects, and she should be good to go. But she had work to do before then—planning, and recon, and food storage. A twinge of guilt pulled at her gut at the thought of stealing from Hank, who was surprisingly trusting of her already. She shrugged. Couldn't be helped. Nori made a mental note to begin dry runs to test her escape. She had to be ready when the time came.

"How much farther?" she asked Kade after a while. She was glad to learn more about the tunnel and search for a potential way out, but they'd been walking for miles.

"Not long now." Kade's long strides forced her to hustle to keep up.

"Couldn't we have taken a bike or something?"

His deep laugh rumbled through the enclosure. "Hank's trusting, but not that trusting."

"Would you really chase me?" she asked.

"If you tried to escape, you mean?"

Nori nodded.

"You bet I would."

Fists flew to her hips. "Why?"

"A deal's a deal."

"Oh, but I didn't make a deal," she argued. "Some jerks kidnapped and sold me to Hank without my permission."

"That's how it works," Kade said with a shrug.

"I can't believe you'd get behind this kind of moral injustice." Nori threw her hands up as the heat of indignation spread from her neck up to her cheeks. She ground her teeth and growled, surging forward with such fire Kade had to catch up with *her*.

"It's just a part of life," he said. "It's not fair, but it's the way it is. Anyway, who's gonna stop it? You see any moral — or civil, for that matter — authority around here?"

"Surely somebody's tried to stop this."

"People have revolted, sure. They've run away. But these guys know what they're doing. They find people like you, and me, and Grant, and Diesel, who have no connections, no family. And who's going to do anything about it?"

"Us!" Nori said with conviction. "We could fight. We could escape."

"Been there; done that," Kade said. "Got the beating to prove it."

"No," Nori breathed. "From Hank?"

"No." He shook his head. "Before I came here. But Hank would make you regret the day you tried to escape, believe me."

She scoffed, but Kade pinned her with a look that said he wasn't exaggerating.

"Is it just me, or is getting humid in here?" Though a general dampness always permeated her new world, this was different.

"We're close to the lake. It's fed by underground springs, so, yeah."

They'd made two right and four left turns since leaving Trogtown. Nori jotted that down in her mental notebook under the heading "Escape Plan."

Some intersections had directional signs indicating the next point. Trogtown - 3 mi, or Incinerator with an arrow. The last fork in the road said Debajo - 67 mi.

"What's Debayjoe?" Nori asked with feigned nonchalance.

"Deh-BAH-ho," he corrected. "Spanish for underneath."

"Okay, what's Debajo?"

Kade ignored her mocking tone. "It's the next town over."

"Surely you can't take this tunnel for another 70 miles," she scoffed.

Kade shone the light toward her and she clenched her eyes shut. "You can take this tunnel all the way to Canada," he said. "How do you not know that?"

Nori kept her eyes closed for several long moments. Keeping her business to herself was more difficult than she'd anticipated. To make this work, she would have to be smarter. And she would have to do a better job of keeping her big mouth shut.

"I just got turned around." She shrugged, but didn't dare look in Kade's direction for fear he'd spot her deception.

If the tunnels went all the way to Canada, she wondered, did they go to Mexico, too?

"Here it is." Kade bent onto hands and knees in front of a three-foot opening. "I'll go in first. You hand me the light once I'm inside, and then I'll help you in."

Nori's heart was in her throat. "You can't be serious."

"Have you been here before?" Kade's right eyebrow shot toward his hairline in a cynical arch.

Nori shook her head.

"Do you know some other lake?"

Another shake.

"Then hold this light while I climb through."

She took the light, grumbling. "Why is the entrance so small? Isn't there another way in on the other side or something?"

"Not that I know of," he said. "This thing is like four acres wide, and it's still intact because it's so hard to get to. People keep a tight lid on it, like a treasure, because it's the source of the stream that runs through town. I still can't believe Bron told you—wait. Yes, I can. Did he try to bring you?"

"Um, yeah."

"But Hank said you should have me take you instead." When Nori didn't answer, he prodded. "Right?"

Kade had pieced Hank's plan together; no sense denying it. She shrugged noncommittally.

"Bron just wants in your pants. You know that, right?"

"Kade!" Nori whacked him with his own flashlight as he laughed and climbed through the narrow entrance.

Nori shoved her light through the hole at Kade, and backed in the same way he had. She shimmied through the narrow entrance feet-first, her boots finding purchase on a rocky but flat surface, and then she slid the top half of her body through, too.

Whatever retort was on her lips was lost as she took in the eerie and exotic beauty.

The cavern was huge, and extended farther than she could see. The rock of its domed ceiling was marbled with millions of years of variegated layers, a deep clay color swirling within grays and graphite. There were no stalactites, as if the underground lake had washed them away over time and left a nearly-smooth finish.

Most of the lake was calm, as still as a cloudless sky. But in a far corner, an underwater current disturbed the water ever so slightly—one of the springs feeding the lake.

"Can't see much, even with these lights." The beam of Kade's spotlight bounced from the cavern ceiling to the serene water, shadows and highlights putting on a show for Nori's singular gift.

"Magical," she breathed, and her chest deflated on a deep exhale.

They stood like that, Nori contemplating the unspeakable beauty she'd never known could exist, and Kade lost in thought as deep as the lake's silent depths.

"Can you… Does anyone ever swim in it?" Nori asked after a while.

A wicked gleam crossed the hard lines of Kade's handsome features, and he pulled the black shirt over his head. He kicked off hiking boots and jeans, leaving him only in shorts as he dove into the watery blackness.

"Wait for me!" She laughed, shedding her own boots before jumping in, too.

Nori laid her head back in the warm, mineral-rich water, her body buoyant. As she floated, she marveled at the masterpiece created without brush or chisel and felt at peace for the first time in weeks. The moment had to end, but she tucked that thought away. No sense stressing about stress. The only sounds were Kade's small splashes, comforting reminders that she wasn't alone in the eerily beautiful space. They were in no hurry to get back, so she closed her eyes and lost herself to the serenity.

When Kade's intermittent splashes stopped, and a bite-like pinch struck her ankle, Nori screamed and bolted upright. Her shrieks echoed around the cavernous space and back toward her, as if a banshee had joined them in the cave.

Kade's face was alight with laughter even before he broke the water's surface.

"Idiot." She splashed him and tried to scowl, but couldn't keep the frown in place. "Seriously, though. Are there any fish, any animals in here?"

"I've never seen them, but I heard there are sightless white fish."

"Sightless? Like, blind?"

"Mm. And some without eyes entirely. They didn't need eyes in the darkness, I guess, and adapted."

Nori's chest tightened as she peered down into the water in search of the little cavefish. They were survivors, making do with what they had.

"Besides this big pool," Kade said as he swam up beside her, "the lake supposedly goes back for miles and miles into crevices we can't see."

"I wonder what's above it," Nori mused. "What we're directly underneath."

"Somewhere beneath the Ozar—" Kade's eyes narrowed and his mouth gathered in an injured scowl. A flash of betrayal puckered his face before he smoothed it back into a practiced mask. "You're stupid if you're still thinking to escape, Nori. I mean it. It's lucky you ended up with Hank. Better the devil you know than the one you don't."

She made a noncommittal grunt. "What if I don't want to keep company with a devil at all? I can take care of myself. I'm smart and fast. I'm a survivor, just like those fish."

"Yeah, well, those fish stay out of trouble—well out of sight, and in groups. You know what kind of fish goes it alone?" When Nori didn't answer, he said, "One that's caught. One that's dinner."

She looked away.

"We need to get back. Hank's probably perforated his ulcer by now."

At the edge of the lake where they'd first entered, Kade's big body towered over Nori's as he held out a hand to help her up. She took it, his warning still fresh on her mind. Despite the peaceful respite, she was far more hopeless leaving the underground lake than she had been coming in.

"We can work on your training some of the day tomorrow," Kade said as he walked Nori to her room. "My fight is Saturday and I need to rest."

She nodded and pushed open the creaky door.

"Kade," she called when he turned to walk away. "Thanks for today. For getting me out of here."

He caught her gaze, but didn't linger. "Thanks for getting me out of my head."

20

WEAK

Weight training, Nori discovered, was something she could really get into. Though she'd only been working to build her muscles for a few days, she already felt stronger. She walked taller, certainly. The endorphins coursing through her body after workouts lifted her spirits, and her outlook. She'd probably keep up the routines even after she found her way out of her current hellhole.

After the morning workout, her never-ending list of chores still had to be done. It was an ever-present weight on her shoulders, but Hank was right: she had food to eat and a place to sleep. Nothing in life came free.

Before coming to Trogtown, to the Pit, she'd been sheltered by her parents. Pampered, even. This was her first job. She set to work with determination and, maybe, a bit of pride.

The Pit had cleared out for dinner by the time she finished, and though the small dining hall bustled with activity, she spotted Kade alone at a corner table. As she passed, Bron stuck out an arm. His gaze lit on her face, which was flushed from the stifling laundry room, and her hair, wild from a day of exercise and physical labor. Disapproval colored his ruddy features but then he seemed to decide her current appearance didn't matter that much.

"Oh, like I care what you think." She snorted and threw his outstretched arm back at him.

"What?" he called as she left him for Kade. "What'd I do?"

"Trouble in paradise?" Kade hid his lips, trying not to smile.

"Ugh. This town needs more women."

"Don't look at me," he teased. "I'm doing my part to alleviate that problem." His eyes were bright and playful for only a moment and then they flickered with pain.

Nori changed the subject before he allowed grief to take him under again. "Schedule says you're fighting Renegade tomorrow, which got me thinking. Is Kade even your real name?"

He barked a laugh then wagged his eyebrows.

"I knew it! What is it?"

Kade scrutinized Nori's face, his internal battle of letting her—or anyone else—get to know him better playing across his bold features.

"Kade's my last name. It's Keagan. Keagan Kade."

Nori tried the name on for size, rolling it around in her mouth. "Keagan. Keagan." She shrugged. "Fits."

"Not a fighter's name, though."

"No," she agreed. "All right, Keagan Kade. Tell me about Renegade."

Kade tilted his head from side to side as he worked to phrase his thoughts. "I haven't fought him before. He's coming all the way from Canyon City."

Nori didn't reveal her geographical ignorance this time, only nodding her interest.

"Hank's seen him. Says he's vicious. And big. The fight's expected to draw crowds from all over. Big matches like this bring out the gamblers, the thieves, and lowlifes of all sorts."

He leaned into Nori, suddenly serious, his sleek brows drawn in concern. "I can't imagine how you've made it this long, as delicate as you are, but you have got to be extra careful this weekend."

Nori stiffened and snarled, "I am not delicate."

"You are." His words were emphatic. "Frighteningly so." His face softened a bit at her injured look and he quickly said, "I know you're strong," he pointed to his own heart, "in here. But it's like you were raised under a flower petal or something. Sheltered. How is it you came to Hank, anyway? Who sold you to him, and where'd they find you?"

Nori shook her head, her nostrils flaring as she tried to control herself. She was working to be tougher. She was. It was why she'd thrown herself into self-defense and getting stronger. Did he mean she needed to be harder, more cruel? Probably. But she didn't ever want to be that. That wasn't who Norman Chisholm had raised her to be. Not who she wanted to be. The world was hard enough.

"You're one to talk," she said, still stinging from his blunt assessment. "You want everyone to think you're this badass fighter, hard and emotionless. But I heard you crying in the shower. And locking yourself in your room all day isn't anywhere near tough."

Kade's head jerked back like she'd slapped him. He opened his mouth and closed it, twice, his jaws flexing under the effort to restrain himself. "I lost someone I loved before you came," he ground out. "Loved. Someone who professed to love me, too, but took his own life rather than live out his days here." He shook his head and shot Nori a look of disgust so pure her heart shriveled in her chest. "Low blow, Nori," he said. "I take it back. You're not delicate at all. You're just weak."

She didn't look up when he left the table, didn't cast a glance in his direction as he slammed his plate down in the kitchen. She stared into her lap, wishing she could take back what she'd said. Maybe he was dead on. Maybe she was weak.

21

FIGHT DAY PREP

After a fitful night's sleep, Nori sought out Kade as soon as she woke. He was already up, dressing for the big day, when he answered the door. He let her in without a word, his back straight and shoulders tense. Before he turned from her, though, she caught sight of his wild gaze.

"You nervous?" she asked.

He shrugged, focusing too hard on combing his dark hair. His face was reflected in the mirror, and when he finally raised his tortured eyes to hers, she melted.

"I'm so sorry, Kade. I don't know why I said that. You've been so good to me, and I... I'm a huge jerk."

He shrugged again, but some of the tension eased from his shoulders. "S'ok."

Nori released a ragged breath. "I really am sorry."

He gave her a little smile in the mirror. "I know," he nodded. "We're good."

"Okay," was what Nori said, but she wanted to thank him —for being a friendly face in a world of strangers, for acts of kindness even in his darkest days and, most of all, for forgiving her mean-spirited attack. "I'll see you out there, champ," she said and backed toward the door.

"Hey now," he pointed a finger at her. "Don't jinx it."

FIGHT DAY, Nori discovered, was a whole other world. A furiously fast, over-populated, bustling, and busy world. From the moment she left Kade's room, she was pushed in every direction, arms stacked full of towels, and gauze, and tape, and extra chairs. There would be five fights, with Kade's bout against Renegade the main and final event.

"Nori." Hank's gravelly voice was hoarse from a morning of wrangling guests, of settling disputes, and of last-minute instruction to his corral of fighters.

Unfolding the last metal chair in the sea of rows outside the arena, she looked up. "You need me?"

"Run to Dave's and get a case of water. Princess Renegade won't drink from our water stores." Hank snorted his disapproval.

"Dave's is…"

"The general store. You were there Wednesday—below Doc Moore's office. Just tell 'em to charge it."

Trogtown bustled with excitement. Vendors were set up along the dim streets, trading and selling supplies like an underground flea market. Alleys that had been deserted before were now teeming with life. Grungy, bearded, mostly-male life. A perfect day to run away, a small voice said in the back of her mind.

"Back again?" asked the man she supposed was Dave. He was the only one working, despite the long line at the register.

"Hank sent me for a case of water."

"Cases are in the back." He motioned toward a door behind the counter. "Go on ahead."

Nori slowly shook her head. Didn't these people know she was thinking about stealing their precious supplies and running for her life? She must really look as delicate and naïve as Kade had said. With another shake of her head, she entered the back room.

Dave's storage room was stacked to the ceiling with water and fuel—and ammunition. Behind it was a locked gun safe. He'd taken that precaution, at least. There were crates and crates of Vitabars, which Nori had never heard of before going underground, but had since learned were a staple food source.

"You find it?" Dave called, stirring Nori from her impure thoughts.

Hefting a case of the bottled water, she thanked him on her way out, only the slightest bit of guilt sliding across her shoulders for the pocketknife she'd swiped.

Nori rounded the corner as she left the store, and the multi-purpose tool and knife weighed heavily in her pocket. She shouldn't have done it. Hank—and Dave, for that matter—had trusted her. And what had she done? Behaved like a common thief; no better than the ones slithering through Trogtown hours before they gambled away their stolen loot.

But she was different. Her freedom had been stolen by those pricks on bikes. They'd sold her to someone. Sold her for labor. No, she would not feel guilty about the knife. It was still heavy and hard against her skin, but it was also a comfort. A reminder that she may've been stuck, but she wasn't stranded.

When she was jerked into the doorway of a dark building,

with no one to witness her abduction, no one to hear the heavy thud of the case of water dropping to the ground as she scratched at her attacker's arms, the knife was more than just a comfort.

A man's hand covered Nori's chin and mouth, thrusting her back against a hard chest as she was dragged from the street. She twisted her body wildly and pulled at the man's hands, but he kept a tight hold. Stomping her attacker's feet did nothing to deter him as she met the hard resistance of reinforced boots.

He was saying something, but she couldn't hear it over the roaring in her ears. Didn't want to hear it, anyway. With all the strength she could find, Nori raised her arm and jammed an elbow into the set of ribs behind her. Her attacker grunted, and the grip on her shoulders loosened. It was her only shot. She twisted to escape, but before she could flee, he threw an arm around her stomach and pulled her back toward him.

Continuing to struggle so he wouldn't notice her intentions, Nori dipped one hand into the pocket of her jeans, inching out the knife. When at last she flicked open the blade, she raised her arm to her side as best she could. There wasn't a lot of leverage with her upper arms pinned to her sides. She readied to plunge the steel into her attacker's thigh, and her thoughts honed to this one shot at freedom.

As she cleared her mind and prepared to strike and run, the man's low, urgent words finally sank in.

"Stop, Nori," he said. "It's me. Stop."

Nori paused the fight for her life, her body as motionless as a snake just before the strike. The attacker's grip on her mouth loosened enough that she could mumble, "Cooper?"

"Yes. For God's sake, would you stop the kicking and

biting?" He let go of her then, and she spun on him, eyes bright with fury.

"I thought someone was trying to kill me. Why would you do that, you idiot? You scared me to death."

"I didn't want us to be seen together. Wallace is in town, too, and I thought you'd probably prefer he forgot about you." Cooper twisted his mouth. "But if you want me to go look him up..."

"You wanted to talk to me, so you abducted me?" She snorted and dusted her jeans. "Super inconspicuous."

"I tried to get your attention before you went into the store. And after. You never even looked my way." Cooper eyed the blade she was clutching so tightly her knuckles were white. "Where the hell did you get a knife, anyway?"

Nori released her grip, eyeing the prized possession she'd nearly sunk into Cooper's thigh.

He snatched it before she could move.

"Give. It. Back." Nori's growl was a promise of death.

Cooper whipped his dark head up at her lethal tone. He studied her for several long moments before giving a slow nod of approval, his mouth sliding into a smirk. "I see you took my advice to get tougher."

He extended a fist and opened his hand, the knife resting in his palm. It was back in Nori's pocket before he took a breath.

"What are you doing here?" she snapped, the frantic pace of her heart finally beginning to slow.

"I thought you might want news on the sunscorch."

Nori's breath snagged in her throat and her eyes found his, pleading for answers.

"Well?" She stepped closer to him. "What have you heard? Are my parents okay?"

Cooper shook his head, his eyes softening at her panic. "It hasn't happened. Not yet."

Nori's eyes closed, and she released the breath she'd been holding since hearing that ominous, awful word. *Sunscorch.*

22

THE BIG FIGHT

"La-dies and gen-tle-men." The three words of Hank's welcome rang out over five full seconds.

Nori searched the crowd and, sure enough, several women had come out of the woodwork to watch the fights.

"Tonight's final bout is a title match for the current heavy-weight champion," Hank said. "The Killer from Canyon City, a rebel you don't want to reckon with, Rennnnn-egade."

The fighter's name, which Hank had called like revving a motorcycle engine, produced cheers and whistles across the Pit. Hundreds of people she'd never seen stood from their folding chairs, fists in the air. Some held dark-colored beer that sloshed over the sides of their cups onto the floor. Nori growled low in her throat—she'd be the one cleaning it up later.

"Challenging for the title of heavyweight champ: the fighting pride of Trogtown, a giant of a man, the quickest, the deadliest ever made, Kaaaaade."

Kade was obviously the hometown boy. Shouts and stomps shook chunks of earth from the rafters, and from the top of the Pit, Nori screamed support for her friend. She was the loudest of them all.

When she finally lowered her fists, emotions high and throat sore, she found Hank looking pointedly between her and two chairs near Kade's corner.

"Me?" she mouthed.

Hank nodded.

Nori made her way down the steps to the bottom of the Pit and approached Kade's corner as if she knew what she was doing. As if she wasn't a girl who, last week, was desperate for even one friend. Nori strutted to the chair and, head high and back straight, started to take a seat.

Kade, inside the ring, waved her over. She cleared her throat and rushed to him.

The man she knew to be a gentle giant looked dangerous as hell. Greased to a high sheen, his massive muscles bulged and glinted in the overhead lights. Her friend wasn't wearing the face she knew. Kade's kind and handsome face was replaced with one of focused, evil menace.

"'Deadliest ever made,' huh?" She snickered, despite the three-hundred-pound pit fighter before her.

Kade's face maintained its intimating glower. "Hank's idea."

"Need anything?"

"Not to get killed."

"Oh, you got this," she said, clenching her jaw with the force of her confidence. "Renegade," she scoffed in an attempt to calm her friend, whose eyes had gone wild again. "Where'd he get those shorts, anyway? Ladies' lingerie? I've seen thongs with more fabric."

Kade's eyes were the only thing on his face that changed, the bulging whites of them lessening as he calmed down.

"Remember your training," Hank squawked behind her. "Jabs and leg kicks. Wear him down first."

Kade nodded and thumped his gloves together.

As Hank pulled her away, the bell to signal the first round expected any second, Nori put every ounce of encouragement she had into her face. "Let's do this," she said.

IT WAS no wonder Renegade was the heavyweight champ. He was a monster. A quick, powerful, relentless monster. But Kade was smarter, and more patient.

The first three rounds were brutal. Kade came away with a nasty eye cut and a swollen knee. Renegade didn't have any visible signs of injury, though Kade had landed several kicks and punches.

At the bell signaling the end of the fourth round, Kade's breathing was coming hard and fast, the rise and fall of his chest more like seizures than breaths.

Hank was in his face before the fighter could slump onto the stool in the corner. "Good. You're doing fine, son. That last kick stung him. See how he's limping?"

Nori's gaze followed Kade's, which slid to Renegade. The fighter was wired and ready for more, like a caged wildcat. No limp in sight.

Hank grabbed Kade's chin, reclaiming his attention. "This is it. The last round. Time to pull out the big guns. You've been chipping at him with those solid jabs and kicks, but now it's time to lay down the hammer. No more chipping. Smash him."

Nori's stomach roiled with nausea. Watching her friend being beaten to a bloody pulp, even if Hank assured her it was going well, was torment. She wasn't cut out for the naked brutality of pit fighting. Nothing in her life had prepared her for it. In fact, the opposite was true. She'd been shielded from anything distasteful by well-intentioned parents overcompensating for the tragic loss of her siblings.

The brutal punches Kade had taken to his body hurt. Nori could see it in the tightening of his eyes, the pinch of his mouth. And with each kick to his legs, he stumbled and stalled a bit longer. His left eye had swelled shut during the last round, costing him precious visibility. He suffered for it, unable to defend himself against several of Renegade's punishing blows.

Still in his corner of the ring between rounds, Hank pressed a cotton swab to the swollen cut above Kade's eye. Blood and clear liquid gushed from the wound. A sudden undeniable urge to vomit goaded Nori's already-nervous stomach without warning. She gagged and retched all over Kade's corner of the ring.

She stood stunned, a hand over her gaping mouth, and the front of her shirt ruined.

"Goddangit, Nori," Hank barked, wiping a hand on his jeans. "Clean up this awful mess before the whole crowd spews in their seats." He muttered a string of curses at her even as he continued to address the damage on Kade's face.

Sobered by horror and shame, she ducked under the ring for towels to soak up the watery pile of vomit. Her shoulders caved forward and she ducked her head, becoming the smallest possible version of herself as she mopped. She imagined the entire crowd of raucous fans laughing behind her, thumping mock toasts with their plastic cups and spilling more beer, which she would be forced to mop up, too.

At last she risked a look at Kade, who eyed her as she

manically scrubbed the last remaining spot. His eyes were dancing with repressed laughter, and his lips twitched in an effort not to smile.

Indignation replaced shame, and she stood up straight, throwing hands to her hips. "You think this is funny?"

Kade nodded, biting his lips not to laugh. "You've got something." He motioned to her chin. "Just there."

Nori swiped at her chin, checking for any remnant of bile. Was he just screwing with her? Her gaze threw daggers, and she briefly considered throwing the filthy towel at his head.

The bell's resonant *ding*, indicating the final round, had Kade back on his feet and in the ring in a flash.

Nori was amazed by how quickly he shifted gears, by the level of concentration he achieved in the span of a moment. Kade dodged most of Renegade's jabs with keen efficiency, if a bit more slowly than he had in the first few rounds.

The two fighters traded punches, a battle of endurance, of will. A battle for the title. Who could withstand the other's punishment longer?

Nori's guts were a twisted mess, the insides of her cheeks shredded as she bit them with each awful blow Kade suffered. The mat on which the fighters performed their violent dance, grungy with old blood, now held smatterings of smeared scarlet.

The crowd was standing, the level of volume in the Pit overpowering Nori's senses as shouts and cheers and grunts formed a deafening chorus. Each kick was a crescendo, each landed punch a forte.

Suddenly, Kade was on the run. He backed away from Renegade, knees near buckling as he endured fist after fist to the head. He held his hands up, but couldn't deflect every punch, couldn't see them all, and a few powerful blows made it through. Spitting a mouthful of blood onto the floor of the ring, Kade breathed deeply and re-calibrated.

Renegade pursued his prey, the bloodthirsty glint in his eyes betraying an intent to kill. He was merciless, focused. He was the champ.

After three quick jabs to Kade's head, Renegade pulled back his arm for the final blow. He wasted a fraction of a second to smirk, as if saying, "Take my title? Like hell."

It was all the time Kade needed. His foot connected with jaw, a spinning back kick delivered so fast Renegade never saw it coming. The champ's head snapped back at the impact. In slow motion, Renegade's shoulders relaxed, his arms fell to his sides, and his body slumped to the bloody mat.

It was over. A knockout.

Kade stood, fists at the ready in front of him until Nori rushed the ring, throwing her arms around his slick waist.

"You did it!" She jumped and shouted over and over, "You did it! You did it!"

Hank joined them in the ring and slapped Kade on the back. "Great job, son. I knew you'd do it. You're heavyweight champ."

"Heavyweight champ," Kade repeated dumbly, his gaze focused on the ceiling somewhere beyond Nori and Hank, beyond the deafening crowd.

23

COOPER AND GRANT

Basking in the glow of victory in his own crotchety way, with a cold beer in one hand and a wad of cash in the other, Hank gave everyone the night off. A license to party—Nori included. She would deal with the disastrous filth of the Pit tomorrow. That was exactly when she would think about it, too: tomorrow. The night was for celebrating.

Actually, in her case, the night was for playing nursemaid to a bruised and battered Kade.

"I thought you'd be more excited." Nori pulled a chair up to the huge silver tub. "About the win, I mean."

Kade shrugged, sending ice chips and frigid water sloshing around him. He clenched his teeth, sucking and blowing air through them so rapidly Nori feared he would hyperventilate.

"Is the ice helping?" she asked.

"Helping?" His voice rose an octave. "It hurts like hell. But it's more a blinding, fiery, stabbing pain than the agonizing aches I'll feel in an hour, so I can't really say."

His hands and head were the only things above the

freezing water. He was submerged to his shoulders and rigid with cold. "How much longer?" he asked.

"Hank said three minutes. You've done half that."

He groaned and forced out a tortured breath, his focus on the wall in front of him.

"Almost there," Nori said, moving a chunk of ice away from his neck. "Tell me the truth," she said to distract him. "Did you think you'd win?"

Kade's gaze left the point on the wall and found her face. "I hoped." He shifted in the water. "I hoped I would win. Otherwise, what's the point?"

He looked away then, an unfathomable sadness replacing the tortured look his face had held. For several dark moments, he stared at nothing, his mind somewhere far away.

"That's it. I'm done," he said, rising abruptly from the ice bath. He stepped over the side of the metal tub, snagged a towel from Nori's outstretched hands, and limped to the showers.

THOUGH COOPER HAD PROMISED to be at the fight, Nori never caught sight of him. She'd scanned the crowd, but after Hank motioned her to the ring, she was too busy, too caught up in Kade's match to worry about Cooper.

With the fights over, the Pit cleared out, leaving only her and Hank and a few of his old buddies. The undercard fighters and the rest of the crowd were either buying celebratory rounds or crying in their beers at the one bar in town.

Nori left Kade to the showers, and heard Hank's dry cackle floating from his office down the hall. At the old man's laugh, a smile pulled at her lips, starting slowly then spreading across her entire face. She was happy. For Kade. For Hank. For herself. After all, it was the first time she'd done something on her own. She'd made a place for herself in the Pit, in this grungy new world. She'd done her job well and made friends. She was part of something outside the little world her parents had created.

Her heart felt full—too full, like it would burst. The sensation was completely foreign to her. Was it pride? Yes, she thought. Despite the dark and terrifying path she'd taken into the subterranean world, she was glad she'd stumbled onto it.

As she approached it, the door opened, and a head of thick, dark hair emerged from Hank's office. Her full heart stuttered within her chest. Cooper. His wide smile revealed a row of perfect teeth, and her own grin grew in response.

Had she seen him smile before? She couldn't recall. Didn't recall much of anything at the moment.

"Hey," he said, striding toward her. He stood too close, but she didn't retreat. "I'm headed out. Just stopped to make sure Hank's getting his money's worth."

At the reminder of her indentured status, Nori's smile soured.

"Aw, now, don't be so serious. I'm just teasing."

"Nothing about this is funny to me. It's my life we're talking about. My parents risked a lot to get me down here."

"Yes, and getting you to Hank probably saved *your* life."

Nori bristled, her lip curling in a smirk. "You'll forgive me if I don't grovel at the benevolence you showed in selling me for slave labor."

A muscle ticked in Cooper's jaw. She'd pissed him off. Good.

"Has Hank been cruel to you?" he asked.

She wouldn't meet his gaze, but answered. "No."

"Is your life…" He struggled for the right word. "Your… safety…threatened here?"

She mumbled, "No."

"Would you rather be on your own wandering through miles of dark tunnel where women are scarce and slugs like Wallace and Jenks can find you?"

Nori shook her head, rolling her eyes.

"Then you're welcome. Groveling not required."

Nori's gaze shot up to find his smile had resurfaced. In a softer voice, he said, "It's not so bad, is it? When I was here, Hank treated everyone well."

She hadn't expected that. "You lived here?"

"Mm. For a minute. Listen, I don't have long. I'm set to go to the Surface tomorrow. I'll try to find your parents. Ralston, right? It's not too far out of my way."

She nodded, stepping into him and clasping the sleeve of his jacket. "Please." She searched his gaze. "Please find them. Tell them I'm okay. They'll be sick with worry."

"I'll do my best. What's the address?"

"Twelve Skyler Court."

"All right. I'll come back when I can."

"Why?" The word left her lips before she even knew she'd thought it.

Cooper's head fell to the side. "Why what? Why will I come back?"

"Why help me?" She still held his arm, the leather worn and warm beneath her fingers. She didn't let go.

Cooper shrugged and looked away. "Because I've been there. I've been in trouble, and alone, and clueless, and scared.

And someone helped me." He smiled then, his mood lightening considerably. "Anyway, I owe you three. This is two."

Nori smiled back and released him, letting her hand fall to her side. "Thank you."

It wasn't enough, but it was all she had.

Too late, she thought to ask who'd helped him.

KADE GROANED and closed his good eye. "Even my teeth hurt."

"If it makes you feel any better, you probably look as bad as you feel."

Kade laughed and loosed a moan from his soul. "Don't make me laugh. Don't make me talk. Don't make me breathe."

His room was bigger than Nori's. And, she noted, he had a chair. A nicer rug, too. The new champ sat slumped in it, his head draped listlessly over the back.

"I've got a surprise for you," Nori said sweetly.

"Leave me alone. I'm contemplating death."

"Oh, don't be such a diva." She crept to his side and stood over him so the only thing he had to lift to see her was an eyelid. "Don't you even want to know what it is?"

He groaned again then, "What?" He didn't open his eye.

"Someone sent booze. A fan. But you're too sore and tired to deal with a gift, right? I'll just take it to Hank. I know he can make use of it."

A single, very severe-looking brown eye pinned her. "You better give me that bottle."

"You sure?" Nori blinked in mock innocence. "You can barely lift your arms. I don't know if you're in any condition to handle alcohol."

"At this point, you could just pour it down my throat and I'd be happy."

"All right." She laughed. "A little or a lot?"

"Mmph," was the only answer. A lot, then.

"You sure you don't want to go out with the other guys?" Nori put the drink in his waiting hand.

Hank's stable of fighters hadn't all won, but they went out just the same, whether to celebrate wins or lament losses.

Kade took a swig from the clear glass and sighed his pleasure. "Nope."

"You don't want to celebrate your big win? People will expect the new champ to go out."

"I really don't care what people expect. And there's no way I'm giving high-fives and taking shots all night. I'm just not up for it."

"Okay." Nori shrugged. "We'll have our own party, then."

"Oh!" Kade moved too quickly and winced. "I didn't think. Go and have fun. You don't have to stay with me. I'll be fine here alone."

Nori scrunched her nose. "No thanks."

"If you're worried about Bron or Diesel, or anyone else…"

"No, no, no. I don't want to go, either. Pointless, really, to go to a bar since I don't drink."

Kade's eye narrowed. "How old are you? I never asked."

Nori straightened. "Seventeen."

"You ever had a drink?"

She looked away and shook her head.

"You want one?"

She shook her head again, but her refusal lacked the certainty it held before.

"You sure?"

A thought struck. "Tell ya what," she said. "I'll take a shot of…whatever that is…if you tell me what you meant when you said, 'otherwise, what's the point' when you were in the ice bath."

Kade said nothing, but took another swig from the glass. He set it onto the table hard, making Nori jump. "All right. Deal."

The clear liquid rippled within Nori's glass. It was denser than water, smoother. And, she thought, sort of lovely.

Tipping the glass to her nose, she gently inhaled—then her head whipped toward Kade.

"God," her face wrinkled in disgust, "has this stuff gone bad?"

He laughed and shook his head, eyes gleaming with anticipation.

"Aren't we supposed to toast or something?" she asked.

Kade shifted in his chair and didn't wince. "That's a good idea. I don't suppose you know any."

Nori gave a crooked smile at the thought of her beloved father. "My dad used to say, 'here's to a long life, and a happy one. A quick death, and an easy one. A good girl, and an honest one. A cold pint…and another one."

"That's good," he said, then groaned. "My God. It even hurts to smile."

"I imagine so," she said, suddenly serious. "You let far too many jabs through. We really need to work on keeping your hands up."

"We do, do we?" Kade mocked her and she nodded. "When I recover, I'll let you show me how it's done."

"Oh, I'm not built for the Pit. Look at these arms!" Nori squeezed a fist and made a muscle. The flat line of flesh from the inside of her elbow to her shoulder illustrated the point.

"I dunno," Kade said. "You're quick. You're working to bulk up. With time and practice, maybe..."

"Are there really female fighters? I bet they all look like Peg."

Kade laughed. Groaned. Nodded. Groaned. "They do. What would your name be?"

"My fighter name?"

"Yeah," he said. "Oh, wait. I know. White Lightning. Cause you're fast. And pale."

She laughed and threw something at him.

"Okay, okay, okay. How about...Javelin?"

"Javelin? Javelin. That's a good one." Nori said it a few times, trying it on.

"Wait," Kade breathed, and she could almost see the light bulb above his head. "I've got it.

"What?"

"Noir," he said with a dark flourish.

"*Noir*? French is not tough," Nori said. "And I've watched a lot of TV."

"It's a play on your name." Kade narrowed his eyes and announced theatrically. "Dark. Dangerous. Deadly. Noir." He intoned the last, his voice so deep the word reverberated within the solid, underground room.

"You know me too well." Nori laughed again then raised her clenched fists to the sky and scowled. "A girl on a mission to make it in a deadly world. Noir: mean as a snake, and just as bulky."

"I said don't make me laugh!" Kade said as he held his brutalized stomach. "You gonna drink that or what?" He nodded to her glass.

"I thought you'd forgotten."

"Nope." He sat up and leaned toward her, raising his own

glass. "To nights we'll never remember with friends we'll never forget."

Nori met his gaze, their connection suddenly intense, and raised the glass to her mouth. She threw her head back, and the liquor into her mouth. As soon as it hit her tongue, her eyes flew wide, panicked. After a noisy swallow, she opened her mouth, fanning it with her hands. "Jesus! Why would you drink lighter fluid?"

Kade turned helplessly onto his side in the chair, laughing as Nori scraped her tongue with her sleeve, gagging and gasping for air.

"Makes you all warm inside, doesn't it?" he said when he finally stopped laughing.

"Oh, yeah. Super cozy." She shivered. "Seriously, though. Do you actually like that?"

"It's a precious commodity. All you need to make moonshine is sugar, water, and yeast, but still, it's a very nice gift. From whom, by the way?"

"I don't know. Hank sent it."

"Another round?" Kade raised the bottle in her direction.

"I'll pass, thanks."

"Suit yourself." He poured himself another.

Though her mouth still tasted of chemical warfare, Nori's shoulders pressed delightfully to the floor. She rolled her neck, which had relaxed considerably. Her brain, too, seemed at ease. She began to see the appeal.

"So," Kade said, bringing her back online. "You wanted to know about Grant?"

Nori didn't recall asking about Grant specifically, but if he was in the mood to talk, she was all ears.

Kade gripped the arm of his chair with his free hand until his knuckles whitened. His big chest raised as, slowly, he took a breath. Held it. He closed his good eye and released the breath so wearily it seemed he'd changed his mind.

"Grant and I had been fighting. A lot. He wanted to leave Trogtown. Wanted me to leave the Pit—fighting in general. Said he wouldn't watch me fight again—couldn't, actually. Said he *couldn't* watch me get beaten to a pulp again."

Kade's hand shook as he raised the glass to his mouth. "Fighting is all I know. It's what I'm good at. And anyway, where would we go? I had a little money saved up, but not enough to quit fighting altogether. He had the idea Hank was going to trade him, send him away. Said he'd overheard Hank negotiating with someone about it. I didn't believe him. I mean, Hank didn't necessarily approve of us, but he never said anything. He's a very live-and-let-live kinda guy."

Nori nodded. "Go on."

"Anyway, Hank is shrewd. Very practical. He wouldn't do something to risk me leaving and taking a huge chunk of his business. I told Grant all of this." Kade swirled the liquid in his glass, lost in his thoughts.

"What did he say?" Nori scooted to the edge of the bed, toward her friend.

"He said I never put him first. That if I didn't believe him over Hank then I didn't trust him. And if I didn't trust him, that's all he needed to know. He said he refused to stay here one minute longer, with or without me. I told him he was being ridiculous and dramatic." Kade threw back what remained in his glass. "Because he was. I never thought—" He choked back a sob and cleared his throat. "I never thought he would do something so desperate. So stupid."

Kade's head fell between his shoulders, and he covered his eyes with his free hand. His shoulders shook, and Nori debated what to do. Hug him? Ignore it and look away?

When he finally lifted his head, his eye was rimmed with red. "I chose Hank over Grant. I chose to stay in this filthy place and abuse my body—to brutalize others. I chose this," Kade sneered and spread his arms wide, "over the man I loved. So if I didn't win, then what the hell is the point of it? Of anything?"

24

IMMINENT DANGER

A sunscorch warning has been issued by the Global Weather Service. All persons are advised to take cover immediately. I repeat: sensors indicate a sunscorch is imminent within the next 24 hours. Take cover in a designated shelter area, or if one isn't available, go now to a basement or storm cellar.

The metallic clang echoed through every corner of Ana and Norman's small house.

"Ana?" Norman raced into the kitchen. "You okay?"

"Did you hear it?" she asked, her eyes wild as she bent to pick up the bowl she'd been washing when the alert sounded on the emergency radio. The tremor that started in her hands spread to her entire body.

Norman crushed his wife to him, absorbing her terror-stricken shakes. "Let's go. It's all right. We prepared for this."

Ana clung to him, fingers digging into the back of his cotton shirt. "D-do you think she'll be okay?"

Of course her first thought was of Nori. So was his. "I do. She's safer than we are." Norman leaned back to find his wife's flushed face. "We got her underground. She'll make it through the sunscorch and then we'll find her."

"But th-that man. I don't trust him."

"Who, Barker?" he asked. "Nate said it would be fine, and we have to believe that. At least she's not alone. Nori's smart. She's quick. If anybody can make it, it's her."

Ana nodded, still pressed to his chest.

"Grab your bug-out bag, hon, and go on down. I'll get mine and meet you in the basement."

Norman opened the front door and squinted up at the afternoon sky. Ralston was a ghost town. After living through the last sunscorch, no one took the warning lightly. Cautious, well-prepared people were the ones who stayed alive.

The experts were right, he thought, taking one last look around. There was no tangible difference, nothing he could reach out and touch, but the air felt strange. Oppressive, like the eerie quiet and choking atmospheric pressure of an impending lightning storm. The afternoon sun filtered through a thick haze, giving it a soft, soothing glow. Like a poisonous flower, the muted sun was beautifully deceptive. Deadly deceptive.

"I'm here, Ana," Norman said, backing down the basement stairs and closing the door behind him. His wife sat on the thin bunkbed they'd prepared for Nori. She stared at the concrete wall, lost in thought.

He didn't sit beside his wife. Not with the nervous energy searing through him. He tested lanterns and flashlights. He sloshed barrels of water to ensure they were full. He inspected the cans of food lining the sides of the basement in tall metal racks. After two tense rounds of their temporary home, he stood beside his wife, the outside of his flexed thigh touching her shoulder. "I'm sure she's okay, Ana. I'm sure of it."

25

THE SUNSCORCH

When Norman dropped the glass jar, Ana bolted from bed, frantically scanning the room for him. A mess of broken glass, green beans, and tomatoes lay at his feet.

His breaths came in pants, but were close to sobs. His fists were balled at his sides, and his body was hunched and rigid with fury. He worked to calm himself, gripping a nearby workbench, whose wooden surface groaned under the pressure.

Ana didn't say a word.

"You might as well try to rest, Norm," she finally said. "We might be here a while."

"Can't sleep." His voice was strained. "It's been eight hours. You think it's not coming?"

Ana cleared her throat and slid her legs to the side of the bed. "They said within a day, but I suppose we could be down here a few days. We're lucky to have had any warning at all."

"I know. Of course you're right." He turned to her. "You think she's okay?"

"Oh, Norm," his wife whispered and held out her arms.

He ran to her side, kneeling by the bed, and diving into her embrace. "We'll find her," she said. "Just a few more days. We'll find her."

Electricity surged, causing the basement lights to buzz and brighten before going out completely. Neither of them spoke as Norman reached to switch on a nearby lantern. The light flickered on, sending the basement into an eerie fabricated twilight as they awaited what they both knew was coming.

Norman had experienced several tornadoes growing up, and recognized the too-full feeling in his ears of changing air pressure. His forearms sprouted chill bumps as his body sensed, too, something sinister on the way. Holding Ana close, Norman kissed her head and murmured into her hair as much for himself as his wife. "It's going to be fine," he said. "We'll be all right. She'll be all right. When this is over, we can find her. She'll be back with us, and we'll never be separated again." He was babbling, but talking helped him, and maybe it helped Ana. At any rate, he couldn't stop.

The heat on his face when the sunscorch struck was like a whisper of death, even buried as they were in the protective basement. It was as if Earth were a giant gas oven, everything on its surface a slice of pizza. Houses and large structures were meat toppings, their fat popping when the temperature rose high enough. Any plant life or plastic was cheese, losing shape and melting into nothing as it cooked. Basements, and bunkers, and structures below the surface were the crust, warming, crisping, but suffering no real change to their makeup.

It lasted only moments, but the damage would be irreparable. The world had already lost so much. During a sunscorch, anything green that had dared to grow was cremated. Electrical fires and gas explosions obliterated entire blocks. Any utility line not buried was incinerated, leaving no lines of communication besides the few battery-operated walkie-talkies and ham radios saved or scavenged.

"Is it over?" Ana whispered.

Norman let out the breath he'd been holding. "I think so. I think that was it."

"What now?" Her lip wobbled, and she swiped a hand at the tear creeping down her cheek.

"Now," he said, "we wait."

***

"ANA?" Norman looked wildly around the room at the sound of earth shifting and falling apart. Their house creaked and shuddered, and the walls of the basement began to crumble sending chunks of concrete crashing to the floor. The low groan of metal pipes as they bent and broke was a grinding chorus, an accompaniment to certain destruction.

"We need to get out of here," he said, shooting from the bed. He lost his balance and fell back onto it when the floor buckled. Scrabbling onto his knees, he pulled his wife behind him, placing himself between her and the newly-gaping crevice in the basement floor.

Norman's brain couldn't reconcile what was in front of him, what had happened to the floor, to their house, to the world outside. A canyon had cleaved their home in two in a matter of seconds. He and Ana knelt together on a bed on one side of the chasm as the other side stretched farther and farther away. The roof caved as they watched, flattening the living room beneath it. Dust and shards of splintered wood plunged into half of the basement.

"Where's your bag?" Norm was already standing, toeing between flat spots in the warped floor.

"What?" Ana stared blankly at the other half of their home.

"We have to get out of here now!"

26

DEVASTATION IN RALSTON

Cooper closed his eyes against the gory scene of destruction in Ralston. The town had suffered a massive earthquake, no doubt triggered by the sunscorch. It had taken him four days to get there once his business in Chicago was finished. Destroyed and impassable roads had forced him to backtrack three separate times. If he wasn't afraid of being found by Sarge, or worse, he'd have just travelled Subterranean.

The Surface was his secret passage, the way he was able to conduct his business. Most of the people living Subterranean believed the Surface uninhabitable. Long-believed lore held that the scorch had rendered the air poisonous. Deadly. Cooper certainly wasn't spreading the truth. It was just a matter of time, anyway, now that Stealth had figured it out. *Stealth*. Cooper hadn't seen him since that night in the alley. The night he'd met Nori. He had no doubt the bounty hunter would resurface. He didn't earn his deadly reputation by letting his marks go free.

There was nothing to stop Cooper from parking his motorcycle in what was once a main road through Ralston. Traffic was a thing of the distant past, at least there.

He ran a hand through the hair at the top of his head and formulated his next steps. Where was Skyler Court? Had anyone lived through the earthquake? He hoped to God Nori's parents had somehow survived. How could he return to her with any other news?

A rumbling tractor engine drew his attention to the east. Thankful for the clue, he straddled his motorcycle and sped toward the sound, the only indicator of any life left in the destroyed little town.

"Hello." Cooper raised a hand to the man on the tractor, who was too intent on his work to notice. The sound of the engine and crash of rubble as the man lifted debris from an old gas station was deafening. Cooper leaned against his bike and waited, watching the man work. There was something satisfying about it, maybe it was simply the instant results of a job well done.

When the tractor operator finally turned his way, Cooper caught the man's eye and raised his head in greeting.

The man hopped down from the machine and waddled toward him, nearly as wide as he was tall. "Haven't seen anybody new in a few days," the man said. "He stuck his arm in Cooper's direction as he walked, clasping his hand when they met and gripping hard. "Name's Durant."

"Cooper. You, ah, you live around here?"

"Yep. This is my station." He removed his cap and rubbed the top of his balding head. "Such as it is."

"I'm sorry," Cooper said, and meant it. He'd seen so much destruction it tended to run together, the whole world morphing into one big disaster. But seeing the haunted eyes of someone who'd lost everything—again—put a very personal face back on the devastation.

The man nodded but didn't say anything else.

"You know anybody named Chisholm?" Cooper asked.

Durant cocked his head. "I did. They lived over on Skyler, I think."

"That's right." Cooper nodded, hope daring to rear its head. "Have you seen them since the scorch?"

The man's mouth pursed, and he shook his head. "I'm sorry, son. No. And there isn't much of that part of town left."

Cooper nodded, his eyes darkening. He'd suspected as much. "I need to go by there."

"Just follow this road as far as you can and turn right at the old park. You'll see the slide and things—bent and idle now—but that's where you turn. Skyler is just around the corner."

Cooper twisted his foot in the dirt, hating to leave the man, who seemed so isolated. "What's next for you?" he asked.

"Aw, we'll start over again, I guess. We've had practice."

Cooper smiled despite his sadness. After all they'd lived through, people still had hope. The human spirit was a wonderfully resilient thing.

"Good luck," Cooper said and mounted the bike.

"Same to ya." Durant waved his cap in salute before donning it again.

THERE WAS HARDLY anything left of Nori's neighborhood, and her street had been hit especially hard. Cooper waded through pile after pile of ash and climbed over heaps of bricks in search of number twelve. He found eight, or what was left of it. The burned-out house looked as if it had simply abandoned hope and lain down to die.

Farther up the street, he rifled through the ash and rubble, through blackened piles of stone and metal mixed with the skeletal remains of the things that make a home. Cookware, melted and misshapen, appliances and file cabinets—all useless now. Finally, beneath a warped picture frame, Cooper found a thin piece of metal. He wiped the ash away with his hand. Twelve.

Shielding his eyes from the sunlight, Cooper looked up to find that a single wall remained erect, as if standing watch over its fallen comrades. The wall and a four-foot pile of rubble were all that remained of Nori's childhood home. Beyond those remains, the menacing mouth of a crevice as wide as a basketball court.

"Jee-zuhs." Cooper whistled low at the breadth of devastation. Entire houses had fallen into the canyon, but one or two balanced over the side, holding on for their lives. Across the crevice was the void where the other half of Nori's home had once stood. His stomach hollowed and seized at what that meant for Nori's family.

"Hello?" He cupped his hands and yelled toward the chasm. "Hello. Anyone here?" Cooper flipped over a piece of metal siding with the toe of his boot, his chest tight as he hoped for an answer. "Hello?"

There were no recent tracks, no signs of life. With advanced warning of the sunscorch, there had been time to prepare. Many people had fled to safe houses and shelters. Those who could afford them migrated to underground bunkers. But Cooper knew Nori's parents had retrofitted their basement as a makeshift shelter and had planned to stay. If they'd been on the other side of that house when it went... Cooper shook his head and, for a moment, allowed himself to think perhaps it was best if Nori never knew the truth. Maybe he wouldn't go back to Trogtown. Sure, she would always wonder, but wasn't that better than the truth?

No. He kicked at the debris again. It wasn't. She deserved to know. It wasn't fair to make her wonder. She needed closure and a chance to heal. Besides, he'd given his word to someone who'd risked her own life to save him. He didn't have many possessions, but his honor still held value.

After a deep breath and a final look around, Cooper abandoned the search for Norman and Ana Chisholm, and headed back to Trogtown with bad news.

27

BAD NEWS BEARER

"What is that?" Kade squinted at Nori's back as he rounded the table in the small dining hall.

"What? What is it?" She whirled, tugging at the tank top she'd fashioned from Hank's stacks of oversized t-shirts.

Kade pressed a single finger to the top of her shoulder. "It is," he whispered. "It's a muscle."

Nori laughed, despite herself. "Oh, shut up," she said. "Not everybody can crush nuts with their biceps. Some of us have to work at it."

"Nut crusher's my new stage name." Kade's grin was blinding. "Seriously though. I can see results."

She could, too. Under the baggy sweats, her body was changing. In the short time she'd been training, her shoulders were leaner and more defined, as were her thighs and calves. She had no arm muscles to speak of, but she could at least do a set of bicep curls without withering to the weight room floor.

It was dinner time at the Pit, and she and Kade had taken their customary place in the dining hall. As usual, Diesel sat with the other fighters but kept his eyes on them, a snarl stuck on his thin lips.

"So, what does the new heavyweight champion do now?" Nori asked before swallowing a spoonful of lukewarm soup. The cook had added thyme to the kale, sweet potato, and lentil mix known underground as olio, but he hadn't fooled anyone. "It's been nearly two weeks since the big fight. Your eye's almost healed. Will Hank schedule another fight soon?"

She meant the questions to spark light conversation. A fighter's timeline wasn't something she was familiar with. None of it was. But at her question, Kade's mood darkened, muscles flexing as he clenched his strong jaws.

"I'll fight again, though not soon enough for Hank and the others, I'm sure."

Nori swallowed, nodding, and changed the subject. "I heard Faust found the guy who beat him in the ring and demanded a rematch, which the guy granted on the spot. Faust went down in two minutes."

Kade's ears almost twitched with interest.

"Hank's furious, but only because he didn't make any money on the deal. He —"

Nori's words trailed off at the sight of someone walking toward their table. The bottom fell out of her stomach as she searched his face for a clue, but found it blank.

"Nori." Cooper nodded, his gaze soft.

"Well?" She didn't bother to introduce Kade or even say hello.

"Can we go to your room?" he asked. "Somewhere private?"

"Just tell me." Her voice was paper-thin.

"Take him to your room, Nori." Kade's words were gentle. "You don't want your business exposed in front of... You don't want to do this here." When she made no move to leave, Kade pulled her to his side and led her away from the dining hall and toward her room. Cooper was close behind.

"I'll be just down the hall." Kade eyed Cooper, but didn't say another word as he softly shut the door behind him.

Nori sat on the edge of the hard bed, her eyes focused on the floor. She couldn't look at Cooper, couldn't stand to know for sure what she thought she saw there.

The light clip of Cooper's boots as he paced the length of her room stopped. He stood in front of her and squatted to her eye level.

"Nori." His voice was tender, pleading. "Nori?"

She closed her eyes and raised her head. When she opened them again, she looked at Cooper, and the lines of his face seemed exaggerated, his expression so tired. "You didn't find them, did you?"

He shook his head. "I found your house, but not your parents. There…" He swallowed. "There was a lot of damage to the house."

Nori raised her clenched hands to her mouth, fighting the scream that wanted out. "The basement? Did you look in the basement?"

"A fissure ran right through the house, Nori, and the basement was sliced in two. I'm so sorry." Cooper reached to embrace her, but she pushed against his chest.

"But they weren't in there?"

"No."

Nori heaved a sigh of relief, her hands dropping back to her lap, though they remained in tight fists. "Could you tell if they made it out? Were they injured?"

"I-I have no way to know. Half—" Cooper rubbed his eyes

and looked away. "Half the basement fell into a canyon, Nori. There was no sign of them."

Everything seemed so far away, as if it were happening to someone else. She covered her eyes as her body folded in on itself. Rocking back and forth, she sat on the bed with her face in her hands. She didn't cry. She couldn't. It wasn't real.

COOPER STOOD silent and stoic for what seemed like hours. He didn't know Nori well enough to comfort her, though he wanted to. But he couldn't bring himself to leave her grieving, and desolate, and broken. So he stood in her room, lending support the only way he could: with his presence.

After a while, Nori looked up. The gravity of her sober gaze took him by surprise. "I have to go to them."

He stepped closer, but didn't touch her. "There's nowhere to go. The whole town was decimated. I saw it."

Her resolve faltered, her eyes shuttering for a moment before she shook her head and cleared her throat. "Doesn't matter. I know my parents. They've made it through somehow."

"I'm sure they were very strong," he said. "Just look at you. But no one could've survived that, Nori. And besides, Hank won't let you leave."

"He can't keep me here!"

Cooper did touch her then, clasping her upper arms. He wanted to shake her, to shake sense and comprehension into her silly little head. "Yes, he can. And he will. He's an honest man with a soft spot for underdogs, but he's a businessman first. He paid a lot of money for you, and he's not going to let his investment go on a fools errand."

"'Fools errand," she whispered. "You think they're dead." It wasn't a question.

Cooper's resolve cracked under her desperate, horrified gaze. He loosened his grip on her arms, but held on. "God, Nori, I..." He let go of her shoulders and ran his arms behind her back, pulling her solidly into his body. She stiffened, too stunned to move, but didn't pull away. One heartbeat. Two. And then Nori crumbled into him. He held her as she struggled to catch her breath between sobs, as her legs gave out and her body went limp. He held her until she took a final sniff, running a hand between the two of them to wipe her eyes and nose.

At last she looked up, her too-blue eyes so swollen and red-rimmed they were eerily reminiscent of the sunscorched world. She cleared her throat, staring into Cooper's gaze so long he started to speak just to end the charged silence.

"I'm going to find them, Cooper," she said. "There has to be a way."

"NO. ABSOLUTELY NOT." Hank had listened as Nori told her story, leaning his head to the side and clicking his tongue sympathetically toward the end.

Though she'd left out a significant part about coming from the Surface, he seemed to her engrossed in the tale of how she'd been separated from her parents, swindled by a stranger, and left to fend for herself before being captured by Sarge and his minions. Hank seemed sympathetic to her situation...until she asked for his help, asked to be released to go in search of her parents.

"Please," Nori begged, putting the fierceness of her love in her words and her eyes. "Please let me go to them."

"I understand your situation, darlin'," he said. "I really do, and I'm sorry. But I can't let you leave. Besides the danger someone like you could get in on your own, there's the pretty substantial fact that I have a lot of money invested in you."

"That's not my fault!" Nori's grief morphed into anger. "You chose to give that jerk your money. That's on you. You can't own people."

"I can, and I do," Hank said. "And whether you'll admit it or not, I saved you the day I gave that jerk my money. There are worse fates than being here. It's honest work under my protection. You're lucky Cooper was there that day. You're lucky he brought you here. And a little gratitude wouldn't kill you."

"Gratitude?" Nori scoffed. "You want me to thank you for holding me hostage? For keeping me here when my family needs me? When they're out there homeless and worried sick about me? They'll never find me in here. That's why I have to go to them."

"They're probably already gone!" Hank's voice boomed through the small office. "Did you think of that?"

Nori jerked and shrank into herself.

"I'm sorry," he said. "I just— This is ridiculous. The answer is no."

Nori scrubbed her face with her hands, taking long, deep breaths to regain her composure. What would she do? What could she do? She went very still. Her mind was resolved as soon as the thought struck her.

"Fine," she said. "Thanks for nothing, you old goat. There's your gratitude."

The slam of the door splintered the silence in the hall. She had no doubt the entire Pit had heard their conversation, but she couldn't bring herself to care.

"Nori, I—"

"Don't even start," she interrupted Cooper. Her nostrils flared as she sucked in an irritated breath. "This is your fault, too. I wouldn't be stuck here if it weren't for you."

Cooper reached out to hold her arms again, but she jerked from him.

His head and hands dropped. "I'm sorry I couldn't help more. But I did what I could."

Nori didn't say another word, didn't say goodbye. She strode to her room and shut the door.

She had work to do.

28

A BAD BREAK

Armed with her pocketknife and loaded with all the water and Vitabars she could carry, Nori closed the door to her room as she left. She regretted not being able to say goodbye to Kade, but he'd admitted he would never let her leave. After a final glance in the direction of her friend's room, she headed toward the Pit and the Subterranean beyond it.

Her temporary home wasn't just quiet as she left, but a vacuum of sound. Her steps and nervous breaths, though she aimed for silence, ricocheted down the hall. Luckily, she'd planned her escape when everyone was asleep, tiptoeing past the cavernous Pit. Sixty yards to freedom.

If she could just get through Trogtown unnoticed, she could hurry down those steps and escape into the tunnel the same way she'd come in. There were twenty-two turns. She'd kept track, despite speeding through tunnels on the back of Cooper's motorcycle. Scribbling down notes at the first opportunity, she had noted turns and infrequent landmarks, sure the information would be useful sooner or later. As she snuck away from the Pit, she was thankful she'd had the foresight to tuck the notes away for just such an occasion.

Breaking into Dave's store for more supplies before leaving town was another risk. Was it worth it? She had food —such as it was—water, and a weapon. That would have to do. She had no need of lanterns or lights, after all, which would give her one advantage over anyone who pursued her.

Would Hank send Kade when he discovered her missing? Diesel and Bron? Would he hunt her himself? Nori shuddered at the thought of being hunted, but pushed her fears down deep. She had to do this. Had to know. Her parents had not died in the sunscorch, she knew it. *She knew it.* She hoped. Oh, God, she hoped they were safe.

Halfway across the Pit. Thirty yards to freedom. She ran a hand across the weight bar Kade had been lifting when she first met him. She would miss having a friend. It had been nice while it lasted. But when she found her parents and they made a new home—somewhere—she would make new friends.

Fifteen yards to freedom. Nori's pace ticked up as she neared the doorway, and she worked to slow her breathing, to calm down and escape as quietly as possible. The double doors were locked, but she'd taken the key from Hank's office days ago. She shrugged. It was his own fault. He'd been foolish to trust her, to think she wouldn't try to escape. In the nineteen days she'd been there, she'd secretly planned for this day. How could she not? That Hank considered her his property made no difference to her.

She'd promised to meet her parents after the sunscorch, and that was what she intended to do. But it had been eleven days since the scorch. She'd never thought it would take Cooper so long. Had she missed the window to reach them?

Had they moved on? No. She shook her head. They wouldn't leave without word from her. Were they waiting somewhere? Trying to find where Barker had taken her? That was most likely, and oh, how she hated the thought of her sweet parents in a panic to find the concealed entrance to the Subterranean.

"Going somewhere?" Hank's voice ruptured the darkness, laced with anger and ego. "You think I'm that stupid, girl? You think I didn't know you'd try to leave if I didn't let you go? You think I haven't been through this same damn thing before?" He stood from a chair propped against a support column. "Turn around, now, and get back to your room. I don't know what punishment you'll get for stealing my food and trying to sneak off like this, but I'll think of something."

Nori's face was hot. He'd been there the entire time, and she hadn't seen him, even with her keen night vision. Tucked behind the column like that, he must've watched her creep through the Pit. He'd probably laughed when she'd cast worried looks behind her, when she'd hunkered down and crept toward the door like a cat burglar. Humiliation sent blood straight to her head and anger resurfaced.

"I have to get to my parents," Nori grated through clenched teeth. "It may not be tonight, but I'll get out of here. Just you wait and see." Spinning on her heel, Nori moved to stalk back to her room. Instead, she nearly collided with Kade. Shame and fear flooded her senses, and she felt two feet tall. She turned her head from her friend, not daring to look up at him.

"I'll buy her freedom."

Nori jerked at Kade's words, and her head snapped up.

"What?" she and Hank said at the same time.

"I'll give you what you paid for her. Just let her go. Let her try."

"You don't have that kind of money," Hank said with a sneer.

"I do." Kade's voice was confident. "With winnings from this last fight and what I've saved over the years through a little gambling of my own, I can do it. I can pay for her freedom. I had planned to use it for something else..." Kade swallowed and looked away. "But, well, there's no use now."

"You'd do that?" Nori's gaze lit on every inch of Kade's face. He was serious. He had the money.

Hank's breath came hard. He was boiling mad. Not just at her escape or the prospect of losing her through a fair purchase, she thought, but at Kade's betrayal.

"I won't let her leave for less than six." Hank's snarl was a vile thing.

Kade stepped toward Hank and towered over the big man. "I know you only paid fifty-five."

"That's my price," he spat. "Take it or leave it."

"I'll take it." Kade's voice was resigned. "But I'm leaving, too."

"Kade, please." Hank's tune had changed fast. "You can't leave. You're the champ now. Think of the money to be made in title fights. You want to buy her freedom, fine. She can go for fifty-five. But don't go. Not like this. Don't give up everything you've worked so hard for."

"It doesn't matter anymore, Hank. None of it does. With Grant gone, I... It doesn't matter anymore."

"I knew that little punk would come between us," Hank snarled. "I should never have let it get that far. Should've gotten him out of here when I could. Now he's a damned martyr."

Kade gasped, shocked at Hank's admission. His eyes shone with the depth of his pain. "You did try to trade him. I didn't believe it. Didn't believe *him*. You promised me, Hank. You promised."

Hank closed his eyes as a look of shame and something else—defiance—plagued his features. "He didn't want you to fight anymore. Came to me and begged me not to schedule any more bouts. Can you imagine? The nerve of that little... He had to go. I saw the way you looked at him. Knew he'd get his way eventually."

"And now he has." Kade clenched and unclenched his fists, the battle between fury and restraint clear. "We'll leave first thing in the morning."

"Just give me my money and get the hell out of here!" Hank said belligerently. "I don't want you here!"

"You got it." Kade nodded to Nori, who followed him back into the narrow hall toward their rooms.

"Kade, are you sure?" she asked.

"More sure than I've been in a long time. He lied about Grant. I should've trusted him over Hank, but I didn't. There's nothing I can do about it now. Nothing but leave."

"I'm sorry," she said weakly.

Kade faced her, his jaws set. "I hope you've got some sort of plan."

"You're coming with me?" Nori yelped so loudly Kade put a finger to his mouth. "Really?" she squeaked more softly.

"I can't stay here." His bitter laugh held no humor. "I've got nowhere else to go. I might as well tag along and watch over you. Believe it or not," he tilted his head in mock serious- ness, "some people find me terrifying."

Nori beamed even as tears of relief threatened. She held them at bay, though, while Kade gathered a few things from his room and stuffed them into a duffel bag.

As Kade packed, Nori took a last look around his room.

JEN CRANE

She hadn't noticed before, but one corner held several paint-
ings. One was propped against the wall with freshly-rinsed
brushes piled neatly beside it.

"Kade?" Nori said. "Did you paint these?"

She flipped through a stack of beautiful sunrises, their
ethereal beauty captured in orange and purple hues.

"How did you paint these?" she asked. "You've never seen
a sunrise."

"Painting isn't just what your eyes see," he said, taking a
moment from packing to glance at his work on the table.
"Sometimes you see with your soul."

Nori's heart neared its bursting point again. She was
certain she could see into Keegan Kade's soul, and that it was
radiant.

"You got it right," she whispered. Then louder, "You very
nearly got it right."

Kade shot her a curious look. "Hold this," he said and
handed her the duffel while he lifted the thin mattress. A hole
had been dug into the rock shelf underneath and he dug
through a top layer of gravel and dirt. He pulled a worn
canvas bag from the hole, opened the drawstring, pulled out
several bills, and stuffed them into the front pocket of his dark
pants. After cinching the bag back up, Kade took the duffel
back from Nori and left the room without a backward glance.
She followed.

The door to Hank's office was open and he was pretending
to work, despite the early morning hours. As they passed,
Kade tossed the canvas bag into the office, sending it sliding
across the desk and into Hank's lap. He fumbled for the bag,
lifting it clumsily and, when he looked up, his face was twisted
with loathing.

"Count it if you need to," Kade said. "There's extra for the

180

food." He stretched to his full height and pointed a finger at the old pit boss. "We're done. You understand?" Kade took a step closer. "You send somebody after us, and they won't come back."

Nori and Kade didn't speak, didn't stop, didn't look back until they reached the steps leading out of Trogtown.

"You think he'll follow us?" Nori asked, jogging to keep up with her friend. "You think he'll send someone to bring us back?"

"No." His voice was smooth and sharp as steel. "He knows he's wronged me, that I meant what I said."

A shiver skittered down Nori's spine at the weight of Kade's threat. Thank God he was on her side.

29

KADE'S STORY

"I wish I had a weapon."

Nori and Kade had been walking for two hours, at least, and those were the first words out of his mouth.

She patted her pockets. "I've got a knife you can have."

"Knife doesn't do much good in a gun fight."

She jerked to a stop. "Who has a gun?"

"Everyone."

Nori thought back to the awful day she was taken to Hank and cringed at the memory of Wallace and Jenks and Sarge. No one had pulled a gun on her, but had they been tucked into filthy riding pants and leather jackets? The militant types she'd hidden from in the alcove that first day had guns, though. "Huh." She shook her head. "I've never used one."

Kade opened his mouth to speak before snapping it shut. His jaws flexed and he scrutinized Nori through narrowed eyes.

"What?" she asked, wiping clean her mouth and nose.

"Something doesn't add up." Kade shook his head. "If I'm honest, it never has. You're...you're too odd."

Nori's shocked bark of laughter bounced down the tunnel. "Wow. Thanks."

"Okay, maybe odd's not the right word. Different. You're too different. You don't know major towns. You're unfamiliar with common foods. I've noticed little differences in the things you say." Kade stopped and Nori met his searching gaze. "I've heard about religious cults and...and I know a bit about abuse." He cleared his throat. "If we're going to do this, I'd like to know you as best I can. Where did you grow up, and how did you come to live at the Pit?"

Nori swallowed past the lump in her throat. Of course he noticed something was different about her. She grew up in a completely different world. No amount of adapting could cover up the basic gaffes she'd made. Should she tell him the truth? He'd sacrificed both his money and his future for her. He'd left a good home and a great living in a very unstable world. He'd joined her team. She owed him the truth, at the very least.

"I grew up on the Surface, Kade."

His face screwed up in confusion and a series of emotions played across his face. Disbelief, mockery, injury, anger, and, finally, resentment fouled his bold features.

"You don't have to lie to me." He crossed thick arms over his chest. "If you don't wanna talk about it, that's fine."

Nori touched his arm. "I'm telling the truth. I grew up in a town called Ralston *on top of* this underground world somewhere. It's why I don't know things." She gave him a playful grin. "It's why I'm odd."

"Whatever, Nori." His brows creased and the twist of his mouth held scorn. But something else found its way onto his face. There, just inside the crinkle of his eyes, was the tiniest sliver of hope. "You seriously expect me to believe that?"

"Yes." She said and shrugged.

Kade opened and closed his mouth several times before settling on, "Why didn't you tell me before?"

"Well, we never talked about where I came from." Before he could object, she quickly added, "And I was afraid of absolutely everything. Of everyone. I thought my best shot at surviving was to keep my head down and my business to myself. I didn't know who to trust. I've read enough books to know the guy who rocks the boat is usually the first one thrown overboard.

"Can I ask you... " Nori struggled for words that wouldn't offend him. "How is it possible you didn't know people lived aboveground?"

"Well, there are stories about rogues and nomads who've gone to Surface, but they're myths. I mean, the earth was decimated after the sunscorch. The air on the Surface is poisoned."

Nori grimaced. "It's not poisoned."

Kade shook his head. "What do you mean?"

"There was a big scorch, it's true, and a lot of people died. Apparently, the only Earth I've ever known is in ruins compared to what it used to be. But people—humanity—survived. We're a resourceful and resilient bunch, my dad always says." She risked a look up at Kade, who hung on her every word. "It's dangerous on the Surface, don't get me wrong," she went on. "In most places, it's either too hot or too cold to live, so people moved to the middle of the globe where the climate is more stable. It's very crowded there."

"I'm not saying I believe this." Kade threw his hands in front of his chest. "But for hypothetical purposes, let's just say I did. Why didn't your family move?"

Nori's steps slowed before stopping completely. She didn't

face him when she answered. "I lost siblings in one of the scorches, and we couldn't…couldn't leave them."

Kade touched her arm. "I'm sorry."

"We have to go now, though, and it kills me. I know it's killing my parents."

"I know that's a hard choice. They must love you very much."

Nori sniffed and cleared her throat. "There are others who didn't leave for their own reasons. They built bunkers and basements to survive. Living aboveground…it's a very close-knit community. People have to rely on each other to make it." Kade nodded and the two began walking again.

"Does everyone believe it's poisonous aboveground?" Nori asked after a while. Well, not everyone, she amended. Cooper and Barker knew. Certainly there were others.

Kade shrugged. "Everyone I know."

KADE'S HEAD whipped up at a sound reverberating through the tunnel. Nori heard it, too, and was already sprinting before Kade made the decision to run.

"Come on!" she called, not slowing.

"That's a jeep," Kade said between breaths as he pumped his arms, his upper body nearly dragging the lower portion. He was fast for a big man, but not nearly as quick as Nori. She led them farther into the tunnel even though they couldn't possibly outrun the vehicle.

The white beams of headlights slithered around a corner before the jeep came into view. Nori risked a look behind her, catching a glimpse of the round headlamps the moment they breached the corner. Kade was on her heels with no signs of slowing, but the vehicle gained ground as if they were hobbled. It was no use. They were too slow. She met Kade's frantic gaze, and he blinked in understanding.

Planting her feet, Nori jerked to a stop. She threw her back against the wall, her breaths quick and shallow, and pulled the knife from her pocket.

Kade put himself between Nori and the approaching jeep, feet spread wide and hands fisted at his sides. He was ready for a fight.

"What...do we do?" she panted.

"People...use these tunnels...all the time." He took a deep breath, straightening and relaxing his posture. "We play it cool. Just because it's a jeep doesn't mean it's Hank."

"Okay." Nori nodded, still working to slow her breathing, and hid the knife in the waist of her jeans. "Play it cool. I got it."

"And Nori?" he said.

"Yeah?"

"If it's Hank or someone who tries to hurt us, remember what I taught you."

"About fighting? Which one—use the force of my body or aim for the soft spots?"

"Either. Both. Everything you've got."

Nori nodded and bent her knees. She was ready as she'd ever be.

The jeep slowed as it neared them then stopped. Nori's heart slammed in her chest. The only remaining sound was their labored breathing. She worked to slow her racing heart, to concentrate, to think.

With the headlights off, she could see the two people inside. The driver had a scraggly black beard and mustache, and his camouflaged hat was in tatters from years of wear.

The woman in the passenger seat had thick, corded muscles starting from her shoulders all the way down her arms. A brown t-shirt stretched over tight pectorals.

The woman looked at Nori and then to Kade with discerning, deep brown eyes. "You all right?" she asked Nori.

"We're fine," Kade said coolly. "Just passing through."

"I wasn't asking you." She put a hand on a rifle stashed beside her leg and turned so only Nori could see her face. The woman inspected Nori's skin, her clothes, her hands, and searched her gaze. "You all right, honey?"

Nori's relieved smile was genuine. "Yes. I'm not in trouble." She touched her chest. "But thank you."

Both the man and woman's postures relaxed, and the woman nodded. "Be careful." She tilted her head at Kade. "Even with one big as that beside you. This place is crawling with monsters."

Too late, Nori raised a hand in farewell as the driver shifted the jeep into gear and sped away.

"Kade?" Nori asked much later.

"Yeah?"

"How is it you came to fight for Hank?"

Kade's shoulders sank toward the ground, and he let out a long breath. "It's a long story. And not a happy one."

"Well, we've got, what, two days worth of walking ahead? We've got nothing but time. Besides, you know my story now. It's only fair."

"All right." He sighed and rolled his neck but kept his pace. "I was born north of here in a big settlement. There are places, Nori—a lot of places—that are rough, and lawless, and deadly. Kill or be killed, like the wild west." He paused and looked down at her. "Is it like that on the Surface?" he asked, eyes lit and voice nearly giddy. "Like the Wild West I've read about?"

Nori shook her head. "No horses."

Kade frowned, but went on. "Anyway, after these settlements were built decades ago, the ones who survived were the meanest, the most ruthless—those who'd do anything to stay alive. One of them was my father.

"He taught me to fight at a very young age. He was very..." Kade leaned his head from side to side, "firm...with me. We sparred constantly. I lost, of course. It's why I'm so good at taking punches. I've done it my whole life." He cleared his throat. "Fighting was our normal, and it came with his attention, so naturally I became a great student. When I was eight, he started pitting me against older boys because I was bigger than the ones my own age."

Nori nodded but didn't speak, afraid to break the spell that had somehow loosened Kade's tongue.

"And then a few years later..." Kade rolled his neck again, but the smooth planes of his face developed hard angles. "I had to defend myself a lot when word got around that I didn't take the same interest in girls as other boys." He swallowed and looked at the ground. "When my father found out why I kept coming home bloody, he beat me himself."

Nori's sharp breath drew his gaze back up, and his mouth twisted before he said, "Then he kicked me out. Said he wouldn't suffer an abomination like me in his house and forced me to leave."

"Oh, Kade." Nori's heart physically hurt for her friend. "Where was your mother during all of this?"

"Died. I was young." His eyes glazed a bit as he said, "I remember the feel of her hands on my face. I remember big, dark eyes, but that's about all." The muscles in his jaws suddenly clenched. "Sometimes I wonder if she took the only way she had to escape my father, but…" He swallowed hard. "I don't think she would've left me with him alone. She loved me. I know that, at least."

"I'm so sorry." Nori's hands ached to hug her friend, but she settled on gripping his fingers and letting him finish the story.

"It was hard being alone at first, but I was happy to leave, honestly. Life with him…it was a cruel and bloody hell.

"I left town. Went south. A gang—though they called themselves a unit, like they were military—found me first. They were impressed with how long I fought them off." He sniffed and straightened. "They sold me to a fighting ring."

Nori's eyes were wide as she watched a range of emotions play over Kade's strong features. She tripped on a loose rock and grunted. "We have that in common, at least."

"That's where the similarities end." His mouth twisted sardonically. "The people they sold me to weren't Hank. Not even close. It was a syndicate of sorts, so there were several people invested in my success—or failure. Several to dole out threats or mete out punishments. We…we were like dogs to them. One owner took a particular interest in me. Reminded me of my father in so many ways." Kade's jaws and fists flexed, chill bumps erupting along his skin as memories resurfaced.

Nori swallowed past the lump in her throat. "How did you get away?"

"Hank brought fighters to a match in my town. I was headed to the locker room and found a woman wandering the halls." The lines around Kade's eyes softened. "She was confused, she'd hurt herself, she…wasn't well. I cleaned her up and took her to Hank, who by then was desperate to find her."

"Janie," Nori breathed, and Kade nodded.

"It was before she got so bad." Kade cleared his throat. "Anyway, Hank knew how the people I fought for treated fighters. Hell, they took pride in their reputation. Hank said someone with a heart like mine had no place with the soulless swine." Kade smiled suddenly. "Isn't it funny the things you remember? 'Soulless swine' he called them. So, he bought me. I wasn't cheap."

Nori shook her head in wonder. "I imagine not."

"A lot of the fighters you know at the Pit could tell you a similar story."

She blinked back the tears that threatened to spill onto her cheeks. "I love that story. And I hate it. Kind of how I feel about Hank."

Kade nodded his agreement. "So you see, fighting is all I've ever known. It's about damn time I try something new, don't you think?"

30

THE LONG ROAD HOME

Nori's stomach growled, drawing a grin from Kade. "Hungry?" he asked.

She shrugged and pulled her backpack around in search of Vitabars.

The two ate in companionable silence, concerned with the road ahead but unwilling—or unable—to voice their fears.

"You hear that?" Nori's voice was a harsh whisper.

"Shhh." Kade angled his head toward the noise. "Motorcycle this time."

"You think it's Sarge?"

"No way to know. Could be anybody. Same as before, okay? Cool but cautious."

Nori nodded and touched the knife in her pocket.

The high-pitched whine of a motorcycle grew nearly unbearable just before it stopped completely. Though the engine had cut off, the headlight remained on, blinding them. Nori imagined Wallace, his weasel-like face pulled into a feral grin at his luck.

Too late, she remembered to hide her eyes, and panic

buckled her knees. Oh God, she thought. Did they see? Did they see? She angled her face down and away from the light, but any damage had already been done.

When the headlamp finally switched off, Nori could just make out the silhouette of the man stepping from the machine. Her heart pulverized the inside of her chest. But it wasn't Wallace, or Sarge, or Jenks, and she blew out the breath she'd been holding.

"What the hell, Nori?" Cooper eyed her suspiciously, angrily as he stalked toward them. "And you," he spat in Kade's direction. "I never thought you'd do something this stupid."

Kade sputtered before finally finding words. "I didn't break her out, if that's what you're accusing me of." He stepped forward, his deep voice sharp and defensive. "I bought her freedom. And my own, long ago."

"Oh, I know." One of Cooper's brows arched haughtily. "Hank told me everything."

Kade straightened. "Did he, now?"

"He did. He was feeling pretty bad about some of the things he said. Didn't tell me word for word, but I got the idea."

"Feeling bad?" Kade snorted. "He send any money back with you?"

"Well." Cooper's eyes danced. "He wasn't feeling that bad. Where, ah...where you two headed?" He feigned nonchalance, but his dark brows crept together, giving away the depths of his interest.

Nori and Kade exchanged glances. Should they let Cooper in on their plans? Kade's shoulder lifted slightly, and she gave him a quick nod.

"We're free to go where we want." Her words tumbled out in a rush. "Kade's going to help me look for my parents."

Cooper's nostrils flared before he schooled his features. He looked back and forth between them for several tense moments. "Fine," he finally said. "I'll go with you."

Nori smirked as her head snapped back. "I don't remember asking you."

"Look," Cooper said through gritted teeth. "I've been to the Surface since you have. It's a mess. A dangerous, disastrous mess. I had to backtrack three times and climb in places. You need my help, whether you admit it or not."

Nori wasn't interested in changing their plans and stepped to Kade's side. She slung her backpack behind her. "We can do just fine on our own."

Cooper's dark eyes held cold irritation. "You know how to get to the Surface?"

"No." Nori spat the word, but it was hardly more than a whisper.

"Do you?" Cooper nodded at Kade, who blanched. "I didn't think so," he said.

"I can find it." Nori's hands flew to her hips. "I marked the entrance when I first came in. If we just keep going, I know I can find it."

"Why?" Cooper shook his head. "Why waste time and effort when I know exactly where to go?"

"Well." She snorted without grace. "Reason number one is that you captured and sold me. I don't trust you as far as I can throw you."

Cooper's nostrils flared again, which Nori was pretty sure meant he was incensed. "You don't trust me? Even after I took you to safety, to Hank. After I went days out of my way to find your parents, and bring you news of them? I didn't have to do any of that."

"You owed me for saving you, and you know it."

"I did. That's true. But you might admit I went above and beyond."

"You said you took me to Hank for protection. What's to keep you from thinking I need it again, from taking me right back there?"

Cooper's mouth twisted wryly as his gaze slid to Kade, and Nori grunted.

"Maybe you're leading us right to Wallace, and Sarge, and that idiot Jenks. Maybe you're going to sell us *both* this time."

"I'd like to see him try." Kade's face was confident, an unabashed challenge.

"I've left their company." A shudder ran through Cooper.

"Why?" Nori asked.

"I don't need them anymore."

"Why?"

"I've learned all I need to know," he ground out.

"What do you mean learned? It wasn't an internship. What, are you wise in the ways of the slave trade now?"

Cooper straightened, and his hands clenched to fists. "Look. I'm going that way." He nodded in the direction she and Kade had been going. "I know where there's another bike. You wanna walk the rest of the way, or take your chances with me?"

Nori's answer was unintelligible as she kicked at a pile of rocks.

"Think about it, Nori," Kade said, suddenly the intermediary. "He knows the way, and we could get there faster on a bike. I don't see the problem here."

Cooper's eyebrows inched toward his hairline, and he nodded thanks in Kade's direction.

She shook her head, preparing to argue again, but the fight was gone. Only fear, and dread, and sorrow remained.

"I guess... " Her words were strained with emotion. "I guess because he's so sure they're dead. And I don't need that kind of negativity."

Cooper's gaze softened, and he started toward her, but stopped at Kade's warning snarl. "Can we just start over?" Cooper asked. "I'll take you there, and you can decide for yourself."

Nori didn't say anything for so long Cooper stepped around to see her face. "I promise to keep my mouth shut about it. Okay?"

Nori ran her fingers along her cheeks and cleared her throat. "Okay."

"Okay," Kade and Cooper breathed at the same time.

"HOW MUCH FARTHER IS THIS BIKE?" Though her leather hiking boots were worn and comfortable, Nori's feet ached. She rolled her shoulders, her neck sore from hauling the weight of a backpack for so long.

"There's a storage facility just ahead."

She had a bad feeling she knew the answer, but asked anyway. "Whose storage facility?"

Cooper's answering grin was sheepish. "Sarge and his Boss's."

Kade cursed. "They don't know we're going to 'use' this motorcycle, do they?"

The muscles along Cooper's wide jaw clenched. "No."

"Why would you steal from your friends?" Nori asked.

"They're not my friends."

The vehemence in his words surprised her, and she exchanged a glance with Kade. "What were you doing with them, then?"

Cooper didn't answer, and Nori stepped in front of him. "Either we trust each other, or we don't. I have every reason not to trust you, yet here I am. Trying. Now it's your turn."

Cooper searched her face until her cheeks heated at the attention. Finally, he took a deep breath, his eyes shuttering. "Fact finding," he said, and pushed his bike ahead without another word.

"So, you expect me to drive this thing?" Kade approached the motorcycle like it was a pit viper.

"It's that or walk another forty miles," Cooper called over his shoulder as he pilfered gas and supplies from the storage facility. "I'm really surprised you can't ride." His voice held the slightest of taunts. "How have you gotten around this whole time?"

"Jeeps can fit through most tunnels. That's how we traveled for fights when I was with Hank."

"There was a Jeep at Hank's?" Disbelief laced Nori's high-pitched squeal.

"Yeah." Kade shrugged.

"You didn't think to tell me that?"

"What, so you could steal it? No, I didn't think it wise to tell you."

She snorted and shook her head. "Unbelievable."

"He let us go, Nori. That's one thing. But stealing from

Hank is another thing entirely. He would've come for us, and you'd never make it to look for your parents."

"He's right," Cooper chimed in then frowned. "Anyway, you wanna learn to ride this thing or not?"

After a series of mind-numbing instructions on kill switches, clutches, and throttles, even Nori had the basics down. An idea snaked through her head. Yes. Later she would have Cooper show her how to ride.

Kade's big body dwarfed the motorcycle like a circus strong man on the clown bike. Slowly releasing his grip on the clutch, he pressed the toe of his boot to shift down into first gear. The bike made a quick jerk then settled, and Kade let out a long, relieved breath.

When he pulled back on the throttle and released the clutch, though, the back tire jolted into gear, throwing him off balance. Kade's eyes flew wide, and his mouth flew open on a high-pitched yelp. His big legs swung wildly, and he grappled with the ground to recover.

Nori started toward him to help, but Cooper held her back. As she watched Kade's clumsy one-man show, she simultaneously tried not to panic and not to laugh.

Finally, Kade released the throttle and braced his feet. The bike stilled, but his panic didn't.

Cooper shook his head. "What do you see in him?"

Nori's surprised grin grew wicked. She had no problem letting Cooper think what he would.

After several more practice runs, the determined and capable Kade Nori knew resurfaced. "All right," he said, though his voice lacked confidence. "I think I'm ready."

She smiled as she marched toward her friend, preparing to mount the bike behind him.

"Oh, no, no, no." Cooper said, his mouth forming a perfect "o."

"What?" Nori asked.

"You can't ride with him. He can barely support himself. You'll throw him off balance and get us all killed. We need to move fast to avoid...anyone, and riding with him will slow us all down."

Cooper was right, of course. Kade looked petrified enough without her on board. With a hopeless groan, she threw a leg over the bike behind Cooper, and remembered with distaste the last time she'd found herself behind him. At least she wasn't handcuffed.

Nori reached under Cooper's leather jacket to find belt loops at the sides of his leather riding pants. She was relieved she could hold on to them without having to get too close. But as soon as her butt hit the seat, Cooper threw the bike into gear without a word, accelerating so quickly her neck snapped back and her body tipped backward. Yelping, she linked her arms around Cooper's waist and held on for dear life.

Muscles moved beneath her clenched hands. He was laughing.

31

YOU CAN'T GO HOME AGAIN

Nori shot occasional glances behind her to check on Kade's progress. After the initial panic wore off, the tightness around his eyes softened, making it almost look as if he were enjoying himself. He worked to keep his mouth closed and dust out, but a grin kept slipping onto his face, his top lip rising to show a row of straight teeth. Nori couldn't help but grin, too.

Just as when she'd first entered the subterranean world weeks ago, there were only grimy rock tunnels for miles and miles. With Kade and Cooper she sped through the underground roadway, the roar of motorcycle engines doing nothing to drown out the thoughts in her head. Was Cooper right? Were her parents… No. She couldn't bring herself to even think the word. What would she do if they weren't in Ralston? Where would she go then?

Nori pressed her forehead to the space between Cooper's shoulder blades and closed her eyes. She wouldn't think like that. They were alive, whether still in Ralston or somewhere else. They were all right, she just knew it. They had to be.

Nori's body surged forward when Cooper geared down and the motorcycle slowed. Grip tight on his gray t-shirt, she leaned around to search the tunnel ahead for signs of danger. Nothing.

"Why are we stopping?"

"This is where we go to the Surface."

A bit farther up the tunnel widened, and the outlines of a path leading left were faintly visible. Her heart rate vaulted, anxiety giving her a fresh jolt. Could it be the same way she'd come in? She whipped her head to the right in search of the arc she'd drawn with a rock that first day with Barker. Even through the odd shadows cast by the motorcycle headlights she could see it. Faint, but there.

Kade pulled up beside them and executed a perfect halt. His eyes danced with pride. "What's up?"

"This is it." Cooper nodded toward the side tunnel. "There's an incline then an iron door. Our bikes'll just make it through. I'll lead."

Nori's breath left in a rush. Her nerves were shot, but she straightened and turned to smile at her friend. Kade's face was bone white. His gaze shot wildly from her to Cooper to the new tunnel. "And on the other side of the door?" he asked.

"Outside. It's still a few miles into Ralston. We'll have to…"

Nori stopped listening to Cooper.

Her friend's throat bobbed nervously. "Kade?" she said. "Are you okay?" He gave no answer, just a panicked stare at the tunnel. "Hey," Nori said low. "It's going to be fine. I grew up out there, and I'm all right." She smiled at him. "Right?"

A fine tremor ran the length of Kade's big body. He was frozen with fear.

"What's wrong with him?" Cooper whispered.

"Everything he believed about the world is about to be turned upside down."

Nori waved her hand to get her friend's attention. "Kade?" she said. "Kade, look at me."

He slowly turned his head toward her, though his body remained rigidly forward.

"I didn't know about your world until I had to find a place to wait out the scorch. My parents and I denied its existence at first. It couldn't be true. A whole world out there we didn't know about? No way." Nori's voice was low but coaxing. Soothing. "But I took one step, and then another. Little steps of faith that ultimately led me to you." She swallowed. "Can you take a few steps for me?"

Kade turned more fully toward her. His grip relaxed on the handlebars, and some of the tension left his lips. He nodded and took a deep breath.

Nori sighed and closed her eyes. "Good," she said. "Good. We can do this."

"Let's go." Cooper didn't wait. He started his motorcycle and inched toward the tunnel exit. Kade followed.

The iron door she'd come through before was rusted and round, and over six feet in circumference.

"Be right back." Cooper's movements were confident as he engaged the kickstand, slid his leg across the bike, and stalked toward the massive door.

A metal turnstile stuck out from the middle of the door, which looked, Nori decided, exactly like the rusty old door to a bank vault.

"Is there a secret code?" she asked to lighten the mood, her voice echoing through the small space.

"Not from the inside," Cooper said. Nori couldn't tell if he was kidding or not.

Cooper strained to spin the turnstile, and when it finally gave, the lock sprung free with a thick click. It creaked on rusty hinges as Cooper worked to pull it wide.

Nori sent a last excited grin to Kade behind her, whose answering smile wasn't really a smile at all.

Closing her eyes, Nori prepared to breathe in the glorious fresh air that awaited just beyond the door. It had been so long since she'd inhaled anything but damp, stale air that was tinged with garbage, or metal, or male sweat. The first gust of wind brought not the sweet scents of home, though, but the sharp, chemical smell of burned things. Nori's eyes flew open, and she strained to see beyond the door frame.

Cooper checked his watch before straddling the bike and releasing the kickstand. "We've got about two hours of dark left. We'll have to search for your parents and get back underground as fast as we can." He eased through the door, waited for Kade to pass, and then closed it behind them before mounting the bike once more.

"If for some reason we get separated—" Cooper stopped, turned in the seat, and found Nori's eyes. "If we get separated, you can always find your way back underground by looking for the signs."

Her head cocked to the side, but she held his gaze. "What signs?"

"Like that one." He pointed to a battered metal electrical box a hundred or so feet from the door.

She looked between Cooper and the spray-painted symbol, her brows wrinkling in confusion. "That's just graffiti."

"It looks like graffiti." He shook his head. "But it's much more."

The red and black eye watched back. It was intricately

202

done, though the final result appeared primitive. The outline of an eye was spray-painted onto the metal in black then covered in red. A translucent orb was left unpainted inside the pupil, giving the symbol near-animated soul.

"Is it always this symbol?" Nori's voice was hollow as she grasped the gravity of the information he'd shared.

"No." Cooper hadn't moved. "This one, the scarlet eye, means beware of watchful eyes. Make sure you're alone before using the passage. Make sure no one sees."

The bike roared to life and they were off, the incline brief but bumpy. Nori gritted her teeth as tires gripped cement ridges and weaved toward the top of a hill.

"This is the dam outside Ralston," she said. "I knew I heard water when I came down."

She peeked back at Kade, whose eyes were as big as saucers and nearly all white. Every time he could manage to look away from the road in front of him, he looked up. Nori searched the night sky for what held his interest. Then it hit her. Kade had never seen the night sky. Though the atmosphere was hazy and dense from the recent sunscorch, the stars were still visible. To never have seen the stars... She shook her head. How very sad. With a wistful smile in his direction, she turned back to Cooper with more questions.

"How long has that entrance underground been there?"

Cooper shrugged as if there must be more to Nori's question. "Since they built it."

"What, the dam?"

He nodded.

"You're telling me that passage underground has been there for, like, sixty years and no one knew it?"

"Oh, people knew it," he said over the roar of the engines. "Just not the people you know."

Nori's mouth pressed into a thin line as the information filtered into her understanding of the world she'd always known. A world wiped out and rebuilt time and again. A world that had lost entire countries, entire populations, entire families. A world that had lost billions of people to environmental devastation that was never even a concern to those living Subterranean.

"Someone knew an underground world existed that could've saved half the population and did nothing about it?" The words echoed through her head, the weight of them pulling her heart, her soul down with them.

Cooper's shoulders rose and fell on a deep breath, but he said nothing.

"How is that possible?" She stared at the back of his head. "Who would do something so horrific? No way you're right about this."

He shrugged again and leaned into a curve as they sped away.

COOPER BREATHED a sigh of relief that he hadn't been going very fast when Nori jumped from the bike. The shoe of her back leg caught on the seat, and she fell hard, but was up again before he could dismount and help her.

Kade pulled in behind them, calling after Nori as she ran toward the wrecked neighborhood.

"You good?" Cooper asked Kade, who nodded and watched Nori wander past chunks of stucco and rusted metal. "This is going to be a bad day," Cooper said. "She's going to need you."

Kade met his gaze, a moment of understanding passing between them. "I won't give up until she does."

Cooper looked away first, and went in search of Nori among the piles of rubble and roofs. The beam of his light found her sitting on a metal bedframe half submerged in a mountain of ash. Her face was covered in soot except for two peach-colored lines running from her eyes to her chin.

He bent on a knee beside her. "It doesn't mean they're gone," he said.

When Nori looked up, his lantern caught her eyes and they reflected blue-greening the light. He stared for a moment, probably too long, before pointing the light away and struggling to decide whether they were more beautiful illuminated or not.

"You don't believe that," she said and swiped at her face, forming a streak of clean across one cheek.

It was true, though his heart ached for her, for the pain she'd endure when she finally accepted her family was gone. "I still believe in miracles," he said instead. "Even after all this time."

At Kade's heavy footfalls behind them, Nori's eyes left Cooper's. She stood and dove into the big man, who held her as she cried. Awkward and unwanted, Cooper cleared his throat and backed away to survey what was left of the house.

"HEY." Kade looked down at Nori. She shook her head against his chest, and he didn't press her. After a while, and several snivels, he tried again. "Hey."

Nori cleared her throat and looked up. "Hey."

"Let's look around a bit then we'll have to get back underground before daylight."

She didn't speak, but nodded and led him forward, a death grip on his first two fingers.

As they neared the crevice that had cleaved her family home in two, Nori's heart faced a similar alteration. One side of her home was just...gone. The other side looked like a diorama of what once was. Inside was half the basement, half the kitchen, half a bedroom.

"Not too close," Cooper called, jogging up beside her. "Everything's unstable."

"I just can't believe it's gone," she said, her voice little more than a whisper. "I can't believe...they're gone."

"I'm sorry." Cooper's face held such pity it sent her into tears again. "I'd hoped something had changed since I was here," he said. "I truly did."

The only shape Nori's lips would take was a wobble, and that wasn't a shape at all. She turned from Cooper and wiped at her face again.

When she finally looked back at the house, Nori worked to gather the nerve to say goodbye. To the kitchen where they'd shared so many breakfasts. To the bedroom that had been her place of solace for so many years. To the entryway table on which her family had always left notes for each other. Nostalgia pulled her toward the table, memories of birthday cards from her father propped against a bowl of keys and mail. And there, as clear as Nori's sight at night, was a shot of blue. On the entry table, tucked between a rock and the old key bowl, was a folded note.

She gasped and raced for the table, Cooper chasing after her.

"Nori, stop!"

She ignored his command, stepping gingerly through the rubble and snatched up the note.

The mound of debris gave a heavy groan under her weight. She and Cooper stopped dead in their tracks.

"Nori?" he said and she turned her head to find his gaze set on hers. "Step back," he said calmly. "Quick but sure. Step back, and then run like hell."

She forced her terror down with a swallow. Forced it down, and then jumped away from the edge of the crevice. She ran straight to Cooper, who caught her and squeezed her arms as he closed his eyes.

"I'm all right," she said, relief flooding her. "I'm okay. It's a letter."

She flipped open the slip of paper.

Three simple words buckled her knees and blurred the rest of the message. She didn't need to see it anyway.

We made it.

It was her father's handwriting. Her parents had survived. She skimmed the rest of the note and let the scrap of paper flutter to the ground as her head whipped wildly, scanning the area around her.

"What does it say?" Kade stepped forward and picked up the note, but she answered before he could raise a flashlight to it.

"They're alive. They found another place to stay, but come back each night to see if I've come home."

Cooper whispered "My God," and joined Nori's search of the dark horizon. "Do you think they've already come tonight?"

"I don't... I don't know."

"Nori."

"Hmm," she answered without abandoning her search.

"Nori. Look at me."

She turned then, her eyes wild and face pale.

"I'm sorry." Cooper's words were heavy with regret. "I'm sorry for what I assumed...that I stole your hope."

She shrugged, but couldn't yet speak.

Kade stepped close and squeezed her hand. "They probably already came tonight. We've been out here a while. We should head back before the sun rises." He smiled and squeezed her hand again. "Scribble a note that you're safe, and we'll come back tomorrow to look for them."

She nodded and ran a sleeve under her nose. "O—" She cleared her throat. "Okay."

32

A MATTER OF TRUST

"Nori?"

The voice was distant, but she would've known it a mile away.

"Dad?" She turned her head, searching for them. "Mom?"

"We're coming, baby." Her mother's voice was strained but determined.

Her parents climbed around what was left of a neighbor's ranch-style home, and Nori tripped over chunks of sidewalk and her own feet as she scrambled to get to them. She bent and hugged her mother's neck first then let her father squeeze her to him. Words tumbled from all three of their mouths so quickly no one could understand the other. Didn't matter. They were together again. Nori didn't even bother to dampen the toothy grin that took over her face.

"Are you really okay?" Her mother's face was beaming, but wary. "Are you hungry? Were you safe? Where did you sleep? Tell us everything."

"Wait," Nori blurted, her mother's condition registering

much later than the fact that she'd found them. "Mom, why are you in that?"

Her mother sat in a rusty metal wheelchair, one old blanket serving as a seat pad and the other draped over her knees. Her father stood behind her, palms gripping ruined handles wrapped in black electrical tape.

"Mom?" Nori bent low to see her mother's face. "What's happened?"

"Oh, I had an argument with a support beam…and I lost."

Nori's stomach seized. "Be serious, mother. How bad is it?" She looked at her father, who didn't meet her gaze. "Dad? Tell me what's going on."

He closed his eyes. "We sheltered in the basement and would've made it fine through the scorch." His sigh was weighted with regret. "But then this," he motioned between the two sides of the wide chasm, "happened. The house split. Your mother and I made it from the basement into what used to be the kitchen." His pained grimace matched her mother's. "Just as I lifted her up, a piece of the ceiling fell on—" He cleared his throat. "Onto her back."

"Oh God, Mom."

"I was able to lift it off," he said. "Not sure how. But then…" Her father closed his eyes, and when he opened them, the blue swirled beneath unshed tears. "She couldn't walk after that."

Nori's stomach roiled with nausea and she pressed a hand to it. "And now? Can you walk now, Mom?" Her mother shook her head, but didn't speak. "Have you been to see Dr. Ginsberg? What did she say?"

Her father wiped his eyes with his shirt. "She, ah, she said it was permanent."

"Permanent," Nori repeated as the word echoed through

her head. "Permanent? What's permanent? Is she— Are you paralyzed, Mom?"

Her mother gave a forced smile. "Just my legs. Still got these." She raised hands and wiggled her fingers.

Nori's butt hit the ground with a thump. She sat, mouth open, staring between her parents and trying to absorb the news.

Cooper and Kade had done their best to remain unnoticed, but at the awkward silence, they fidgeted.

Nori's father caught sight of them first. "Who're your friends, Nor? Where's Barker?"

That got her attention, and she snorted. "Barker. That asshole dumped me the moment we got underground."

Her mother gasped. "Nori, language!"

"Sorry," she said, but her tone indicated she was no such thing. "Mom, Dad, this is my friend, Kade, and this is Cooper." She waved a hand between the two men.

"Pleasure, sir," Cooper said and stepped forward to shake first her father's hand and then her mother's. "Ma'am."

"Hello." Kade nodded from where he stood but didn't move to greet them.

"How did you all meet?" Her father asked her, but it was Cooper who spoke.

"I ran into Nori in the tunnel—" He was cut off by Nori's bark of laughter, but shot her a dark look and continued. "I took her to stay with a friend of mine."

"And," Kade said nervously, "I met her there."

"Uh-huh," her father said, though his face revealed anything but comprehension. "The bunker Barker led you to must'a been bigger than we thought."

"Oh, you have no idea," Nori gushed, her troubles

temporarily forgotten. "It's a whole other world down there. Cities, Dad. There are cities."

Her father opened and closed his mouth.

"Well," her mother cut in, genteel and gracious, "thank you gentlemen so much for helping our daughter find her way back to us."

Both Cooper and Kade shifted nervously and waved off any attention.

Nori's father checked his watch for the fifth time since finding her. "Sunrise is expected in thirty-five minutes, Nori. We've got to get you inside fast."

Her gaze shot up to his, comprehending for the first time she'd be separating from her friends. Her thought process hadn't extended beyond finding her parents. They hadn't discussed it. Dread and nervous energy formed a hard ball in her stomach and her mind raced for the next move.

No, she wouldn't leave Kade. He would stay on with her and her family—she would insist on it. But Cooper would likely leave in search of other young girls to aggravate. Her smile at the thought was short-lived, and turned to a scowl.

"Where will we go?" she asked them. "Where have you been staying?"

"Nate and Deanna took us in after the earthquake. Since their new house was built with those concrete forms and they live on the north side of town, their house was okay. There's room in their scorch shelter, and we've been staying there. We've got you a bed all set up and everything."

Nori smiled automatically, but it quickly faltered. Was that her new life? Relegated to living in someone else's basement with her parents?

Had she never known the freedom—indentured status notwithstanding—of living underground, of the possibility of having an actual life, she might never have dreaded it. Now, though, the thought of being trapped in a tiny room all day, every day for the foreseeable future made her chest constrict like she was the one trapped beneath rubble.

"Nori?" Her mother touched her arm. "Nori, what's wrong?"

"Nothing. I'm fine," she muttered, taking a deep breath and attempting to shake off the outward signs of her panic. "When, ah, when do you think can we make the trip to the 25th Parallel?"

Though they made no move to answer, her parents' eyes met in shared understanding.

"What?" Nori looked between them.

It was her father who finally spoke. "There are still only two or three hours of dark each night, sweetheart. And you can't stand the light of day even when you're covered head to toe. You know that."

"So, what?" Nori's voice rose as her worst fears were realized. "You're saying we can't make the trip? Ever? You expect me to live in Nate and Deanna's basement for the rest of my life? With you two?"

Her parents recoiled at the cruelty of her words.

Nori massaged her temples with a thumb and finger. "I didn't mean it like that. I... God, it's just...that's not a life, you know?"

"We don't know what else to do." Her mother's voice caught on the last word.

Nori's insides roiled with self-disgust. Paralyzed, her mother's life wouldn't be much different than her own. She hated seeing the parents who loved her in such pain, and she hated herself for adding to it.

"I'm sorry, Mom." Nori rushed to her and squeezed her

tight. "Whatever it is, it'll be fine. We'll be fine. We have each other."

"Ah," Cooper's smooth voice was, for once, unsure. "Excuse me for interrupting, but I think I might have a solution."

All four gazes slid in his direction.

"Well?" Nori asked impatiently, and her mother tsked at her rudeness.

"We can get to the 25th Parallel underground. Why not go that way? I mean, it'll take a while and there are rough patches, but at least you're not at risk from the sun...or any more scorches."

Four pairs of eyes stared at Cooper for so long that he looked down and found something on the ground more interesting.

"You mean we could get all the way to Mexico in those tunnels?" Nori's suspicions were confirmed.

"Well, there are some tricky parts." He shrugged. "But yeah."

For a split second, Nori's chest eased. It just might work.

But when she looked to her parents, reality hit home: there was no way her mother could travel in those Subterranean tunnels. Not with her injuries. Even if there was another bike, she could never sit astride it. Jeeps fit through some parts of the tunnel, but all the way to Mexico? No way. Her heart plummeted, but she accepted the reality of her situation.

"We can't." Nori's mouth twisted. "But it was a good idea."

"Why not?" Her father cut in, and Nori's head jerked in his direction. "Why can't we make the trip underground? If he says there's a way, and you can't withstand the trip here on the surface, why wouldn't we take the route?"

Nori's gaze left his and drifted toward her mother in silent communication. When she looked at him again, his body sagged, but then he straightened and nodded.

"Have you made the trip?" her mother asked Cooper, voice sharp as a chef's knife.

"Yes, ma'am," he said. "Once or twice."

Her eyes narrowed. "Is it dangerous?"

"A little, yes, but given the circumstances..." Cooper's voice trailed off as he turned to meet her pointed glare.

"Ana," her father said. "What are you asking?"

She ignored him, directing her attention only to Cooper. "Do you feel confident you could get my daughter to the 25th Parallel unharmed? Would you take responsibility for her safety?"

"I do, and I would. There are risks, like I said, but the only way she'll have any kind of life — the only way she'll survive is by leaving here for good."

Nori's mother searched Cooper's face for too long, but she must've liked what she found there. "He's right," she announced. "They should make the trip underground."

Her father balked. "Be serious, Ana. There's no way I'm letting my only daughter make a fifteen-hundred-mile trip underground alone with two boys I don't even know."

"What's the alternative, Norm?" she snapped. "What kind of life will she have if she doesn't?"

"At least we're guaranteed she'll have a life. I can't protect her if she's not with me."

"You can't protect me if I am." Nori's voice was as soft as a whisper, but the effect of her words might have come from a bullhorn. Her father turned his head and closed his eyes, the truth of her statement breaking his heart in two.

"We've been here a while," her mother said. "And the sun's

not far off. Whatever we decide, we need to get Nori to shelter. Soon."

The squeeze of time both hushed further argument and rushed the decision. Nori looked at her mother and father, both too overwhelmed to speak.

"We'll take care of her," Kade said softly. "She's the best friend I've got—the only friend." He took tentative steps toward Cooper in solidarity. "She's pretty tough on her own, but she also has us on her side, and that's something."

Nori smiled at him and mouthed 'thank you.'

He shrugged his big shoulders and looked at the ground.

"Ana's right. We don't have much time." Her father's voice was thick with emotion. "Nate and Deanna leave for the 25th in two days. That's the reason for the extra room in their house." He cleared his throat. "They have a van. Your mother would be comfortable. I guess…I guess we'll take them up on their offer."

"Okay." It was all Nori could come up with despite the fact her head swam with a million things she wanted to say.

Her father grabbed her by the shoulders and pulled her into him for a fierce, desperate hug. "What do you need? Everything we have is yours. Food, supplies, gas."

"I've got that covered," Cooper said. "But we'll have to find you once we get there. There's a town called Esperanza south of Monterrey, right at the base of the mountains. People hang padlocks from an old bridge. Attach a note with meeting instructions to one—a blue one—and we'll find it. If we get there first, we'll do the same."

"How will we ever find a blue padlock?" Nori scoffed. "We can hardly find food."

The muscles of Cooper's wide jaws flexed as he stared

down at her, still under the protective wing of her father. "We'll paint it if we have to. You got a better idea?"

A cold finger of shame touched Nori's spine, and she looked down, shaking her head.

Cooper extended a hand toward her father and said stiffly, "Thank you for trusting us with her."

"Thank you for seeing her safely there," he replied and kissed the top of Nori's head before returning Cooper's handshake. "She's special."

"I know," Cooper said, a twitch at the corner of his mouth.

"Don't let me down, son." Her father looked away and blinked several times. "Don't let her down."

"I'll do my very best." Cooper stared straight into her father's eyes and nodded. *Amazing,* Nori thought. In just those few moments, he'd somehow gained her father's trust.

Nori swallowed past the lump in her throat and reached for her mother. "I love you." She held on tight, eyes full of unshed tears. "See you down South."

Her mother's returning smile, suffused with confidence and love, was burned into Nori's memory for the rest of her days.

33

INTO THE GREAT UNKNOWN

T he trip back was a blur, and not just metaphorically. Nori wept most of the way with her head buried in Cooper's back. They made it to the entrance before the sun rose, shutting themselves underground, and the heavy iron door behind them.

Kade had been uncharacteristically quiet, but breathed a gusty sigh when Cooper sealed the door. "I don't know about you two," Kade said, "but I'm glad to be back."

Nori turned in her seat toward him. "Back Subterranean? Why?"

An uneasy tremor ran the length of his body, and he shivered. "I don't know. Being up there, I felt...exposed. Too much open space. I couldn't see all of my surroundings." He shook his head. "Huh-uh. Give me Subterranean life any day over that." He said the last as if talking about rotten meat.

"You up for this?" she asked him.

"What, a road trip?" He scoffed and straightened. "I'm a free man. Besides, I promised your mom, so..."

Nori smiled and held out her hand, which Kade squeezed. "What now, Captain Cooper?"

"Oh, don't call him that," Kade groaned. "His head already has trouble fitting through the tunnels."

Cooper laughed. "Now we ride to the 25th Parallel. Viva la Mexico!"

Nori rolled her eyes. "Do you have a plan to execute this idea of yours? Where will we sleep? How will we eat? We sure can't make it two or three days on what we brought, despite what you told my parents."

"Two or three days?" His face was severe. "More like two or three weeks."

"What?" Nori's screech bounced off the tunnel walls. "You can't be serious."

"It's not a straight shot," he said, suddenly indignant. "And we're traveling underground, if you'll recall. Nothing's going to be easy about this. Or very fast. But my guess is it will take your parents longer since the roads—hell, the whole world— is jacked up."

Nori massaged her forehead again. She was so tired. "All right. So, can we at least find somewhere to sleep tonight and get a fresh start tomorrow?"

"The lady asks me to take her to bed." Cooper waggled his eyebrows. "I cannot refuse. I know just the place."

Nori's jaw dropped. "That's not... You know I didn't mean... Ugh" she finished weakly and Kade giggled. "Oh," she said, turning to her traitorous friend. "You're no help at all."

"What is this place?" Nori's top lip inched toward her nose as Cooper locked the door behind them.

They'd ridden another twenty miles through the grungy tunnel, one mile indistinguishable from the next. After turning down a nearly-invisible ramp just off the main path, the three eventually pulled up to a single door painted to blend into the tunnel. There was no knob, no hinges, no evidence of a door at all. But Cooper had toggled a hidden latch and sprung the lock on a metal-clad door.

Nori followed the two men as they walked the motorcycles into a bunker the size of a school auditorium.

"What is that God-awful smell?" She swung her head to Kade, whose face held the same disgust.

"That, my friends, is food," Cooper said and at their obvious repugnance, he grinned. "Come and see."

"It's an indoor garden." Nori's mouth fell open. "Hydroponics, artificial light. Vegetables!" She ran to a rectangular plant bed framed by thick railroad ties. "Fruit! Oh my God! Where on Earth did they get these seeds?"

"This place was built long before the scorches." Cooper pulled a shiny strawberry from a plant trailing down a thick plastic tube. "People have been farming down here for decades. They brought plants and seeds with them, and have subterranean farming fine-tuned to an art."

"Why?" Nori wheeled around.

"Why what? Why did they grow food? Is that a trick question?"

"No, why did they move underground? Why did people build this massive system of roads and cities? The money and manpower it must've taken... The years spent planning, and hiding, and sneaking around. And how? How did that many people keep the biggest secret since, I dunno, Area 51 — which, by the way, wasn't kept very well at all."

Cooper opened his mouth to speak, but she went on.

"It's almost like they knew," she said and shook her head.

"Like they knew what level of devastation was about to hit, and they built a way to survive it."

"No one would do that." Kade's mouth turned down. "People wouldn't keep a secret like that and save only themselves."

"So, it's just a coincidence that the entire Subterranean was created before the one above it combusted in cataclysmic solar blights? Is that what you're saying?"

"Well, when you put it like that..."

She turned to Cooper, who'd slipped toward the raised beds. "How was an underground world built beneath the one me and my family live on—and we never knew about it?"

"Who's hungry?" Cooper asked with an armful of summer squash.

"Whose place is this?" Nori wiped her eye on a sleeve. The fresh onion she was chopping was particularly strong. She turned away from it both to avoid the smell and to pressure Cooper into finally talking.

He shrugged. "Belongs to the CCC."

"What's the CCC?" Nori asked as Kade joined them in the small kitchen.

"You find it?" Cooper asked him.

"Yeah," Kade answered. "Did you know there are about six dozen cases of water down there? That storage area is stacked to the ceiling with supplies."

"You snag some?" Cooper grabbed a handful of chopped onions from the pile Nori had made and threw them into a skillet of hot oil.

"Loaded up the bikes," Kade said. "Vitabars, and batteries, and extra flashlights. Few other things."

"Good. We'll need to fuel up, too. There are cans along the back wall."

"Cooper." Nori's raised voice was resolute.

"Hmm?" He didn't face her.

"What is the CCC?"

He turned toward her from Kade, but his eyes followed later, as if he had to drag them to meet her gaze. "It stands for Council of Concerned Citizens." At her raised eyebrows, Cooper took a deep breath and words tumbled out. "The CCC started out as a philosophical group. A bunch of racists with radical views on overpopulation banded together to rid the world of the people they thought were depleting Earth's resources." He cleared his throat and looked down. "Over time, it morphed into much more."

"They like to think they run things," Kade said. "Even though everyone knows life down here is anarchy."

Cooper's tone was grave. "The CCC *does* run things. They encourage chaos and lawlessness to further their own goals, while enforcing strict regulations on their own people."

"So, these guys are what?" Nori shrugged. "The Subter-ranean Mafia or something?"

Cooper twisted his mouth as he considered. "Something like that. Except with advanced technology and resources. And more hired thugs."

Nori's head whipped toward Cooper as pieces of the puzzle fit together. "Are Sarge and Wallace and Jenks a part of that?"

Cooper nodded.

"The same jerks you were in cahoots with?"

"Who says cahoots?" Cooper smirked and looked to Kade for backup, but the fighter didn't bite.

"Don't change the subject," Nori said through gritted teeth. "Are you or are you not involved with this CCC?"

"I am not."

"Then why were you with those losers? How do you have access to these supplies and facilities—to their vehicles?"

"Because they *think* I'm in cahoots with them." Cooper groaned and threw the spoon dramatically into the pan. "Aw, now look," he said. "You've got me saying it."

"And why would they think that?" She would not let him distract her this time.

"Because I'm a very good actor."

"Cooper!" Nori seethed. "Give me a straight answer!"

"What do you want me to say?" He turned from cooking to face her. "Listen, I'm not really a member of Sarge's little biker gang or the CCC, and I don't support its maniacal mission. I just let them think I do."

"Why would you do that? Are you some sort of spy?" Cooper scoffed, but she wasn't about to let him off easy. "I think that's exactly what you are," she said slowly. "What are you really up to? And what were you doing in Chicago?"

"I'm just trying to get by, all right?" Cooper said. "These guys, they've got a network of people and supplies that runs in and out of these tunnels like veins to a main artery. If you want to survive, you've either got to be in with them or have friends big and bad enough to scare them off."

"What were you doing in Chicago?" Nori's voice was hard as steel.

"That's what I'd like to know." Sarge's sinister rasp ran like rivulets of ice water down Nori's spine. He stood just outside the door with one leg propped behind the other and one elbow resting on the doorframe in feigned nonchalance.

Two heartbeats. *Ka-thunk. Ka-thunk.*

"Nori, move!" Cooper flung the hot grease—squash and all—at Sarge's head.

She fled to the other side of the bunker, Kade close on her heels. There was nowhere to go but the garden.

"Get on!" Kade bellowed and pointed to the motorcycles parked along the wall.

"I can't drive this thing!" Nori considered it for a split second, but it was hopeless.

"Get on!" It was Cooper, and she blew out a relieved breath before doing just that.

Cooper mounted behind her and kicked the bike to a start. As they neared the single doorway out of the garden, he muttered, "Tuck in tight."

Sarge skidded into the door and time suspended in anticipation of the ultimate game of chicken. Sarge's chest heaved as he breathed, his face red and raw from grease burns. He set his feet wide, as if he could actually stop a motorcycle.

Nori followed Cooper's lead and huddled low on the bike.

In the end, it was a simple choice: live or die. Sarge could move and survive, or stand his ground and get plowed by an engine-powered hunk of hot metal. He chose life.

Nori turned and saw Kade ride through behind them. Sarge grabbed for Kade's shoulder to swing him off the bike. He was wiry, and mean, but Kade had bulk on his side. He tossed off Sarge's grip, shoved him into the wall, and kept his seat on the motorcycle.

Cooper kicked aside dining chairs as they slowly maneuvered the bikes back through the kitchen and toward the front entrance. Nori swiped their backpacks from the table as they passed and tucked them between her and Cooper.

They made it through the open doorway, but barely had time to breathe before Jenks and Wallace came running toward them. Their faces looked like a pair of bad actors miming first confusion, then shock, and then murderous intent. Nori clenched her eyes shut as Cooper laid on the throttle, but when she turned back to look, Wallace had pulled a rifle that was slung behind his back forward.

"He's got a gun!" she screamed. "Kade!"

Gunfire exploded. One after another, the shots popped and echoed like firecrackers.

When the shots stopped, the only sound was the high-pitched scream of her ringing ears. Nori screamed for the friend trapped between her and gunfire. "Kade!" she screamed. "Kade!"

"Go back!" Nori beat Cooper's shoulders with her fists. "Go back, go back, go back!"

Cooper didn't respond besides stiffening under her beating.

"You can't just leave him back there," she yelled over the engine.

"Fine," she said when Cooper didn't respond. She raised her left leg, putting her weight onto her right side.

Cooper whipped around. "What are you doing?"

"I'm going back for him whether you stop or not."

"Like hell you are." He reached behind him to jerk her down by the jacket. "Sit down."

"I can't just leave him." The adrenaline rush was gone, and

Nori crashed. Tears fell and she swiped them with the back of her hand. "We can't leave him, Cooper."

"You want me to turn around and go toward the guns?" he said. "Is that what you want? For all of us to get killed? Cause they'll do it."

"But we can't just leave—" Nori spun in the seat when she detected the whine of a motor behind them. "Kade?" she whispered, her body sagging with relief when her friend's face came into view. He was leaning to the right, but he was alive.

"He's okay," she said, beating on Cooper's back again. "He's okay."

34

A CAVERN OASIS

"Can we stop for a while?" Nori asked.

The motorcycle headlight cut a v-shaped beam into the darkness, but there was nothing to see. They'd driven through miles and miles of rock losing Sarge, who was probably nursing serious grease burns.

Cooper turned his head toward her to speak over the engine. "It's not much farther."

"I really need to stop now," she said, squirming.

"Trust me," Cooper said, and caught her gaze over his shoulder. "I'm sick of being on this bike, too. About five more miles, and we'll be there."

"Where's there?"

Cooper stretched his long neck first to one side and then the other. "Newman County. I know where there's a lodge built inside a cave. We could all use a rest."

Though life Subterranean was perfect for her particular disability, speeding through blurs of blackness mile after grimy mile bored Nori to oblivion. Straddling a speeding motorcycle for days wasn't all she'd thought it would be, either. The insides of her legs were sore and her butt just plain hurt.

She turned in the seat to catch a glimpse of Kade behind them. His mouth was set in a thin line, and he arched his back before rolling his shoulders. He was tired, too.

"God, I thought we'd never get he—ahhhhhh." Nori nearly collapsed when she stepped off the motorcycle. With a hand braced on the rough wall of the cavern, she flexed and shook her legs until they gathered their senses and remembered how to walk. "I'm fine," she said sarcastically. "No need to help me."

"Where are we going?" Kade shone his flashlight past her. "Is that a creek?"

"Yeah, this whole area of karst was naturally formed," Cooper said. Nori looked to Kade, who obviously shared her confusion. Kade shined his light toward Cooper, who hissed and threw up a hand.

"Oh. Sorry, man," Kade said and turned the light to the ground.

"Anyway," Cooper said "karst is landscape formed by water carving into rock. You know, caves, fissures, sinkholes." Nori and Kade finally nodded their understanding, which only encouraged the geology lesson. "This whole area was formed by a natural spring," he said. "They've rerouted much of it now into a reservoir just behind there." He nodded past Kade.

"Why?" Nori asked.

"To have a water source."

"For drinking, you mean?"

"And bathing," Cooper said with a wink.

A bath sounded like the best thing in the whole world, and

Nori lost herself for a moment thinking about sinking into a steaming tub and melting the ice that had frozen to her bones.

Cooper was still talking about caves. "Native Americans once lived here then it housed munitions in the civil war. Even the James Gang is rumored to have hidden out here."

"No." Kade stopped dead in his tracks and pointed the flashlight at Cooper's face again. "Don't mess with me."

Cooper raised an arm in front of his face. "For God's sake, stop shining that in my eyes."

"Sorry." Kade clicked off his light. "Are you serious about the James Gang, though? I've read every book I could get my hands on, and I've seen all the Jesse James movies. Train robberies, mountains, gunfights, snow." He closed his eyes and looked on the verge of a seizure. "It's what I imagined life on the Surface was like."

"Like a Western?" Cooper asked with a laugh.

"Don't ask." Nori said.

"O-kay." Cooper shrugged. "Oh, and someone operated a couple of stills here during prohibition."

His dreams of the Wild West momentarily forgotten, Kade's eyes gleamed with mischief. "You think they forgot any?"

"Oh, we can do better than that," Cooper said smugly, stepping into the creek water and disappearing under a wide, low-hanging stalactite.

Nori followed him, ducking beneath the sharp, cone-shaped rocks hanging from the ceiling careful not to impale herself or break one. Kade splashed heavily behind her. On the other side of the mineral deposits, completely hidden from view, was a bridge across the widening creek leading to a metal door.

Nori pegged Cooper with a murderous glare. "This belong to the CCC too?"

"No." He pushed back the chunk of dark hair that fell into his eyes when he shook his head.

Nori moved both fists to her hips. "Who then?"

"Someone who can't enjoy it," he said almost sadly. After unlocking the door with a key found beneath a rock, Cooper pushed open the door, extending a hand like a butler welcoming guests. Nori crept forward, but was flung to the side by a very eager Kade.

"After you," she groused, but her friend wasn't listening. He was already to the end of a narrow hall.

Cooper switched on a set of lights before locking the door behind him. Nori cringed and blinked in an attempt to adjust. Cooper and Kade were having the same trouble. Artificial light didn't usually affect her, but after the ease of seeing in the darkness, she'd realized her visibility in actual light wasn't great. And there was a lot of light in the room. Too much, like whoever installed it wanted to forget they were underground.

"Ah, Cooper?" Kade's face wrinkled in confusion as he surveyed the main living space.

"Yeah?"

"I'm pretty sure the James Gang didn't appreciate contemporary design. And no way did they have smart TVs."

"Well, they weren't the last ones to live here." Cooper shot Nori a look that said 'Where did you get this guy?' which she ignored.

Nori craned her neck to take in the expanse. The walls and ceiling were all natural cave that had been coated with some kind of shiny epoxy, but the floors were a pale, polished cement that ran beneath tasteful high-end furniture. The kitchen island alone seated six in sleek silver chairs.

"What is this place?" Nori couldn't keep her mouth closed as she opened pantry and closet doors stacked high with food and supplies. "Is it someone's home? Do you know them? Is it okay we're here?"

"It was actually built by some hedge fund manager after reading an end-of-days novel," Cooper said. "He thought the apocalypse was coming and built this place to shelter his family."

The man had been right. Nori wondered if he and his family had made it here in time for the first sunscorch. A wave of nausea snaked through her. If they had, wouldn't they still be here now?

"This is the nicest place I've ever seen," she said. "I had no idea people lived like this."

"Woulda been better if they'd preserved some of the history, though," Kade mumbled.

"Like what, shell casings? Spittoons? You and this Wild West hang-up." Nori grinned at her friend.

"You say that now," Cooper called to Kade from a spiral staircase. "But you haven't seen the wine cellar."

Kade had grown quiet after his initial enthrallment with the luxury bunker. He'd stopped mid-sentence of wondering aloud whether Jesse and Frank had stood in the very spot he occupied, staring off into the distance. His eyes had gone glassy, and his body slumped, like he was stumbling around, lost inside his own head. Nori could always tell when he was thinking of Grant.

Getting shot at was worth it, Nori thought, as she adjusted the thick towel she'd tucked between her head and the garden tub. She'd had to drain and re-fill the bath twice to get rid of all the grime that washed from her body.

Running her toes under the hot water cascading from the

chrome faucet, she sipped from a glass of pink wine. Compared to her first experience with alcohol, the wine was sweet, tasty. More than anything, it made her feel both normal and pampered, and she closed her eyes in supreme bliss.

Cooper had shown her to a bedroom suite, complete with her own bathroom, before heading off to his own. Fine throws and blankets were placed throughout the room, which was as frosty as the rest of the underground world. A chill was part of Subterranean life. Nori had learned to accept the fact, though she didn't like it. Wrapped in a thick towel she'd found in a drawer, she perused the room, basking in the luxurious details, and pressed a button beneath a large rectangle. An electronic screen flashed to life, revealing a thick forest of ancient trees and a lush carpet of ferns beneath them. Breath left her in a rush, and for a moment she forgot where she was. No way was that real. The screen pixelated and changed to a deserted beach at sunset. Nori backed up to the thick, soft bed and sat down to watch the show. It was an artificial window, no more than a screensaver, really, but held gorgeous landscapes she'd never get the chance to see in real life.

"How was it?" Cooper asked when Nori finally emerged from her personal oasis.

"A dream," she gushed. "I was never allowed to use enough water for a bath like that. Ours were shallow—and infrequent. Hot water was just something my mother heated on the stove. How is it even possible?"

"A tankless heater makes it on demand. Electricity comes from a big windmill on top the side of the mountain. Guess it made it through the scorches. They took every precaution. Pretty nice, huh?"

"It's unbelievable. I almost wish we could stay here forever." Nori lowered her voice like she was revealing a secret and tugged at a tuft of cotton on her robe. "I mean, I found a bar of dark chocolate in the pantry."

Cooper's answering grin was smug, like a caveman who'd provided for his woman's every need.

"I...ah...I found their stash of DVDs," he finally said. "You wanna watch a movie?" He flipped through the album of discs, but stopped after a while. "Nori?" He looked up at her and patted the couch beside him.

She sat a modest distance away. "Mmm?"

"We will have to leave," he said. "Sarge and those guys won't stop until they find us. They don't know about this place, but we can't stay long." His expression was apologetic, but his words firm. "And your parents. We have to meet your parents at the 25th Parallel."

"I know. But it's nice to dream." She sighed but then sat up straighter. "What would they do with us if they caught us, anyway? I assume there's more to the CCC than those three?"

"There are more." Cooper took a deep breath. "A lot more. Sarge is just a henchman. And there are more dangerous threats than Sarge out there." He shook himself. "But let's not think about that today. We have this beautiful lodge, all the food, hot water, and wine we could want. Let's make the most of it and think about our troubles tomorrow," he said and Nori laughed. "It's not every day I get to lounge on a leather sofa and watch a movie with a pretty girl."

"Well." The color of Nori's cheeks matched her wine. "What should we watch?"

35

A SHORT DETOUR

Nori woke to a dragging gasp. She didn't remember falling asleep, much less who might be snoring nearby. Smacking her dry lips, she cut her eyes in the direction of the sound...and jolted wide awake. Her head was nestled in Cooper's waist as he lay slumped against the edge of the sofa.

Oh God, she thought. *Oh God! How did this happen?* Nori wanted to curl up and die. At least she had the curling up part down already.

This was bad. Riding behind Cooper on the bike was one thing. Falling asleep on him and snuggling into his warm, muscled—Nori shook herself and harnessed her erratic thoughts. Anyway, yes. This was too intimate. Much, much too intimate.

If she craned her head, she could just see his face, still relaxed in sleep. His dark hair was clean, and laid messily across his forehead. His eyes were closed, and Nori could see movement beneath his lids as he dreamed. He'd shaved, and the skin of his cheeks and chin was smooth. Touchable. Nori's hand twitched to do just that, but she got control of herself in time.

What should she do? Pretend to be asleep and stay still? She couldn't do that for long. Not with the way her thoughts kept wandering. She did try, though, and laid her head tentatively back onto Cooper's side. His breathing softened, and hers synced with it. For a while, she closed her eyes and allowed her body to rise and fall in time with his.

Too soon, nature called, and Nori needed up. She squeezed her eyes shut and held her breath, making slow, precise movements to peel off of him and sit upright.

Just as she disconnected the last inch of her side from his legs, a green-gold eye popped open. He found her face immediately, as if he'd known exactly where she was.

"I'm sorry I fell asleep on you," she said in a rush. "It was the wine—I'm not used to… Oh, never mind."

Cooper's grin was lazy. "No problem." His gaze snagged a little too long on her sleep-swollen lips and mussed hair.

"What time is it?" she asked, suddenly very anxious.

He stretched, raising his arms above his head and flexing to the side, then checked his watch on the way down. "About 7:30."

"In the morning?" Nori smoothed the skin under her eyes and the wild hair buzzing around her face.

"Yes, in the morning."

"I'll never get used to the days and nights down here," she said. "Always the same. It's maddening. At Hank's, I never knew when I was supposed to sleep. The lights went out at nine, and I could follow meal schedules, but it's hard when there's no sunlight. Ever."

"Even if you were on the Surface, the days are so messed

up it's not like you could set your sleep schedule by light and dark."

"That's true." She shrugged. "So, how do you do it? How can you live down here?"

The shuffle of bare feet preceded Kade as he rounded the corner into the living room. "Morning," he said crisply. Freshly showered, he stopped to look between them. Nori was suddenly very aware of her disheveled hair and loose robe, and Cooper's faint, smug smile.

"Morning." Nori cleared her throat and stepped away from Cooper as she pulled her robe tight. "Sleep okay?"

"Yeeeaaaah," Kade said slowly, brows rising toward his hairline as he looked between them. "You?"

"Like a baby," she said. "Being cold and wet and filthy gets old. But this place...with heat and hot water...a palace compared to Hank's." Nori cinched the belt of her robe. "Speaking of, I'm going to take a shower. And yes, I know that's extravagant after my bath last night, but at this rate, it may be a week before I get another."

"Oh my God," Nori said later around a mouthful of bacon. "This is the best thing I've ever put in my mouth."

"Where did you find this?" Kade's top lip crept toward his nose. "There's no telling how many years it's been here."

"I don't care," Cooper said, closing his eyes on a bite of the meaty strip. "It's divine."

"I'm a vegetarian, you know."

Cooper grunted. "You're a vegetarian because you've never had bacon."

"Well, we're not gonna get very far if you two get food poisoning." Kade crossed his arms over his chest and looked down his nose at them as they fought for the last slice.

"If I die," Nori shut her eyes in bliss at the crisp, salty

goodness of the only fried pork product she'd ever had, "I'll die happy. And full."

"So, what's the plan?" Kade frowned as he popped bites of dried cereal.

"The plan," Cooper swallowed, "is to clean up after ourselves. Leave no trace we were here. Sarge and the boys will be looking for us now, so we have to be careful. I found this place on my own, so they may not even know it's here. There are a lot of places we could've gone, but they'll be on our trail. We need to keep moving."

Nori was already moving. "Our laundry should be about finished. I'll check it."

"I'll clean up the kitchen," Kade said, "but I'm not touching that bacon."

NORI'S BUTT HURT, and she was stiff, and sore, and grumpy. They'd ridden for at least six hours.

She fidgeted and flexed to relieve her strained muscles, finally whining, "Can we stop?"

At Cooper's sagging shoulders, guilt stabbed her. He must be sick of her complaints. She tried not to fuss, she really did. But, my God what she wouldn't give to get off the motorcycle and stretch her legs. To run.

She glanced back at Kade, who lifted fingers from the handlebars in a silent hello.

Cooper turned his head toward her. "There's a town in twenty-five miles. I know you're sick of riding. Me, too. The road gets tough. Have to get through a pass before we stop again."

Nori slumped against Cooper's back in defeat. Besides a

sore backside, it was what she hated most about riding the stupid bike. She had a hundred questions, but Cooper only answered in short, cagey sentences when shaking his head wouldn't do.

Finally, when she was sure she couldn't ride a single mile more, Cooper slowed to a stop.

"What are we doing?" she asked as he dismounted.

"We walk from here."

"Surely you don't mean through there." Kade nodded toward a hole in the wall as Cooper walked his bike off the main path. "Why are we leaving the main road?"

"This is the way we're going," he called over his shoulder. "The main road is quicker, but more dangerous, too. It gets treacherous around here, and I'm not just talking about the terrain. The Deep South has some low people. I told you this trip would be tricky. This is where it starts."

"Starts?" Nori balked, jogging to catch up to him. "You don't count our little run-in at the hydroponic farm as dangerous?"

Cooper shrugged and kept pushing.

"That hole's not big enough for our bikes," Kade said. "Hell, I'm not sure I can fit through there."

"We'll fit. I've done it before." Cooper took off his leather jacket and stuffed it into the bike's saddlebag. "Nori, you'll have to go first."

Fear skittered up her spine like tiny spiders. "Ah, no. No way."

He growled low in his throat. "Kade and I have to push the bikes through. You need to go first to see if there's anything blocking the path. If there is, you can remove it, and we can push the bikes past. We have to keep moving."

"Oh, God," Nori groaned as she pulled her hair into a

ponytail. "I can't believe you're making me do this. There are probably spiders in there. I *hate* spiders."

"You know," Cooper cocked his head dramatically, "I already miss the bike. I could barely hear your whining over the engine."

Nori's mouth fell open before she found words. "I am not whining. I'm just saying this sucks. And that I hate spiders."

Cooper stopped pushing the bike, and she closed in on him. She could see the gold flecks in his eyes even in the darkness. They were always more visible when he was upset. He let out a heavy sigh. "You're right, okay? It sucks. A lot of this sucks. But what's the alternative? You wanna go back to the lodge and wait for Sarge and those guys?"

"You know, that very thought had crossed my mind," Kade muttered from behind them.

Nori went first. Of course she did. Making her parents wait and worry was out of the question. Allowing Sarge and his crew to catch up to them wasn't an option either. So she closed her eyes and repeated the mantra she knew so well. One breath at a time. One step at a time. One day at a time. Then she ducked into the tiny offshoot to join the creepy crawlies.

Nori kept moving, cursing each time a jagged rock snagged her hand or tripped her. Cooper was right. She could see, and she could help them make it through the tight space. He and Kade were nearly duck-walking, the tunnel just tall enough to scrape the motorcycles through.

"Why couldn't we take the main road?" she asked. "It would've been so much easier."

"Remember how Sarge found you that first time?"

Nori whipped around to look at Cooper, forgetting where she was, and struck her head on the low ceiling. She rubbed the newest knot with bloody fingers and glared at him with murderous intent, though he couldn't see her face.

"Oh yeah, I remember. I remember you were with them."

"God, can we please not argue this same point again?" he said, and she didn't answer. "Anyway, there are other people who would be just as happy to find you. To find us. We're trying to avoid them."

She turned away from him, tired, and angry, and frustrated, and the shadows changed in the tunnel ahead, as if the detour were ending and they could finally get back into a bigger passage. As usual, the smell of wet, damp earth permeated everything, but she also scented fire. Smoke. She sniffed. Sniffed again. Yes, definitely smoke.

In hindsight, it wouldn't have changed anything if she'd told Cooper about the smoke. There was no way they could've backed all the way through the tiny passage in time. There was never really an escape. The moment she stepped from the jagged shortcut back into the main tunnel, there was a flickering orange light of fire, of flames, and then nothing. Blackness.

36

SWORD OF YAHWEH

The sound of a child's soft humming dragged Nori to consciousness, though she regretted it immediately. Apparently, someone had mistaken her head for an egg and cracked it. She groaned and opened one eye, but squeezed it shut again at the pain ricocheting through her skull.

Finally, she gathered the strength to open both eyes. The child sitting in front of Nori was a filthy little thing, her clothes rags concealing only the important parts. No shoes. Her tiny feet were covered in so much black she might've had no skin beneath it.

Cooper and Kade. Nori searched the small room but they weren't there. The cold fingers of fear first touched her spine then quickly suffused the rest of her body.

"Hey," Nori said softly and caught the girl's feral gaze. The whites of her eyes were the only thing on her face not sooty and black. She blinked, but didn't speak. "Where am I?" Nori asked. "Where are your mom and dad?"

The girl's eyes narrowed, and she stood, chewing her lip as she crept toward Nori.

"Good girl," Nori cooed. "Come here. I won't hurt you."

Without a word, the girl kicked Nori square in the ribs.

"You little — Why did you do that?" She rubbed her side. "Was it you who hit me in the head?" The girl glared, still silent. "Do you know where my friends are?"

The girl backed away, one side of her mouth pulled up in a spiteful half-smile. She squatted in a corner of the room and watched, only moving to scratch her head or pick at her feet.

Nori sat locked in the tiny room with no idea how long she had or would be there. Or why. Her stomach fussed for food, so it must've been several hours. She was already feeling weak.

The girl continued to watch her, eyes narrow slits of disapproval, never acknowledging Nori's repeated questions.

"You've got something," Nori rubbed a finger along the side of her nose, "right there. Little black smudge of something..." Nori circled her face with a finger. "Alllll over your face."

A scowl wrinkled the girl's face, and as if she could no longer withstand the temptation, she finally swiped a hand along her nose.

"Aha!" Nori yelped, forgetting her throbbing head until it threatened to burst again. She rubbed the knot and stared down the girl. "You can understand me," she said. "I knew it! How long are they going to keep me down here? Where are my friends?"

Nothing.

"Okay, can you at least untie me? These ropes are rubbing raw places on my wrists."

A smirk.

"I know you can hear me, you little monster."

Though Nori tried to reason with her, the girl never

complied. Never engaged. It was like talking to a robot, or one of those British palace guards in old movies.

Mumbling outside the cell caught Nori's attention, and she sat up straighter. The women who entered were not much cleaner than the girl. The older woman's hair was shorn close to her scalp, but the younger woman's was matted and stuck to her head in places.

"Hi." Nori aimed for civil, reasonable. "Where are my friends? We don't want to hurt anyone. We're just passing through."

The older woman wouldn't meet Nori's gaze, instead motioning for her to stand and twisting her finger in a circle in the universal turn-around signal. When Nori turned, the woman grabbed the rope around her wrists, punishing her already-raw skin.

"Ow!" Nori whined. "Can you just take these off? Please. I'm not going anywhere. I don't even know where we are."

The younger woman motioned to the girl, who scampered out of the room. The older woman pushed Nori in front of her and out into the hall, where there were other cells like hers. Were Cooper and Kade inside one of them?

"Kade?" she called frantically. "Cooper?"

The old woman twisted the ropes, and Nori sucked air between her teeth at the pain.

"That hurts," she growled, swinging her head toward the woman. "Where are you taking me?"

The woman's answer was a swift kick in the back, which sent Nori stumbling forward.

Down, down, down, Nori was ushered deep into the earth. She kept her eyes peeled for a wider opening, for a place to escape, but there was only the narrow tunnel lit inter-mittently by torches.

Though she'd learned to withstand it, Nori hated the cold. It was the one thing she feared she'd never get used to in the Subterranean. Wet, biting cold chilled her to the bone, and no amount of dry socks could warm her feet enough. But something was changing. The air was more like the mist above a jacuzzi—heavy with warm moisture—and the farther down they went, the warmer it was. Down, down, down. Down into the belly of the earth.

And the deeper they went, the greater Nori's terror. A violent shake started at her knees and sent a fine tremor all the way up her body. She wasn't sure what they had planned for her, but it clearly wasn't good. Her emotions overrode her attempts at bravery, and tears brimmed over her eyelids.

With her hands still restrained, Nori had to bend her chin to a shoulder to wipe her nose. She stole a look at the women, who had yet to speak. Their faces were like whittled stone, staring straight ahead, unemotional, unfazed even as she begged to be let go.

Around one last bend in the path, stifling air hit Nori like a furnace to the face, and she worked harder to breathe through the thick air. She was in a tomb-like space, little statues on ledges and scenes of people on their knees carved into the rock face. Three or four benches...no, Nori thought as her stomach dropped. Three or four *altars* were carved from stone, and placed throughout the room. The tomb was lit by torchlight, fire feeding from thick black oil soaked into rags on old-fashioned stakes. The air was obnoxious with the smell of sulfur, and she gagged and blinked back more tears.

Panic suddenly clambered past despair, and Nori kicked and screamed, trying to turn and run from the strange temple back to the dirty cell. Though she struggled with every ounce of strength she possessed, the women managed to shove her through a wide opening, revealing, with terrifying clarity, the heat's origin.

Nori sucked in a breath at the ominous beauty. Sandstone columns glowed as they absorbed the fiery light of lava. Nori stopped fighting her captors, frozen with fear at the sight of red-hot magma bubbling a hundred feet below. The older woman twisted the ropes tying her hands again, a reminder to keep moving forward.

The entire temple was built to frame the cauldron of lava. Half-arches were carved from the earth around it to form windowed walls. This was it, Nori thought. She'd finally seen the scariest thing in the Subterranean. And then, when she couldn't possibly comprehend another shock, she looked across the fiery pit and found a dais and throne.

Twelve men in gray robes stood on the dais, their eyes keen on Nori's face as she approached. Panic surged at the sudden attention, and the thick breaths she took through the stale air turned to shallow pants. Lightheaded, dizzy, bound, and alone amidst a collection of grungy apostles, Nori closed her eyes and prayed for a miracle. This was it. This was the day she was going to die.

Among the twelve, a single man stood out. He wore a charcoal robe, and worked to hide the pleasure pulling at the corners of his mouth. His eyes were narrowly set, and yet the most prominent feature of his face. His nose was too long and his lips too thin—if he pressed them together, he might've had no mouth at all. Sandy hair was tied back, his hands clasped behind him.

Nori stopped walking. Stopped moving. Stopped breathing. "What's going on?" she said, and her voice was high with panic. "Where are my friends?"

The women forced her around the last arched window,

where she caught sight of Cooper lying unmoving beside the dais.

"Cooper!" she screamed. "Oh my God! Cooper!" Nori tried to run to him, but the older woman still held her restraints and jerked her roughly back. "Let me go!" she said. "What have you done to him?"

The narrow-eyed man approached her with a graceful, ravenous intent. He sized her up as he walked, gaze beginning at her hiking boots, slowing as they moved over her knees and thighs, up to her waist, and absorbing every twist and turn of her body. She shivered and longed for a shower. Finally, the man's eyes rested on her face.

"Welcome," he said. "These are the Disciples of Yahweh." He waved an arm toward the men. "And I am the Sword, though you may call me Lonnie. You've met Marta, Dawn, and Nayem, the Matron, the Maid, and the Daughter."

Nori's first impulse was to laugh at the absurdity of it all, but they were serious, which made her want to cry instead. What did they want from her? Why had they forced her to the wicked-looking temple? Cooper's unconscious—or dead—body was a clue their intentions weren't benevolent.

"What have you done to my friend?" Her voice was weaker than she would've liked.

Lonnie looked down at Cooper, a snarl flashing across his beatific face before it disappeared. "Your friend did not accept our invitation."

"Please just let us go," she begged. "We don't want any trouble."

"We lead simple lives here," he said. "Simple, but purposed."

Lonnie stepped into her personal space, and she tried to

back up but Marta—or Dawn— stood behind her and she couldn't move.

"What do you want from us?" Nori asked, stalling until she could form a solid plan. "Why have you hurt him?"

The breath Lonnie exhaled reached Nori before his hand did, and she shivered at the too-familiar touches of both. "Sometimes we must open the eyes of those who will not see."

Nori's stomach turned as her suspicions landed their first piece of evidence. "Where's my other friend?"

"All in due time, child. All in due time."

Nori started to argue, to scream, to ask what in hell he was talking about, but she was distracted by Cooper's twitching foot. Relief flooded her. Maybe he knew who the wackos were —and how to get them out of this mess.

Unfortunately, Lonnie saw it, too. He knelt beside Cooper, whose hands were tied firmly behind his back. "He awakens." Lonnie motioned to one of the robed men still standing stoically on the dais. "Shall we see if he can be saved?"

The robed man stepped forward. He never looked up before bending to lift Cooper's prone body and helping him stand. Nori searched Cooper's face for some clue what to do. He held her gaze then closed his eyes in…regret? Defeat? The muscles of his jaws clenched when he turned away from her.

"Cooper?" Nori moved closer to him, and away from Lonnie. "Cooper, what's going on? Who are these people? What do they want from us?"

"Excellent question, dear one." Lonnie motioned again, this time to the woman behind Nori, who untied the knot at her hands. She rubbed her wrists and rolled her neck, while keeping an eye on Lonnie. He approached her again, clasped both her hands in his, leaning so close she could barely breathe. "Long have we, the Sword of Yahweh, borne the burden of sharing the Lord's message," he said. "Long have we borne the burden of safeguarding the manifestation of his eternal salvation. Long have we borne the burden of sharing the way with those we meet."

Cooper shifted, his body going rigid, and Lonnie shot him a venomous warning glare. Lonnie held Cooper's gaze, but spoke to Nori as he rubbed her hands intimately between his. They were cool, and soft, and clean. Her body shook in a disgusted shudder.

"If you ask the Lord to cleanse your soul," he said, "you may live among us. You may join us, and share his abundance as one of our own."

Nori risked a look around the room. The men surrounding Lonnie, the silent female servants who'd brought her down, they all bought into it. They all subscribed. It wouldn't be smart to insult their religion, but there was no way in fiery hell she was staying to join them.

"And if I don't accept?" she asked. "If I decline the offer to join you?"

"Well." Lonnie splayed his hands in front of him, a peaceful gesture incongruent with his words. "If you will not join us, you will sustain us. All the Lord's gifts are accepted here."

"Sustain?" Nori's gaze shot to Cooper, whose face was less defiant than it had been a moment before, and noticeably afraid.

"Listen, Lonnie," Nori said with forced bravado. "Thank you for the offer, but we can't stay. Maybe next time we're back this way we'll stop and talk redemption."

"Entertaining." Lonnie nodded toward Nori, but spoke to

Cooper. "She is entertaining. But I fear you both may suffer the fate of your friend, who also denied the Lord's invitation."

A cold chill raced down Nori's back, taking the strength of her legs with it. Her knees buckled as she looked down into the pit of lava. A metal vest emblazoned with a crucifix was suspended by chains just above the lip of the crater. The vest was fitted around a person, a man, and with ominous clinks the contraption began to lower into the steaming red liquid.

Nori screamed. A metal mask covered his face, but she knew. She knew it was Kade. "No," she begged. "Pull him up. He'll do whatever you ask—just pull him up." She clasped Lonnie's hands and stepped into his embrace. "I'll do whatever you want. We'll do whatever you ask, just pull him back up!"

Cooper scurried toward the pit, sending rocks and dirt tumbling into the lava. He stopped just short of the edge and looked down, then frantically up at the ceiling and walls, his gaze finally snagging on a lever high above their heads.

"I am sorry," Lonnie said, though he looked no such thing. "Your friend made his choice. He declined the Lord's offer, and now will serve as a sacrifice for our continued blessings." Lonnie made a dramatic gesture to the person manning the lever in an overhead chamber. The chain extended with a creak, slowly lowering Kade toward the scalding liquid.

Nori and Cooper's screams joined those coming from the metal contraption, which only lasted a moment more.

37

A CHANCE IN HELL

Nori slumped to the ground, though Lonnie still held her hands in his. Rubbing, rubbing, rubbing with a light, cool touch so incongruent with the steaming pit. She wasn't thinking clearly. Couldn't reconcile what had just happened. She stared numbly at the pit with no emotion. Had her brain splintered somewhere along the way?

Lonnie's long, dramatic breath was almost meditative. Nori looked up at him, her feelings swirling between horrified, and confused, and afraid. When he opened his eyes again, they were alight with wicked pleasure.

"Ah." He patted her hands and bent to place them in her lap. "We have another postulant," he said. "Let us see if he wishes to accept the gift of salvation."

Nori's gaze shot to Cooper's. If he stood beside her, bloodied though he was, and Kade had been lowered into the lava, who were they bringing? She wiped her eyes with her palms to see, and when he came into view, she questioned her sanity again. "What?" She looked at Cooper, at the prisoner, and back again. "What?"

"It wasn't him," Cooper breathed, his voice tight with disbelief.

"Kade." Nori hiccuped a sob and searched the face of her friend. He hadn't been touched. He was unharmed. Alive.

When Kade's eyes met hers, they closed. Relief. He'd been worried, too.

"I have just been explaining to your friends our calling," Lonnie said. "The Lord has charged us with growing his kingdom, with glorifying his name, and with nourishing both his spirit and our own. Will you accept him and learn our ways, sharing both our bounty and our lives?" Lonnie waved a hand toward the lava pit with gentle grace. "Or will you face the fate of your friend, who has nourished our immortal souls?"

Kade's eyes shot wildly between her and Cooper, whose face had gone bone-white.

Kade struggled to get words out, swallowing several times.

Cooper cleared his throat and stood upright. "Lonnie? Ah, *Brother* Lonnie? We find ourselves suddenly open to your offer. Can you tell us more about your work here?"

Lonnie's face transformed to one of passion and light. "Yes, Brother. I hoped you might see the light. We are honored to share with you the blessings of our fold."

The women didn't untie Cooper and Kade right away, but they did lead them from the volcanic pit. Small victories, Nori supposed, her pulse slowing a little. As they shuffled past the dais, she motioned toward the metal rigging, which was once again suspended above the pit and burned clean. "Who was that?" she asked.

Cooper shook his head, but didn't look at it again. A tremor ran the length of his body.

"What do we do now?" she whispered, earning a censorious look from the dreadlocked Maid.

Cooper shook his head, his mouth a tight, straight line.

The sound of machine gun fire was deafening, like her eardrums had burst after the initial shot. Nori only heard white noise after that, but instinctively threw herself to the ground, landing hard on elbows and knees. She tried to crawl, straining to search for her friends. Kade had dived behind a column. Cooper was nearly lying on top of her. She wiggled and pitched her body to throw him off.

"Get off me," she said through gritted teeth.

He did but rolled his eyes. "You're welcome, by the way." "This way," he said. "Follow me."

Nori, Cooper and Kade ran toward a tiny alcove behind the dais and waited.

"What the hell's going on?" Kade demanded.

"They fried someone in that pit before they brought you out," Cooper said in a rush. "They thought we were all together. Maybe whoever that was had friends."

A spine-chilling cackle drew Nori's attention toward the temple entrance. She would've known that laugh—and that face—anywhere. Even through the steam and gunpowder smoke, she recognized Jenks's slimy sneer. He and Sarge took cover behind columns as they mowed down the men on the dais, who weren't armed. The battle was easily won.

"We have to get out of here," Cooper said. "They'll come for us next. Quick, untie us."

With Cooper done and finishing the knots at Kade's back, Nori spotted Jenks across the way. A smile spread across his face that was so evil she shivered. He'd caught sight of the little girl, Nayem. Spiteful brat or not, no one deserved Jenks's particular attentions.

She snuck behind Jenks as quietly as she could. He was too busy firing on parishioners pouring out of the hallway to notice her. She dipped behind an arched wall and waited for him to pass by. Nori didn't breathe for fear he'd see her, but he didn't. When he was finally close enough, she launched herself, throwing her arms around the column. She held on for dear life and kicked Jenks in the gut as hard as she could. He swung his arms wildly to stop the momentum, but it was too late. He plunged into the boiling pit. A split second later, Nori gasped, blinking as she came to terms with what she'd done. Jenks was a vicious, evil person, and he'd had his sights on a child. Bile rose in her throat anyway. She'd killed someone.

Nayem's movements drug Nori's attention away from the lava. The girl ran away, but Nori didn't chase her. Instead, she hung her head and considered letting herself break completely down. The rush of panic and fear had left an empty space that needed to be filled. Her eyes stung and her sinuses threatened to burst, but she sniffed and shook her head. Dwelling longer on Jenks or his idiot friend Wallace, who'd suffered the same fiery fate, was a waste of time they didn't have. She scrambled back to Cooper and Kade, who watched her with barely concealed shock.

Lonnie had somehow avoided the bulk of the gunfire, and rose onto his knees. "How dare you sully the House of Yahweh?" he intoned around a mouthful of blood.

Sarge, whose face sported angry red burns, cocked his head and stared at the man, then looked at the dozens of people he'd just slaughtered. He examined them one by one, his stony expression never wavering. And then he aimed the gun at Lonnie and shot him one last time. Lonnie fell back awkwardly, legs bent beneath him.

"Looks like it's just you and me, kids," Sarge said too brightly, his voice pitched to a maddened high. "Well, and my gun. Now, unless you three really are ready to meet your maker today, I suggest you keep your hands to yourself and go back the way we came in."

He pulled a pistol from a holster at his waist and nudged it into Cooper's back, who jerked angrily away from it. "Followed you idiots here," Sarge said. "Don't you know how to avoid the Sword of Yahweh?" he said with a snort. "I know you do, Cooper. Taught you myself. Couldn't believe our luck when we tracked you to this pass."

Nori's head whipped in Cooper's direction. "You knew about these psychos, and you led us right to them?"

"Of course I didn't lead us to them." Cooper blew out an exasperated breath. "I mean, I knew about the Sword, but this was the way to avoid them."

"Old information," Sarge sneered.

"You didn't think that was something we should know?" Kade accused. "You didn't think you should tell us murderous zealots were waiting to boil us alive if we didn't forfeit our souls?"

"Well, I really hoped to avoid all that." Cooper gave a jerky shrug. "Obviously."

"How did that work out for you? For us?" Nori ground her teeth and fisted her hands. "I thought I was gonna die, Cooper. I thought you were dead. And Kade..." She looked away and worked to calm her breathing.

"They woulda fried you suckers, too," Sarge said. "If I hadn't gotten here." The black metal of his gun glinted in the torchlight. He pointed it at each of them, sparing neither a glance nor an obvious thought for his two fallen comrades. "We're gettin' out of here. Place gives me the creeps."

No one argued the point, but they didn't move.

"I said let's go!" He shoved the pistol into Cooper's back

again, but before he could even grunt at the pain of metal to his spine, Cooper spun and threw his elbow, catching Sarge in the middle of the throat. Sarge gave a strangled gag and his eyes bulged before he righted himself and leaped onto Cooper. Gravel — and the pistol — scattered as they fell to the ground.

The meaty sound of fists to skin had Nori jumping to pull Sarge off Cooper. She slung her arm under his neck and squeezed it toward her, using the other arm to form a solid vice around his throat. Sarge twisted and bucked beneath her, cursing with venom and skill, but she held on. When he faltered, Nori ground her teeth and squeezed tighter.

She didn't anticipate the headbutt, and only registered Sarge's greasy head speeding toward her face after she heard the bones of her nose grinding to slivers. She lost control of her limbs — and all consciousness.

When Nori came to, she closed her eyes again to reboot. She blinked three, four times, which did nothing to change the scene before her. Nayem's tiny hands shook under the weight of a gun. Kade was on his knees holding his right shoulder. Blood seeped through his fingers and soaked into the dirt floor. Sarge watched the girl through narrowed eyes, his intention to take the gun from her clear. Cooper's eye was swollen, and a streak of drying blood marred his bottom lip.

"Wait, no!" Cooper's desperate yell threw Nori's attention back to Nayem. He leaped toward the girl, whose little face contorted when she squeezed her eyes shut and pulled the trigger.

The sound of gunfire cracked through the tunnel, and Nori pressed palms to her ears. It all happened so fast. One minute, Nayem's shaky aim was headed straight for Nori, and the next, a blossom of red spread from Sarge's gut. He fell into the wall, gasping. Nayem's little mouth formed an "o," and her breaths whistled through the tiny opening.

"Is there anyone here?" Nori asked her. The girl didn't flinch, didn't look at Nori.

"Nayem," Nori asked urgently. "Is there anyone coming for us?"

Nayem's dark eyes swung viciously toward Nori. No, they wouldn't be alone there for long.

Cooper swiped the back of his hand over his bloody lip. "Kade, can you ride?"

Kade nodded, wincing as he trudged toward them.

"Where are our bikes?" Nori asked. "And what about Sarge? Do we take him? Finish him?"

"There's nothing we can do for Sarge now," Cooper said. "He looked the man over, but showed no emotion. "We have to get out of here before the rest of them find us."

"We came in through there," Kade's voice was strained as he motioned toward the passageway with his good arm. "Hopefully, it's the way out, too."

Nori didn't have a name for the emotion pulling at her heart. "Wait!" she said and ran toward the chamber, where Nayem stood. She crept toward the girl, whose savage gaze shot up to meet hers. A tremor started at the girl's grubby feet, and before long, took over her entire body.

"It's gonna be all right," Nori said. "I promise." She aimed for calm and soothing, though she felt anything but.

The girl didn't acknowledge her at all, but stood looking wildly around.

"Nayem? Come with us, okay? We'll get you out of here. You'll be safe with us, I promise."

The child's narrow lips thinned until they disappeared, and she shook her head. There was something not quite right about her eyes as grim determination crossed her gaunt face.

"Nayem?" Nori repeated.

Without a word, the girl lurched toward the center of the chamber, arms dangling behind her as she ran. She climbed into the windowed opening of the arch overlooking the fiery pit.

Nori's stomach dropped and her breath wheezed out.

"No!" Nori screamed as Nayem leaped into the bubbling pool of lava without ever looking back.

38

THE BIG MAN GOES DOWN

Cooper closed his eyes and shook his head, his stomach twisting with nausea. He'd give Nori time to recover if he could. This had all been too much, too fast. She wasn't used to this pace, to the harsh environment, to the danger and death.

He ground his teeth as regret washed over him in angry waves. He should've found another way around Yahweh's territory. He'd made a mistake, and they'd nearly paid for it with their lives. Nori had stunned him, though, with her attack on Jenks. Good. She'd need to be tough, to think quickly to survive down here, and there was no better way to learn a lesson than the hard way.

"Nori?" He lifted her from the chamber floor because her legs didn't seem to be working. "Nori, we have to go."

Her face was drained of blood, the blue of her eyes like cerulean saucers against a white tablecloth.

"Why would she do that?" Nori whispered. She turned to face him and clutched his arms. "Why would a little girl do that?"

Pity flooded his heart, and it wasn't all for Nayem. "We'll never know what she endured here," he said. "Maybe she found her own way out." He allowed Nori one more moment then set her onto her feet. "I'm sorry," he said. "We really have to go."

"It was...a lot...easier...when we were...coming down," Kade said through ragged breaths. Despite the long, steep incline from the pit of despair back to the main tunnel, he was exhausted too quickly for someone in his prime shape.

Nori searched his face. Too pale. The front of his jacket was soaked in fresh, red blood.

Cooper was looking, too, then he turned to her. "Just a little farther."

She heard something. Voices—male. And they were getting closer.

"Kade, man, we've gotta move faster." Cooper ducked under the fighter's good arm and hefted him up the steep path.

The shouts came louder, the tone violent.

There was only one other way to go. "Through here," Nori said and led them through a shallow doorway carved into the earth. There were no torches in the rooms, but that was no impediment for her.

"Lead the way, Nor." Cooper's voice and muscles were strained under the weight of Kade's big body.

She jogged into the darkness, Cooper and Kade limping behind her, falling farther and farther behind.

"Hold on," Nori gasped and slowed. "I smell gas."

"Keep going," Cooper called and waved her on. "Maybe it's the bikes."

When they caught up to her, Nori had found the motorcycles and reattached their supplies.

"Can you ride out of here on your own?" Cooper asked her.

"What?" She blinked, uncomprehending.

"No way Kade can operate a bike. I'm worried he can't even stay upright behind me."

"What?" she said again.

Cooper's jaws clenched as he helped Kade onto the back of the bike she'd ridden with Cooper. "Nori, I need you to ride his bike out of here. You can do it. I know you can."

"I mean, yeah, I can ride, but I'll never get it kick-started, and you know that. I've tried fifty times."

Cooper's face took on a different kind of strain. A guilty one. "Kade's bike has an electric starter. You don't have to kickstart it."

Nori sucked in a shocked breath. "You're not serious," she said. Cooper looked at the ground and nodded. "And all this time...when I was learning to ride...you didn't tell me. You made me kick, and kick, and kick your stupid bike."

Cooper still hadn't met her gaze.

"Oh, you suck, Sam Cooper. Did you get some sick enjoyment out of watching me struggle? That's just cruel."

"You're right, okay?" He finally looked at her, and he at least seemed sincere. "I'm sorry. But we do need to go. Now."

Nori fisted her hands and narrowed her eyes at him. "Okay. But this is not over." Cooper nodded guiltily at her before he mounted the bike in front of Kade.

"Okay," he said. "See that little black button?"

"Yeah."

"Push it."

The motorcycle roared to life beneath Nori's thighs. With a final shake of her head, she put the bike in gear and followed Cooper out of the Sword of Yahweh's den. She didn't look back at the fanatics pouring out of the tunnel after them. She couldn't look back. Not ever. She would only see Nayem.

Kade lost consciousness without warning. His thick arms fell heavily to his sides and his big body slumped into Cooper's back. The motorcycle was already weighed down beneath the two men, and the added instability sent it wobbling. Cooper held the handlebar with one hand and reached behind him to grab Kade as they slowed to a stop.

"Wait, and I'll help you," Nori called as Cooper stopped to maneuver the fighter to the ground. "Are we far enough away?" she asked, hefting Kade's big legs. "Will they come for us?"

"I haven't heard anything since we left." Cooper said and carefully laid Kade's torso and head down.

"That's probably because I yanked tubes from every vehicle I saw while I waited for you and Kade to catch up."

Cooper's mouth fell open, and, after a second, he laughed. "Impressive," he finally said. "Anyway, their MO is lure and capture, not hunt, so we're in the clear." Nori breathed a sigh of relief until he added a mumbled, "I hope."

She knelt and skinned Kade's bloodsoaked jacket from his body, pushing his shirt away. He hadn't been shot in the chest as she'd thought, but in the outside muscle of his shoulder.

"Did it go through?" Cooper's voice was urgent as he sifted through the bike's saddlebag.

"Ah." Nori's hands shook as she hefted her friend's shoulder off the ground. She'd never been squeamish, but seeing Kade bloody made her lightheaded. "There's a bigger hole on the back side of his upper arm."

"Good," Cooper said. "That's good."

"He's lost a lot of blood. He needs a doctor, Cooper. What are we going to do?"

"He'll have to make do with us." Cooper pulled disinfectant and gauze from a first aid kit they'd lifted from the lodge.

Oh, to be back there again with a hot shower and movies, Nori thought. And a bed. Lying on the cold stone floor wouldn't be good for Kade—a gaping gunshot wound was sure to get infected in such conditions.

"The biggest threat right now is blood loss." Cooper was still speaking while she daydreamed. "Press his coat into that wound and stop the bleeding while I make a tourniquet."

Nori held the fabric to her friend's wound, and Cooper knelt beside her and tied a strip of fabric so tight around Kade's arm and shoulder she was glad he was unconscious.

"What's that?" Nori asked as he poured a thin liquid over the bloody holes.

"A sterile solution to wash the wounds." He opened a packet with his teeth and extracted gel-like sponges. "And these will help stop the bleeding. Hopefully." He packed the sponges into both the entry and exit wounds, which had continued to seep bright red blood. "The location of the wound isn't ideal for a tourniquet, but I did the best I could."

As they watched, the flow of Kade's blood slowed. Nori blew out a breath and took her friend's hand in hers. Cooper gave an encouraging nod, but she didn't feel much encouraged.

"What now?" she asked.

"Now," Cooper said. "We hope for the best."

"Shouldn't he be awake by now?" Nori paced beside Kade's prone body.

"He lost a lot of blood. I don't know."

"We've got to get him to a doctor," she said. "We can't just sit here and do nothing." She kicked the hard stone wall and regretted it as pain shot through her toes. "We've got to do something."

Cooper closed his eyes and let out a breath. "You're right. Change of plans. We're making a detour."

She nodded. "What do you need me to do?"

It was a struggle to lift Kade's dead weight onto the bike, but they finally found a working method by making one move at a time. Sit him up. Lift his legs. Lift his trunk. Carry him toward the bike. Maneuver one leg over the bike. Push his trunk onto the seat. Hold him upright.

Once they finally had Kade astride the bike, Cooper slid in and leaned the fighter's heavy head onto his shoulder. Cooper's idea to prop Kade on the seat in front of him, facing him, had seemed like a good one at the time. But the result was the two embracing like lovers. Nori tried, but couldn't contain her giggle.

Cooper whipped his head toward her as far as he could, his eyes throwing darts. "A little gratitude would be great right about now."

Despite the seriousness of Kade's condition, Nori's giggle spread to a full-on belly laugh, and she had to work to catch her breath. "Sorry," she squeaked, making a real effort to tone it down. "I think I'm a little hysterical."

Kade's body jerked like he was waking from a bad dream. "What?" he mumbled, his eyes unfocused. "What's happening?"

"Hey." Nori eased toward her friend and ran a hand down his arm. "Everything's okay. We're taking you to a doctor."

Kade winced but sat up on the bike, which put his eye level at Cooper's forehead. He scowled, and the fine muscles of his jaw feathered. "Anybody care to explain why I'm sitting in Cooper's lap?"

In the end, Kade was able to sit behind Cooper for the trek to the nearest town. The injured arm rested in his lap, and he braced his good hand on the seat behind him. Nori grinned at the awkwardness between the two and hoped they didn't make any sudden turns.

"Where are we?" she yelled as the tunnel subtly widened.

"We had to go a bit farther west than the route I'd planned. This is Bannera."

"What's in Bannera?" he asked.

"Hopefully, a doctor."

Each person they passed along the way turned to watch them until they were out of view. They were certainly a sight to behold—two big men sharing one bike, and a girl trailing on her own behind them. Nori sat up straighter and saluted a particularly obvious ogler. Might as well give 'em a show.

They stood their bikes next to several others along a long wall just outside of town. Kade's face was still pale, and he had a pretty high fever, but he was holding it together. Cooper strode toward the entrance of a general store, and the two followed.

"Hello." He nodded to the wiry woman checking out a customer. "My friend's been hurt. Any doctors in town?"

The woman took in Kade's bloody clothes and arm. They all looked a mess, even by Subterranean standards. The woman squinted her dark eyes, and her lip curled. "Bannera's a peaceful town. We keep it that way by limitin' the influence of outsiders."

"We're just looking for some medical help, ma'am." Cooper widened his eyes in feigned helplessness. "My friend's badly hurt. We'll move on just as soon as he's able."

Cooper elbowed Kade in the gut when she wasn't looking, and the big man groaned. "He's getting worse," Cooper said, feeling Kade's cheeks and forehead.

Nori shook her head in wonder at Cooper's performance. If the crusty old woman didn't take pity on them, she had to be a walking corpse.

"Hmph," the old woman said. "Doctor died last year."

Cooper's facade faltered. Maybe he was more worried about Kade than he'd let on. Kade made a sudden fuss of coughing and groaning, and Nori rolled her eyes.

"But," the woman eyed them again, "a newcomer says he has medical experience. You might try him."

"Thank you so much, ma'am," Cooper gushed when she gave directions.

"You sure this is the place?" Kade was skeptical, and rightly so. A shack, no more than three pieces of tin fastened together, was propped against the side of another building.

"The lady said to look for the lean-to." Cooper shrugged.

"Lady." Kade snorted.

"Let's just knock," Nori said. "We'll never know till we ask."

"Hello," Cooper called toward the front piece of tin. "We were told you could help with a wound."

Something rattled inside the shack before its occupant pushed open the tin door.

Kade's mouth went slack, and he stared at the man inside the shack.

Nori ran to him, afraid he would pass out again. "Kade? Kade, are you okay?"

When he finally found his voice, Kade uttered a single word. "Grant?"

39

BIG SURPRISE IN BANNERA

The man's slim fingers fell away from the makeshift door. Without saying a word, he turned and extended an arm to invite them all in.

Nori's gaze shot to Kade. His face had gone pale again, and not just from blood loss. His eyes fluttered shut milliseconds before he crumpled to the floor.

"What happened to him?" Grant bustled about the small space, collecting medical supplies as Nori and Cooper moved Kade to the small but neat bed.

"He's been shot," Nori said.

"What?" Grant gasped, his sleek brown eyebrows drawing together. "When?"

"Hours ago," Cooper said. "We think it went straight through."

"God," Grant moaned, his hazel eyes filling with tears. "Oh God, Kade."

Nori and Cooper looked at each other, but didn't say a word about the elephant in the room.

"What do you know about gunshot wounds?" Nori asked.

"Will he be okay?" She rubbed a sheen of sweat from Kade's brow. "Wait. Do you even have medical training?"

"I have more than anybody in this town since their doctor died," Grant said. "And I took care of Kade for years. I'm the best shot he's got."

Grant gently but efficiently treated Kade's wounds, his gaze roaming his patient's face as frequently as his shoulder.

"Who are you, anyway?" Grant asked, risking a look away from Kade.

"I'm Nori. I...ah...I took your place at the Pit." Grant blanched but nodded. "This is Cooper," she said with a shrug, not sure how to describe him.

This wasn't ideal, Nori thought. Kade needed serious medical attention, a real doctor. But Grant was right—he was all they had.

"How bad is it?" she asked him.

"The wound's infected," he said, "but he was lucky. It went through a muscle. I cleaned the wounds pretty well, but he'll need antibiotics, and those are hard to come by. I have something, but it's not very strong. Still, he's strong, and in good health. It'll be fine." He looked away and said much quieter, "Please God let him be fine."

Cooper stood. "I'm going to look through the bikes to see what meds we brought from the lodge."

Nori watched Grant fuss over Kade a few minutes more. "What happened?" she asked.

Grant shot her a confused look.

"Between you and Kade," she said. "He told me about you. How are you here?" She shook her head. "How are you alive?"

Grant's body sagged and he released an exhausted breath, as if he simply couldn't carry the weight anymore. "We were supposed to be the most important person in each other's lives," he said. "But he never put me first. Not really." He laughed bitterly. "Story of my life. Anyway, I wasn't happy at Hank's or in Trogtown. We couldn't be together, not really." He stood to throw something in the trash. "For years, we were stuck in the same place, and I wanted to go forward. Together. That wasn't possible at Hank's, so I thought it was time to leave." He closed his eyes and ran his hands through his hair. "Kade wouldn't. I wanted to start over somewhere new, but he wouldn't go." Grant's nostrils flared with a sharp intake of breath. "He didn't choose me," he said and sat roughly on the bed at Kade's feet.

"Yeah, that's pretty much what Kade said," Nori nodded. "But why...why do something so gruesome, so dramatic as jump from a gorge? Why make everyone think you were dead? It just seems so cruel." Nori searched Grant's face. "I care about Kade, and you destroyed him. Why would you do that?"

Grant's head hung between his shoulders, and he put his face in his hands. "I was hurting. I was desperate. Heartbroken. I was in pieces, and when he wouldn't believe me, when he wouldn't leave with me, I just wanted him to feel as broken as I did."

"Well," Nori said, her tone razor sharp as she stood. "You got your wish."

The cool air that blew into the shack at Cooper's return brought Kade back to consciousness. He gasped and tried to sit up, but Grant was there with a hand on his chest. "No, no. Lie back down. Everything's all right. You're all right."

Kade lay back down, but his eyes remained on Grant. Though he was injured and weak, his body was tense.

"What the hell are you doing here, Grant?" His breaths came hard, but not because of the fever. "What the hell?"

Nori cleared her throat and motioned Cooper outside.

"Why did you call me out here?" Cooper asked once the tin door/wall had closed. "I thought Grant was dead, too." He moved to go back inside. "I want some answers."

"Wait." Nori grabbed the sleeve of his leather jacket. "Let's give them a moment."

Cooper eyed her as if she were ridiculous.

"Fine," Nori relented. "Grant escaped from Hank's and led everyone to believe he was dead. Even Kade. He started over, and landed here, I suppose."

"That's messed up," he said. "I mean, I can see why he'd orchestrate the whole thing so Hank wouldn't come after him, but not to tell Kade... They seemed close. Poor Kade, man. What a shock."

"Poor Kade is right." Nori nodded. "It shattered him. And to find Grant here, alive..."

Cooper's head tilted to the side as he worked through his thoughts. "So, Kade and Grant..."

Nori nodded.

"Not you and Kade?"

Nori shook her head.

"Ah." Cooper's Adam's apple bobbed beneath a hard swallow.

"Anyway," Nori said. "Looks like Kade will be fine after some antibiotics. What now?"

"Now?" Cooper did a rare thing. He smiled at her, and she nearly gasped at the beauty of it. "Now, let's go see if we can scare up a hot meal. They have a lot to talk about, and if I have to eat another Vitabar, I'll jump from a gorge myself."

Nori laughed and Cooper ran an arm across her shoulders as they walked toward the town's main street.

"KADE? Grant? We're back, and we brought real food." Nori knocked, and Cooper rattled the food containers he held.

When Grant let them inside, the mood was much changed. The tension was gone.

"You guys were gone a while," Kade said. He still lay in the bed, his skin pale, but appeared to be past the risk of death, at least for the moment.

"Nori had to have dessert," Cooper teased.

"They had chocolate," she said. "And real coffee. Like I was going to pass that up."

"Please say you brought me some. I'm starving." Kade winced as he sat up in the bed.

"No-bake chocolate oatmeal cookies. And real food! Look, potato pot pie. It's still warm."

Kade fed himself with his good arm, closing his eyes at times.

"It'll be a while before we get another hot meal, I'm afraid," Cooper said.

Kade exchanged a nervous look with Grant.

"What?" Nori and Cooper asked at the same time.

"I…ah…I've decided to stay here. With Grant."

Nori looked between the two. "No… But… Why?"

"You know why." He looked at Grant as he spoke. "I made the wrong choice once, and it nearly killed us both. I won't do it again."

She understood. She did. "Come with us," she said. "Both of you."

"I can't ride with my arm like this, Nori."

"You can make it with one good arm, and you know it." Her voice broke when she said, "And you promised my parents."

Kade blew out a deep breath and looked away from her. "I do hate that part. But Cooper knows everything about this trek. I'm just there for moral support."

"And muscle." Cooper's attempt to lighten the mood had little effect.

"Kade, are you sure?" Nori asked as she sunk beside him on the bed.

"I'm sure." He squeezed her hand. "I'm sorry to leave you, sorry to break my promise. But finding Grant here—it changes everything."

"I know," she whispered. "I know."

AFTER A CROWDED NIGHT on Grant's floor, Nori and Cooper woke early and readied the bike to leave.

"Here." Grant stuffed a few packs of non-perishable food into her arms. "You're going to need this."

"Thanks," she said absently, watching Kade and Cooper exchange goodbyes.

"No." Grant squeezed her arm. "Thank you. For saving Kade after what I did to him."

She shrugged and cleared her throat, hiding her emotion from Kade as he approached. He stood in front of her, holding his injured arm, but she suspected it wasn't physical pain forming the clouds behind his eyes. She was barely holding it together herself.

"Cooper's a good guy," he said. "You can trust him. He'll make sure you get to your parents."

"I know. And I'm glad you found Grant. I just…I just wasn't ready to say goodbye." Kade clasped her to him in a bear hug, and she squeezed his waist. Her cheek barely reached his chest. "I don't have many friends, Kade. I never have. I hate to lose you, is all."

"Hey." He pushed her back to arm's length and searched her gaze. "Hey. You're not losing me." At her doubtful look, he said, "You're not. You can't get rid of me that easy. When I get better, and we save some money, who knows? Maybe we'll join you in Mexico. We can all get a big house together. I'll cook bacon every morning, and you can be in charge of laundry." That got a laugh, and he squeezed her one final time. "I'll miss you, Noir."

Her smile was only for show. "I'll miss you too."

Nori waved goodbye one last time before clinging to Cooper like she never had before.

40

COOPER OPENS UP

"I can't feel my toes anymore," Nori said. Standing on the bike's foot pegs did nothing to increase blood flow to her feet. "Can't we break for a minute? My head hurts, and I just want five minutes of silence." The roar of the engine, the constant vibration of her body left Nori on edge; she needed peace, if only for a moment.

"We need to make up at least some of the time we lost in Bannera," Cooper said over his shoulder. "Let's go another forty miles then we can stop."

She pounded her forehead against his back, but didn't argue anymore. Without warning, the bike slowed to a stop and Cooper dismounted. He didn't say anything to her before stalking around a bend.

"Thank you," Nori said when he returned. He shrugged and looked away. "Tell me about where you grew up."

"I thought you wanted quiet."

"I needed a break from the bike, okay? I needed to walk, to talk. We've been riding for hours, and I can't hear you over the engine."

Cooper didn't answer, and she didn't speak for several charged moments. Finally, the silence was too much.

"So, where did you learn to ride?" she asked.

A smile flashed across his lips. "My mother."

Nori blinked. "Your mother taught you to ride a motorcycle?"

"She taught me everything."

Nori nodded for him to go on, and he sighed, relenting.

"I grew up in what was basically a commune. Everyone worked together toward the same goal. We shared resources and responsibilities. You've heard that phrase 'it takes a village to raise a child?' I had a village, though we called it the Settlement. It was a happy little life, actually, and at the helm of the ship was my mom. She was so smart, so independent. She made her own way without worrying about what people thought. The rules didn't apply to her, you know?"

Nori nodded, engrossed in the tale of a mother he obviously adored. It was the first time he'd opened up...about anything, really. His eyes brimmed with pride and love as he spoke, and Nori leaned toward him, elbows on her knees, anxious to hear more.

"I never knew my father, though Gramps served that role as well as anyone could. He and Gran were steady figures in my life. They were both climate scientists who came to the Settlement during the first sunscorch."

"Climate scientists," Nori repeated. "That must be fascinating in a world like ours."

Cooper nodded, but frowned. "Anyway, that's the gist of me."

Nori barked a laugh. "Ah, I think you're leaving a few things out."

"Like what?"

Her eyes widened, and she threw out her hands. "Like, how you got mixed up with Sarge. Like, why you pretended to be in with them. And you never answered me about Chicago."

Cooper stretched his neck and avoided Nori's gaze.

"Cooper?"

"Yeah," he said too lightly.

"You wanna come clean about any of that?"

He shook his head and gave her his most charming grin. "Not really."

"Fine."

Cooper's eyebrows shot up. "Really?"

"No," she said, stomping toward the motorcycle. "We're sleeping here tonight, and I'm taking the blanket."

Cooper muttered to himself as Nori snuggled into a corner with the only blanket they had. After a while, he sat at her feet and rested his head on bent knees.

Nori woke surprisingly snug, considering she'd slept on rocks. Breath on her neck was like a welcome heater, warming skin not covered by the blanket.

She jolted as comprehension dawned, her head slamming back to smack Cooper in the forehead.

He moaned a muffled "ow" before fear overrode his pain. He jumped to attention. "What's wrong?"

"What's wrong?" she said. "You spooning me in my sleep, for one thing."

"Is that all?" He dropped the gun he'd apparently been holding in his sleep. "I got cold."

"And so, of course, you just snuggled right in." Nori's sarcasm didn't go unnoticed.

"Yeah, well, you had the blanket." He turned, unfazed, to walk down the tunnel and out of her sight.

"Hey!" she yelled after him. "Where are you going?"

"A little privacy?" he said, his tone dripping with scorn. "Really, Nori, you need to work on boundaries."

"Oh." She threw a handful of gravel at him. "Oh, *I* need to work on boundaries. You have got to be kidding me."

WHEN SHE'D FIRST CONSIDERED the prospect, navigating a secret subterranean roadway to another country had sounded thrilling. To a girl whose disability had kept her indoors, days on the road with the wind in her hair and a powerful machine beneath her was a dream come true.

What Nori had failed to consider was that when traveling underground, scenery rarely changed. No pit stops for tourist traps. Besides an occasional swath of graffiti, it was just rock, rock, and more rock. Some parts of the path were smoothed by time or hand, and there were occasional veins of silvery minerals, but by and large, it was just a bunch of uninterrupted rock.

Nori was so sick of it she thought she might be the first case of death by monotony. A whole new kind of stoning, she mentally snorted. Yeah, she definitely needed a change of scenery.

"How many more days do you think we have to go?" she asked. "And any chance we'll see something besides this stupid tunnel? Any towns?"

Cooper turned and talked over the motor. "Drove through south Texas yesterday. Takes a while to go around big settlements like San Antonio and Laredo, though they have the best infrastructure. With any luck, we'll pass into Mexico today."

"Cooper!" She punched his ribs. "I'm dying here. I need a shower. And real food. Why would you drive around a town?"

"Generally better to go unnoticed," he said. "Towns mean trouble. Gangs. Remember the Sword of Yahweh?"

"That wasn't a town, it was a cult," she huffed. "Bannera was okay."

"We risked Bannera because Kade's gunshot was infected. And it turned out okay because of Grant, who that town needs since there are no med schools and doctors are dying of old age. The important thing is getting to the 25th. Finding your parents. Don't forget that."

"Of course I haven't forgotten," she snapped. "This is just...tougher than I'd thought it would be."

"I know. And I hate to tell you, but it's going to get worse before it gets better."

She sat up higher on the bike. "What do you mean?"

"The passages we've taken—all of the ones running under the US—were funded by the government decades ago."

"That's not true." Nori shook her head. "I never heard that."

"Oh, and you know so much?" he said sarcastically. "Did you know an entire population of people lived underground?"

Her face scrunched into a scowl. "Point taken."

"Anyway," he went on, "the tunnels I've seen in Mexico aren't as...structured. There are main arteries to and from important areas, but they're patrolled by pirates or militants. The tunnels we'll have to take are sometimes no more than mud-caked wormholes. We'll be lucky if we're able to ride the bike the whole way."

Nori banged her head on Cooper's back at the thought of walking—or crawling—the rest of the way to the 25th Parallel.

He twisted in his seat. "For what it's worth," he said, "I think you've been a champ." Nori risked a look up at his face. "I'm serious." His green-gold eyes were intent on hers even when a chunk of his dark hair blew in his face. "This is a hard trek. There's a reason not everyone makes it."

She closed her eyes and mumbled "thanks," but then sat up. "Cooper?"

"Hmm?"

"Thank you for bringing me all this way. I don't think I've ever said that. Thank you for helping me find my parents."

"That's it." Cooper downshifted. "We're stopping."

"What? Why?"

"I think you've got a fever."

"Ha ha." She punched him again, but playfully, and though he faced forward, she could tell he was smiling by the crinkles at the corner of his eye.

"DAMN." Cooper squeezed the brakes, bringing the bike to a too-quick stop. Nori braced her arms to keep her body from slamming into his, but avoiding contact was as futile as searching for the sun.

After so many days of riding tandem, Cooper and Nori had developed a rhythm. When he leaned into a turn, she leaned with him. At accelerations, she reached for the waist of his jeans and the solid hip bones beneath it.

"What's wrong?" she asked.

"Road's blocked." Cooper dismounted and strode toward a pile of rocks, which bordered some sort of cave-in.

Nori stretched her aching back before running to catch up with him. "Could we get through if we moved the rocks?"

"You and I together couldn't move that one." Cooper motioned to a boulder the size of a chair before massaging his temples. "And there are probably bigger ones behind it. The tunnel's collapsed."

They'd encountered several challenges since entering Mexico, but this was the worst one. A surge of frustration shot through Nori, and she tossed aside some of the smaller rocks in the front of the pile. Bigger ones awaited just behind them. She wanted to scream, to jump up and down and have a full-on fit, throwing handfuls of rock and dirt. She allowed herself one angry, low-pitched growl then slid to the floor and stared at the opposing wall.

After a while, Cooper sat down beside her, sliding his hand to her knee and giving an encouraging pat. He left his hand there, but she didn't mind. Touching Cooper had become second nature. A comfort. Maybe it was to him, too.

"All right," he finally said and squeezed her leg. "Let's get back on the bike."

Nori leaned her head back and groaned. "How far do we have to backtrack? How far to one of the towns we passed before?"

"We're not going to a town. Not that far." He stood and offered a hand to help her up.

"Where, then? Did I miss a turnoff? I haven't seen anything since..." Nori's voice trailed off as she pieced together Cooper's plan. "We're not going to the Surface, are we?" She shook her head. "Cooper? We're not going to the Surface?"

His eyes softened as he considered her fear, but his voice was confident. "It's our only choice. Anything else will set us back days, Nori. Days."

Cooper slowed the bike some time later and Nori caught a

glimpse of a painted symbol someone had wiped free of grime. "I saw that on the way through," she said, "but it didn't click." She sat up straighter on the bike. "I recognize it now." The stamped symbol was a bleeding red. Simple but aggressive. "That's the symbol for biohazard. Right?"

"Basically, yeah. Only this one has that sunburst in the middle."

"You're right." She dismounted and crept closer to inspect it. "What does it stand fo— No!" She traced three "C"s whose stems met in the middle. Does that mean what I think it means?"

"That depends," Cooper said and walked the bike through a narrow entrance and behind a camouflaged wall she hadn't seen until that moment. "If you think it's a symbol for your friends at the CCC then yeah."

"Why a biohazard warning, though" she wondered.

"Oh, it's all very calculated. See how the sunburst looms ominously behind the circle of "C"s?" he asked, and Nori nodded. "It's not just their symbol, but a warning, a way to perpetuate the "Surface is poisonous" hysteria."

Nori chased after him, fear creeping into her bones. "You don't think those psychos are up there watching this exit, do you?"

Cooper pushed the bike past a series of rusty doors. "No," he said, his voice overly-light. "They're just the ones who built the exit. There's nothing to worry about."

As they ascended a muddy path far narrower than the main tunnel, she could've sworn she heard a garbled, "Probably."

41

EL GRAN DESCONOCIDO

"Cooper?" Nori asked.

"Yeah?"

"What if it's not dark out?"

Someone had put a thick padlock on the door leading outside. Cooper used the gun he'd taken from the last run-in with Sarge as a lever to dislodge the lock from the latch. It didn't work.

"Can't you smell it?" he asked.

"Smell what?"

"The night air."

"I smell something," she said. "Burning—no, burned."

"That's just everything left after the scorch. Try, though," he said. "Picture the night sky as you breathe, see if you can tell the sun's gone."

Nori cocked an eyebrow at him, but tried anyway. It had been so long since she'd inhaled anything besides exhaust fumes. Maybe her chemoreceptors were fried.

Cooper's vicious kicks at the door only minimally

distracted her. "You're right," she said, eyes popping open as a gust of night air hit her. "I can totally tell."

He laughed out loud, and for a moment her heart expanded almost painfully. "I'm just messing' with ya," he said. "I looked at my watch." Cooper stopped his laughing and met her gaze. You slug, she said. "You slimy, septic slug. I hate you. You know that?"

"You do not." His words held more meaning than she was comfortable with.

"What are you banging on?" she finally asked.

"See," he said proudly. "Stick with me, and you'll learn something."

"I've learned a lot already, actually," she said, and then finally looked at him. "What are you banging on?"

Cooper's guilty grin turned wolf-like when her gaze snagged on the metal squares in his hand. "The lock was new and wouldn't budge. Glad I snagged those tools from the lodge. I dismantled the hinges."

"OH. MY GOD." Nori covered her mouth with shaking hands, horrified by what lay just behind the metal door. Her watery eyes turned to real tears as she took in the husk-like remains of bodies piled around the door. "People," she whispered. "These are people." She turned to Cooper, whose face had gone white. "There must be a hundred of them." She shook her head, and her voice rose with each word. "Oh. My God. My God, my God, my God."

"That new padlock." Cooper's whispered voice was savage. "Someone locked them out of the tunnel. Someone murdered all these people."

"Who would do that?" she bleated. "Why?" Nori's heart physically hurt, and she rubbed her chest.

Cooper didn't speak again as he mounted the bike. He looked straight into the night. "I don't know," he finally said. "But there's nothing we can do for them now."

"Shouldn't we bury them or something?" Nori asked. She couldn't bring herself to get on the bike, to leave the tortured, soulless bodies.

"If we bury them, no one will see. No one will know." Cooper gripped the handlebars so tight his knuckles turned white.

"You think these people knew about the Subterranean?" Nori asked. "You think they were locked out? That this was intentional?"

"I can't see how it's not," Cooper said. "They'll pay for this. I'll make sure of it."

"Who? Who'll pay? The CCC? Guys like Sarge and Wallace?"

"All of them. Every single one of them."

Nori had never heard Cooper's voice so violent before. She was beginning to suspect a well of barely-leashed rage bubbled just below the surface of his playful facade. Nauseous, furious, they left the victims behind. But Nori's horror stayed with her for a very long time.

"Have you ever seen anything like that before?" she asked after a while, her head stuffy and voice nasal.

"No." Cooper cleared his throat. "No, I haven't."

Nori nodded and changed the subject. "Any idea how much night we have left?"

"We'll be okay," he said, though his voice was more hopeful than confident. "The road is at least passable. Keep an eye out for that symbol on any old road signs or utility boxes.

The scarlet eye. Hell, watch for any graffiti. It's our best shot at getting back Subterranean."

It was blissfully dark out, at least for the time being. The wind in Nori's face as they raced down the old highway tried its best to scrub away the horrific scene she'd witnessed. But each time she closed her eyes, she saw them, the charred husks of people seeking shelter underground and finding none.

Who had put that lock on the door? What kind of monsters could sentence people to die like that?

Though the temperature was mild, sweat rolled down Nori's neck and soaked into her t-shirt. She hadn't seen a single graffiti mark since going to the Surface, which she guessed was over an hour before. If the sun caught her unprotected, she wouldn't survive—simple as that. Any part of her body that came in direct contact, and sometimes even indirect contact, with the sun would burn like she'd waded into fire. Infection followed, and in the conditions she faced...well, an infection like that was a death sentence.

"I'm getting worried, Cooper."

He nodded once, but didn't speak. She kept her eyes peeled for markings, for signs, for graffiti of any sort—the key to getting back underground where she would be safe. With her night vision, it was she who had the best shot of seeing them.

"How long you think until the sun rises?" she asked.

He shrugged tight shoulders.

"I'm just... I'm worried. We've been riding at least an hour, and I don't know when darkness fell before we got aboveground. The sun could rise any minute, and I'll fry, Cooper. I'll fry like those people, but it won't take a sunscorch."

"I know that." His voice was rough. "Don't you think I know that? I took a risk going aboveground, all right. I risked running into people, though we haven't seen any, and I risked the sun—"

"Cooper?" Nori tapped his shoulder, but his words didn't slow.

"I risked you, and I'm so sorry. I hoped the detour would work out, that we'd find a way back down before now."

"Cooper?" she repeated.

"God, this was so stupid."

"Cooper!" She squeezed his waist and shook him, and he finally turned to her.

"What?"

"I found the scarlet eye." Nori pointed to an omniscient red eye painted on a rusted water tower.

He closed his eyes and exhaled a quiet, "Thank God," as he turned toward the bike.

When they neared the water tower, Cooper thrust his legs out, and ground the bike to a stop.

"How will we know where to find the entrance?" Nori scanned the landscape around them for secret hatches.

"It's supposed to be within fifty yards of a sign," he said.

"But that's pretty big. Maybe we should split up. You take the bike and start at the outside of a fifty-yard circumference. I'll start from the tower and work my way out. We meet in the middle and whoever finds the entrance first will whistle."

Cooper grinned at her. "You're enjoying this, aren't you?"

"A little," she admitted.

"It's a great plan," Cooper said and went in for a fist bump.

"It's mine, isn't it?" She met his fist and dropped an imaginary mic.

———

"Okay," Nori said to herself as she stalked through debris just off the highway. "The entrance has to lead down. That much is obvious. The first was by the dam outside Ralston then the one we came out of…" She stopped to look up at the night sky that she could swear was lightening with every passing second. "…nearly two hours ago, was beneath an old bypass, and this one has to go beneath that mountain."

Cooper's motorcycle whined on the other side of the peak. He'd had the same idea. Or, she acknowledged with a groan, he'd suspected it was near the mountain the entire time, but let her think it was her idea. Didn't matter. She would find the entrance first.

Running over the rough terrain, she found a cliff cut into the side of the mountain. A barely visible path started at the side of the cliff and led to an outcropping above her head. She struggled, pulling herself up and onto the rocky ledge. Her hands were scraped and bloodied by the time she made it up, but it was worth it. There was a small landing just outside the mouth of a cave. Has to be it, she thought, and whistled for Cooper, but not before doing a little victory dance that sent rocks and dust skidding down the cliff.

The sound of the motorcycle engine grew louder as Cooper approached. He didn't see her at first, so she stepped onto the ledge and waved down at him.

"How did you get up there?" he asked.

"There's an old trail," she yelled back and pointed. "See? Better walk the bike. It's pretty steep."

Cooper's cocky smile was visible even from a distance.

"Cooper?"

He revved the engine.

"You are not going to ride that thing up here." Nori's hands fisted at her hips, but flew in the air when he sped recklessly toward her.

"You could've killed yourself," she said as he skidded to a stop beside her. "And what would I do then?"

His eyes danced above a wide grin. "Oh, I imagine you'd manage just fine." He patted the seat behind him. "Hop on. Not much dark left."

"Well," she said and mounted, "while I could live without you, I wouldn't get far without the bike, which would probably be damaged in the process."

Cooper barked a laugh. "You're right. I'm sorry. In the future, when I try to kill myself, I'll make sure to leave the bike behind."

"Thank yo—" Her words cut off as Cooper goosed the throttle. She grabbed for his waist as her head flew back, and out of the corner of her eye, she caught the flash of a headlamp. Nori's grin died on her face. "There's another motorcycle. Close. Too close."

Without another word, Cooper killed the ignition. He turned his head and listened for a while before propping the bike just inside the cave entrance. Backing into the wall, he made his body as invisible as possible and pulled Nori with him. There were no doors this time, no padlocks. Just a rock-hewn corridor leading down. They didn't dare speak. Didn't move.

When the motorcycle engine stopped, Nori's gaze shot to Cooper's. They sagged with relief, and he nodded to her to get back on. That was when they heard the voices. Two male voices. Their words were unintelligible, but the tone was sharp, argumentative. The voices stopped, and an engine roared to life, but so much closer.

"Get on!" Cooper yelled.

Nori scrambled toward the bike, her butt hitting the seat a fraction of a second before Cooper thrust them into the tunnel. She held on to Cooper for dear life when the bike slid to a stop.

"Which way?" she asked as he eyed a fork in the road.

"I'm not sure."

"What?"

"I haven't been here before," he said.

"What do you mean you haven't been here? I thought you'd made this trip before."

"I have. But with a big group of badasses, and we didn't have to avoid towns and take these crappy little offroads."

Nori groaned and closed her eyes. They were finished. Maybe the Sword of Yahweh had finally caught up with them. Maybe the CCC had found out about Sarge and his men and sent more cronies after her and Cooper. Maybe it was some new foe altogether, this one worse than the last.

"Left," Cooper said and kicked the bike into gear.

"Why did you choose left?" Nori asked once they were on their way again.

"Just a guess," he said.

"Well, is it right?"

"What, left?"

"Yes," she replied.

"Let's hope."

Every few seconds, Nori turned to see if they were being followed. When a swath of light cut through the darkness, her heart seized in her chest. They were in trouble.

"Somebody's coming, Cooper. I see headlights."

He growled and surged forward.

"They're gaining on us!" she said. "How are they gaining on us?"

"Faster bike?"

The headlamp was blinding as the pursuers closed in. Nori turned her head and squeezed her eyes shut. "They're yelling at us."

"What?"

"They're yelling something at us, but I can't tell what."

"Well, I'm not gonna stop and find out." Cooper leaned forward, as if he could move the motorcycle faster by sheer force of will.

"I can only make out *stop*," she said. "Two riders. Back one is waving his hands."

"Yeah, no chance of that," he scoffed and leaned toward the handlebars.

"Hey, Cooper?" Nori said after a minute.

"Yeah?"

"I really think Kade's driving that bike."

Cooper wheeled around to look for himself. "What? What makes you think that?"

"Built like him."

"World's full of oversized bad guys. That's how they stay alive so long—bigger than everybody else."

"No, I really think so," she said. "They keep flashing the headlight, and the last time it flashed off, I could swear I saw two men. And the front one looks like Kade."

"How sure are you?" he asked.

"I don't know."

"Give me a percentage."

"Eighty?"

"Is that a question?"

"Okay, I'm eighty percent sure that's Kade and Grant behind us," Nori said. "And no one has shot at us yet, so..."

Cooper stretched his neck to either side, cursing under his breath. Nori held her breath when he finally down-shifted and steered the bike to a stop on one side of the tunnel.

Brakes whined as the other bike came to a sliding halt. The tunnel erupted in dust, and Nori pulled her shirt over her nose.

"What the actual hell, guys? Why wouldn't you stop?"

"It *is* you!" Nori yelped, hopping off the bike and running to Kade.

"'Course it's me." He shook his head. "Who else would chase you that long?"

"We didn't know. I mean, we weren't expecting you, of all people. What are you doing here? How did you find us? What happened to Bannera?"

"Well," Kade said. "Turns out Princess Buttercup," he nodded in Grant's direction, "was more attached to the idea of a grand gesture than actually staying in Bannera. He came clean after just two days. By that time, I'd healed a bit, and, well, here we are."

"Two days?" Nori repeated. "How did you catch up to us?"

"We came on the Surface," Kade gushed. "On actual roads, beneath the sun in the open sky!"

Nori laughed with him. "You're not serious."

"I am. Now that I know how to ask the right questions, someone who owed Grant a favor knew how to get to the Surface. We exited somewhere outside Bannera and just followed the roads South all this way."

"You're lucky you weren't killed," Cooper said hotly.

"We almost were outside Laredo," Grant said with a shiver.

"You went through Laredo?" Cooper threw up his hands. "What were you thinking?"

Kade stalked toward Cooper, who had to look up to meet his gaze. "I was thinking of finding the fastest way to Esperanza. The fastest way back to help you and Nori."

Cooper breathed hard for several tense moments. "Yeah, well," he said. "It's dangerous out there. A wolf-eat-wolf world. People are looking to take all they can from you."

"That's one benefit of being me," Kade said seriously. "The only people who ever mess with me are trying to prove something, not take something. And usually too drunk to fight."

"Did you love it?" Nori cut in. "Did you love the feel of the sun on your face as you travelled the open road?"

"At first I hated it," Kade said. "It felt like someone was always watching me, like I was too exposed. But once I got used to it," his eyes glazed over, "I knew it's how people were meant to live."

"I wish we could've seen it before," Grant said. "When there were trees and birds and animals. It would've been something to see."

"I always wanted to ride a horse," Kade admitted.

"You and this cowboy hangup." Cooper said and shook his head.

"You never know," Kade said defensively. "Maybe someone built a Subterranean Ark or something."

After the things Nori had seen these last few months, the idea wasn't nearly as preposterous as it once would've been. Maybe there was a stable of animals out there somewhere, just waiting for the Earth to heal. The idea gave her hope, at least. "Well, where to now, boys?"

"To the 25th Parallel. To Esperanza. To Norman and Ana," Cooper said and pretended to cheer with his water canteen.

The thrill of having her friend happy and by her side again, combined with a sliver of hope for the future, and topped with the knowledge they weren't far from her parents filled Nori with a rush of joy she couldn't contain. She jumped and threw her arms first around Kade, then Grant, and finally Cooper, who went rigid with shock. Finally, finally, he relaxed enough to squeeze back. He clutched her to him until she let go then cleared his throat, but his grin remained.

"Even with four of us now," Cooper said, "we'll have to go around Monterrey instead of through it to get to Esperanza."

"That'll take longer, I assume," Nori prodded.

"It will. And we'll have to navigate beneath a mountain range. But we can't risk Monterrey..." He cocked an eyebrow in Nori's direction. "Not to mention your solar restrictions."

She bristled, but let it go. It's hard to argue with the truth. "What's so bad about Monterrey?"

"Monterrey's the gateway to the 25th Parallel," Cooper said. "Both Subterranean and Surface. If you want to get there, it's the quickest, easiest way." He kicked at a pile of rocks. "And when people want something, there's always some jerk there to make it harder to get. Gangs, pirates, coordinated syndicates, the CCC... You can't spit without coming across raiders of some sort."

"Yeah, but, nobody's gonna mess with us," Nori said. "Not with you and Kade around." She shot an apologetic look at Grant. "No offense."

"None taken," Grant replied. "It's true I'm not known for my thuggery."

Kade thrust his chest out. "Oh, and I am?"

"Is there any answer that'll keep me out of trouble?" Grant asked.

Kade's grin was easy. "No."

Their happiness nearly lit the dungeoned depths of the tunnel. The realization hit Nori so hard breath abandoned her in a rush. She wanted that. To adore and be adored. She wanted a partner with whom to share tiny moments of joy, with whom she could dare to hope in a cold, dark, apocalyptic world. The thought had never occurred to her in the cocoon of her parent's house. She didn't have many friends. Any friends. Her parents were all she'd ever had, and ever needed. Romantic love wasn't even on her radar. Was she only thinking of it now because she missed the warmth and adoration of her parents? Probably. She tried to dismiss the idea, but it didn't go away easily. Would she ever have it? Was it even possible for her?

"I'm sorry for the extra miles," Cooper's cool voice cut into her thoughts. "Believe me, I'm tired of the bike, too. But it's safest to go around."

Nori nodded and tried to shake off her disturbing musings. "You think my parents will be okay?"

"I'm sure. They're going with a group. They'll take the right precautions."

As she rode deeper into the earth toward Esperanza, Nori's thoughts remained with her parents traveling on the dangerous landscape above her. She hoped Cooper was right.

42

UNA SORPRESA DE MONTAÑA

Nori stood on the bike's foot pegs to speak close to Cooper's ear. "Something's different."

He turned, his face close to hers, and the corner of his mouth pulled up in a smile visible even in profile. "It is. Can you feel it?"

"It's...pressure," she said. "What is it?"

"We're going under a mountain. Creepy, right, to think of all that rock on top of us?"

"More like terrifying." Nori's shiver was due to more than the increasing cold. "How far, you think?"

"Under the mountain range? Probably thirty miles or so." Her grip tightened on Cooper's waist, and he put his hand over hers and squeezed. "The good news is the road to Esperanza is on the other side."

She nodded and forced a smile. Her parents were just on the other side of the mountains. She could withstand anything for a few miles if it meant finding them again.

The four developed a system of communication. Since they

rode second, if Kade and Grant wanted to stop, they flashed the headlamp three times. If it was Nori and Cooper who needed a break, they simply stopped, and the other two pulled alongside.

It was when Kade and Grant's headlamp flashed off that Nori saw so far ahead. She stood on the foot pegs to see over Cooper and slapped his shoulders. He laid on the brakes, bringing the bike to a sliding stop as Kade and Grant skidded in beside them.

"Thank God you finally stopped." Grant hopped onto one foot as he extricated himself from the bike before Kade had even moved. "My navel's trying to eat my backbone."

"How someone so wiry can eat so much, I will never understand," Kade said, smiling and shaking his head.

"I know you're not talking about me. You eat enough to feed a militia."

Kade shrugged. "I'm a big guy."

Grant's snort echoed through the chamber.

Nori barely registered their words. She and Cooper had left their bike, creeping farther into the tunnel.

"What is that?" she heard Grant say.

Cooper's headlamp reflected on a smooth blackness draping over the road.

"Is that water?" Kade said behind them, jogging to catch up, but Nori and Cooper had already bent to take off their shoes.

"How deep?" Kade asked.

"Don't know," Cooper said and tossed his boots to the side. "One way to find out."

"Wait for me," Nori squealed, hopping on one bare foot.

"You guys go ahead with that," Grant said sourly. "I'll work on lunch. Or dinner. What time is it anyway?"

"Time to eat," Kade agreed, trudging back with Grant to unpack the only food they had left: dry protein pellets.

"I think it's a *cenote*," Cooper said, touching the fresh water to his lips. He waded into the pool, and Nori followed. It was shallow at first, but deepened enough to swim as they left the path and made their way toward a door-sized hole low on the rock wall.

"What's a seh-no-tay?" The water was freezing, but Nori relished the feel of something besides caked dirt on her skin. She was radiant, alive. Frigid, but alive. She scrubbed at her face and hair as she swam, taking the opportunity to de-grime.

"Sinkholes from collapsed bedrock. They're all over this area. It's groundwater. Fresh."

"You think our bikes can get through?" she asked.

"It's shallow along the path and deeper here. This hole letting water in is probably new, where the limestone's collapsed even more." He held his hand in the air. "Feel that? There's a breeze. Chimney effect." He nodded toward the jagged hole in the wall. "I bet there's an opening that goes aboveground somewhere through there."

"Let's go see it." Nori's excited jump sent waves in Cooper's direction. "It must be dark out or we'd see signs of sunlight."

Cooper frowned and eyed her, but didn't answer.

"Oh, come on, Cooper," she begged. "Please?"

"I don't think —" he began, but she cut him off.

"Fine. I'll go myself."

"Oh, no you won't." Cooper's voice was stern.

Nori's chest inflated. She did *not* take orders well.

"Let's go eat," he said softly "Aren't you starving?"

"Starving?" she scoffed. "For a little scenery, for a little fun? Yes!" Nori's heart pounded with excitement as she climbed through the hole and into the cavern before Cooper could argue.

"I didn't bring a flashlight," he said through clenched teeth, ducking through the hole after her.

"I'll see for both of us, don't worry."

Nori's view of the breathtaking cenote at night was a privilege worth the risk. A thousand tiny stars shimmered and twinkled down through the cloudless sky through a hole in the ceiling big enough to drive a car through. She pushed onto her back in the limestone void and hung weightlessly in the cool, calm water.

"My God. So gorgeous." Cooper's words whispered over her as he drew closer.

"Isn't it?" she said. "I feel like I could float right up to the stars and polish the ones not glowing as brightly as the others."

Cooper turned his head to the side, and a line formed between his brows. "What an odd thing to say."

Nori glanced away self-consciously, and he quickly added. "No, I mean, it's an interesting thing to say. Why worry about the dull ones?"

She lowered her feet to stand in the chest-deep water, and her shrug sent ripples between them. "I like to see everyone have the same chances," she said. "Some things just need a little extra help."

Cooper's lips pulled into a crooked smile, and he nodded. Even in the dark, Nori could see approval, and maybe even admiration, in his eyes. She was suddenly glad of the darkness, for it concealed her flaming cheeks and fidgeting hands.

She found a wide, shallow ledge and leaned back, hands behind her head to watch the natural light show through the earth-framed hole.

"As much as I'm enjoying this," Cooper said after a while, "we'd better get back."

"I knew it couldn't last," she said. When she sat up and looked away from the stars, for the first time she noticed a partially obscured marking in a corner of the *cenote*. "Cooper?" she said.

"Hmm?" He was more relaxed than she'd ever seen him. Maybe the side trip had done both their souls some good.

"Why would there be a CCC sign, logo—whatever —down here?"

"There wouldn't."

"There is."

Cooper went still as death and followed her line of sight. "I can't see anything. Are you sure?"

"Yes." She nodded. "The one that looks like a biohazard warning. It's the same one."

Cooper's hand flew to the top of his head and he rubbed it nervously.

"Why would it be down here?" Nori asked again.

He didn't answer, but his breathing changed. Exhalations came quickly, forced. Relaxed Cooper was gone.

"Cooper?" She watched his face as it hardened. "What are you thinking?"

Intense, gold-flecked eyes shot to hers. "I'm thinking we've got to get out of here. Now."

"What? Why?" she whined. "No one could find that. No way someone's looking for it. You said yourself the hole letting water into the tunnel was new. Unless someone came through it like we did and brought a waterproof flashlight, they'd never see it."

He was already halfway across the water, swimming for the hole that led back to the tunnel.

"Wait," she called. "Tell me what's going on."

"They wouldn't be coming from the tunnel like we did," Cooper said, snatching up his boots.

"I don't understand."

"We gotta move," he ordered, stomping toward Kade and Grant.

Kade was up in a flash. "Where's Nori?"

"Coming," she called, not yet out of the water.

"Grab your stuff," Cooper said. "We're leaving."

The biceps of Kade's thick arms bulged as he locked them across his chest. "Explain."

Cooper let out an exasperated growl and looked between Kade and Grant, who had yet to move. "Fine. Nori," he glanced her way as she trudged up the tunnel, "found a symbol on an obscure wall inside the *cenote* —"

"What kind of symbol?" Kade cut in.

"One we've seen before, one used by the CCC."

"But," Nori shook her head, joining the conversation, "why would the CCC post a symbol where no one could find it? That doesn't make any sense."

"I think…" Cooper let out a long breath. "I think this might be a back door to their headquarters."

Nori's wild glance shot to Cooper as Kade and Grant sputtered disbelief. "You can't be serious," and, "Wait a minute, now," preceded her frenzied, "What?"

"I think the hole above the cenote is either some kind of escape hatch or secret back way into the CCC's headquarters — or both — located somewhere within this mountain range."

"Nori, are you sure that's what you saw?" Kade asked.

"I… Yeah. I've seen the symbol before. It was there on the wall. Small and smudged, but it was there. I mean, I'm pretty sure. No, definitely. It was definitely there."

"Let's go," Kade said, pulling a flashlight from the bike's saddlebag.

Cooper's head snapped toward the fighter. "Where? Back in there?"

"Yeah. Let's take a closer look."

"Nooo." Cooper stepped between Kade and the water and held out a hand. "We need to get across the water, to the other side of the tunnel, and keep moving."

"Why are you in such a hurry?" Grant narrowed his eyes. "And what makes you so sure they have a headquarters under this mountain? Or a headquarters at all. How could you know that?"

Cooper's head fell back as he heaved out an impatient breath. "I know wherever there's a CCC symbol, there's trouble. This one is obviously meant for a very specific audience, and we're not it. Let's keep moving before we find trouble again."

Kade was watching Cooper suspiciously, too.

"Oh, come on!" Cooper's typically cool demeanor evaporated.

"I'm going to look for myself," Kade said with finality. Grant grabbed his own flashlight and followed him into the water.

"Ah, I'd better make sure I saw what I thought I saw," Nori told Cooper in a rush, abandoning her effort to don dry socks.

"Fine," he seethed. "We'll all go. But follow my lead. And for God's sake," he shot a look at Grant, "be quiet."

43

A HIDDEN AGENDA

"Told ya," Nori quipped, relief warring with dread as Kade's flashlight illuminated the stenciled red emblem.

Cooper cursed.

"What now?" Kade pointed his light from the symbol to Cooper's face.

"Now we go back to the tunnel and get the hell out of here," Cooper said, "like I wanted to do in the first place."

"What *is* your hurry?" Grant asked again. "Don't you think we should investigate? See if it really does lead to the super secret headquarters?"

"No," Cooper said. "I don't. There's no way I'm taking the three of you in search of a secret entrance to a den of psychotic militants."

"Oh, don't be such a drama queen," Grant scoffed.

"This is serious, people." Cooper's voice was clipped and angry. "The CCC is dangerous. I've seen it, lived it. Believe me when I say they would kill us without a second thought."

"Ah, guys?" Though she could still hear them arguing, Nori had wandered away from the group. A shiver snaked through her at the implications of her latest discovery. "Cooper?"

"What?" he snapped, his murderous gaze still set on Grant's face.

"I think I found the way in."

"No. Absolutely not." Cooper clasped Kade's forearm when he started toward Nori and held on even as the big man stared him down. "This is not a game, Kade."

"What if there's a store room, though?" Grant asked. "We need food again. And Kade's shoulder is still pink. We could use better meds."

"I said no!" Cooper's voice boomed through the cavernous *cenote*.

"Shhh," Grant admonished, and Nori worried, truly worried, that Cooper might drown him right there.

Closing his eyes and working to release flexed fingers, Cooper uttered a tense, "Out. Now."

The voices were so clear Nori could make out every word.

Her gaze shot to Cooper's, desperate to know if they were dead already. His mouth was open mid-word, but in the time it took to blink, he snapped it shut, and the group to order, with a finger to his lips and a motion toward the wall.

Maneuvering silently through the water was impossible, though they tried. The men's voices were bouncing down the corridor she'd spotted, though, and off the water. As the approaching strangers continued to talk, Nori closed her eyes in silent gratitude. They hadn't been heard.

"Lindgren said to prepare for combustion, I'll prepare for combustion. Know what I'm sayin'?"

"This place gives me the creeps. I hate coming down here."

"Yeah, well, the cenote *cover is stuck. Lotito and Ealy are going in*

from up top, but we gotta check if there's something obstructing it from below."

"My dream job. A glorified flashlight holder."

From the *cenote* ceiling a hundred feet above them, a beam of light cut into the darkness.

Backed into the eroded wall, Nori, Cooper, Kade, and Grant barely breathed, desperate to remain unseen. The light flashed over Kade's head. If fear had force, Nori's would've sent tsunami-level waves through their watery grave.

But the beam of light swept past Kade, catching a reflection on the stamped red symbol and landing on two men in gray jumpsuits. The men stood at a flat embankment between a corridor and the water of the *cenote*, gas masks covering their faces. Their flashlight beams lit the cavern ceiling, revealing the heads of two other men bent into the car-sized hole.

A voice came through radios attached to the first men's suits. "Henderson, you and Jules see anything?"

"Not from down here," the taller of the two said into his radio. "You?"

"No. Wait. Yeah, I see it. Rock's jammed and won't let the door slide. We'll have it out in a minute."

"You don't need us down here, then?"

"Nope. Got it."

The taller one, Henderson, turned to the one who must've been Jules. "Commander Mills says we got forty-eight hours till the next scorch. They'd better hope they get that door fixed and back inside. Now," he said, elbowing his partner, "who's got the dream job?"

And then they were gone. Henderson continued to talk as his voice faded and disappeared completely behind the heavy thunk of a closing door.

For a small eternity, neither Nori or any of the four spoke.

Blood roaring in her ears, she finally broke the silence. "They can't know when the next scorch will be. Right? How could they possibly know that?"

"Just a couple of idiots," Kade said.

Cooper hadn't said a word since they first heard the men approaching. Nori turned and opened her mouth to speak, but his eyes were glazed, his mind somewhere else.

"Cooper?" When he didn't answer, she said louder, "Cooper."

Jarred from wherever he'd been, he finally focused, and seemed surprised to find himself in the *cenote*. "Ah." He cleared his throat and looked away from her. "I have to go."

"Yeah, I think we should go, too."

"Sorry about before," Grant said, sheepish.

"No." Cooper finally met Nori's gaze. "I have to go. Back to Chicago."

"Chicago?" The three repeated at the same time.

"What do you mean, Cooper?" Panic sent Nori's heart into overdrive. She stepped closer and touched his arm.

He looked down into the water. "I can't take you to meet your parents, Nori. I'm sorry, but this is bigger than you, than any of us. I have to get word to Chicago about the scorch."

"You mean about what those guys said?" She stepped toward him. "You think they're serious. That they're right?"

"I do." He nodded, and his admission came slowly. "I know more about the CCC than I let on. This location...that intel about a scorch in the next 48 hours...about Commander Mills...it's exactly what we've been looking for. I have to tell my people."

"But, they can detect scorches now," Nori argued. "I saw it on a broadcast. You don't have to go. You can't leave us." She stepped closer to Cooper. "You can't...you can't leave *me.*" She pursed her bottom lip to keep it from trembling as tiny tentacles of betrayal took hold inside her.

Cooper shook his head slowly, avoiding her gaze. "It's more than that. We've been looking for the CCC headquarters, for this Mills, for years. And it's not just a lead. I've found an entrance. I have to report it as soon as I can and get people down here."

"Who's we?" Nori asked, her stony gaze demanding an honest answer.

"It's a long story."

"Tell us, Cooper." Her voice was sharp. The betrayal, his willingness to break his word and leave her, stung. "You owe us that much. I'm the one who found that symbol, who found the entrance."

He inclined his head, closing his eyes before returning her hard stare, daring her not to take him seriously. "I'm part of a group committed to stopping the scorches, to stopping the CCC from destroying what's left of our world."

Her mind sifted through a thousand thoughts, piecing together what she knew with with he'd revealed. "You're telling me that all the sunscorches..." Nori swallowed, and her eyes welled with tears. "The one that took my siblings...so many families... You're saying somebody did that on purpose? That the scorches are man-made?"

Cooper nodded, his lips a tight, thin line.

"How is that even possible? And why, for God's sake? Why ruin the Earth over and over? What could someone possibly gain from such death and destruction?"

Cooper shook his head. "Like many great tragedies," he said, his jaws flexing, "it started as ideological. One group of people wanted to stop another from threatening their way of life. Only this group, the CCC, was made up of some well-funded xenophobic radicals. They hired the best scientists, the most strategic military minds. Over time, they devised a way to rid the world of who they saw as the biggest offenders. They took their employees and their families underground, and let the rest of the world burn."

"Nobody would do that, crazy xenophobes not." Nori would not believe it.

"They'd come close in the past," Cooper said. "Maybe you've read about a little something called the Holocaust? Xenocide isn't new. Whole populations have been targeted before, though this was the first time someone took the world with it."

"Yeah, but they could never get away with that," Nori argued. "Taking all those people underground would call too much attention. They'd be found out."

"The people who knew were kept on a tight leash and strict surveillance," Cooper said. "If they were caught breaking silence, their invitation was rescinded." He shrugged. "A lot of people disappeared, let's just say that."

"How can you possibly know all this?" Grant asked what Nori had been thinking.

Cooper cleared his throat. "The place I grew up... Ah... There are some people there who'd been on the other side."

"You mean people who'd worked for the CCC when they planned this extermination?"

"Well," he said, "they were a part of a partnership early on. One that quickly dissolved, but not before helping the CCC with what they needed to destroy the world."

"What do you mean?" she asked. "Who were the other people?"

Cooper kicked at a pile of rocks. It was obvious he didn't like talking about this part of it, but Nori didn't know why.

"They called themselves the Architects of Global Climate Governance, or AGCG." Cooper looked up then quickly back down. "Years ago, after the last round of global climate talks failed, this secret group of environmental hardliners'd had enough. Many were scientists; there were government officials from all over the world. They wanted to wake up the world to the effects of climate change, to do something so drastic people would finally understand the apocalyptic future of continuing down the same path."

"That's ridiculous," Kade scoffed. "Ruining the world to save it?"

"They were desperate," Cooper said. "Misguided, to be sure. For a while, AGCG found a common cause with the CCC. Some of the worst environmental offenders were also the most overpopulated. China, India, and South America were both destroying the Earth and gobbling up its remaining resources. So, together, the AGCG and CCC worked on a plan to scare the world into behaving."

Nori hung on every word of Cooper's fantastical tale, but doubted the truth in it. It was too far-fetched. Then again, he had so many details. And the fact was, the world lay in waste above her. The reason for the sunscorches had never been determined. There were theories, sure, like the Sun was in the beginning stages of death, and the scorches a catalyst for the next Ice Age.

"What was this plan?" Nori asked, confusion warring with fury and sadness inside her. "How did they supposedly create the scorches?"

"They planned to decimate the ice sheets, both in Greenland and Antarctica, and then ignite the massive amounts of methane that escaped."

Nori gasped, and Cooper touched her arm. "Wait, though.

The AGCG backed out. They wanted no part in it. They tried to put a stop to it."

Nori covered her mouth with her hand. "Oh my God. Why didn't they?"

"The CCC was too powerful. And vicious. They'd already gone too far. When the AGCG started backpedaling, the CCC knew they'd ruin their plan. They took nearly every member of the AGCG out."

"My God," Kade breathed.

"Someone made it out, though." Nori looked from Kade and Grant to Cooper. "You said you know someone who was with the group."

"I do." Cooper kicked at the rocks again. "And so, even though I've always lived Subterranean, I know the history behind the scorches. I know about the CCC—its past and present. And we're working to stop them. There's no one else. You see why I have to get word to Chicago. This is the lead we've been waiting years for."

"You can't make it from here to Chicago in two days," Kade said.

"No, but if I go to Surface, I can make it to a comms post in one day. We can get word out about the scorch and save thousands. Maybe more."

"What will you do about the headquarters?" Nori's voice was hollow. "About the CCC?"

"They're the enemy, Nori. Not just mine, but mankind's."

She inspected Cooper's face, which seemed older somehow. While he was making concessions, there was another thing Nori wanted to know. "And the man chasing you the night we met in the alley, was he with the CCC?"

Cooper let out a long breath. "Might as well be. He's a mercenary they hire to take care of their more... slippery problems." Cooper smiled, but his face held no humor. "He'd been tailing me on the way back from Chicago. I went to Surface in Ralston to try to lose him, but he cornered me. I jumped a metal fence to escape, and that's when I hurt my leg." His gaze darted to Nori's and she swallowed hard. "I've never heard his real name, but everyone knows him as Stealth."

Nori shivered. "It fits."

"Stealth?" Kade croaked. All the blood had drained from his face.

"You know him?" Cooper asked.

Kade cleared his throat and looked away. "Heard of him, yeah."

"He is one bad mother," Cooper said. "He's still out there somewhere."

Nori's heart lurched to her throat and she grabbed Cooper's arm. "You think he's still looking for you?"

"Oh, I'm sure of it."

44

BARBARIC EXTREMISM

Council of Concerned Citizens World Headquarters
Sierra Papagayos Mountain Range
Free and Sovereign State of Nuevo Leon, Mexico
Latitude: 25° North

"Lindgren, give me an update," Mills said. The aging commander's broad shoulders no longer stood at attention, but his razor-sharp gaze and the hard lines of his mouth still demanded respect.

"Zhe sediment-water interface at Alaska's North Slope has been set for extrication," Lindgren answered. "Our testing indicates very high levels of CH4 just below zhe sediment's surface—"

"So I can understand it, you smug Swiss tripe."

Lindgren narrowed his eyes at the insult, but swallowed any retort. He simplified his report without comment.

"Due both to previous sunscorches and zhe change in tilt of Earth's axis, zhe increase in Alaska's temperature has melted the ice molecules making up methane hydrate, leaving very large deposits of gas locked just below zhe surface. Our blast will liberate zhe $CH4-$" Lindgren closed his eyes and stretched his neck. "Our blast vill liberate zhe *methane*, and allow it to escape into zhe atmosphere. Ve add a few key ingredients and zhen remotely ignite it."

"We're still on for the eighth, then? Your team will be ready?" CCC Commander Orval Mills's posture was loose, confident, but his eyes, ice blue and bordering on maniacal, told another story. One of austere and unflinching determination.

"Ve vill." The scientist's gray jumpsuit was filthy, wrinkled from too many nights spent sleeping on the hard sofa in his office. A smudge of something partially covered the embroidered logo that read Dr. Hugo Lindgren, Council of Concerned Citizens.

"You think this scorch will rival the first one?" Mills asked. "How will it compare to the last?"

"Nozhing could rival zhe original sunscorch. Ve haven't yet found a deposit comparable to zhe $CH4$ zhat escaped vhen ve destroyed zhe ice sheets. Ve likely never vill."

The commander's pinched mouth tightened a fraction more. "Find it. That's what you're here for."

Lindgren closed his eyes and let out a breath, along with the question he'd been holding in for months. "Excuse me asking, sir, but vhat for? Our initial scorch eradicated billions. Zhat doesn't include millions lost to coastal flooding, cold, droughts, starvation. And zhen zhe last two scorches have picked away at populations across zhe globe. Surely zhe threat has been mitigated."

"'Vhat for'?" the commander repeated in a mocking sneer.

Black military-issue boots snapped together as he stood to his full height, looming toward Lindgren. "When the CCC aligned with those tree-hugging idiots at the AGCG, our mission was to put an end to overpopulation, to rid the world of those sucking it dry."

He stalked toward the scientist, who subconsciously conceded the space, backing up until he hit the cinder block wall behind him.

"Look around, son. You see an abundance of food? Of resources?"

Lindgren cocked his head and opened his mouth to speak, but Mills wasn't finished.

"No," he snapped. "A barren wasteland is all we have to show for our efforts, for our sacrifice. You think I'm gonna quit now, when we're so close? The CCC will endure. We're ordained to fight this fight. Some day soon we'll look up and be the last ones standing, the custodians of the world. That's what we're fighting for."

Lindgren's gut clenched at the baldness of Commander Mills's objective, though he wasn't surprised. He'd joined the CCC knowing full-well what he was getting into. The cause was one he supported. Watching countries like his, where people worked hard to support their families but the government sent millions of dollars in aid to countries whose people lived in squalor had infuriated him. Don't spread my wealth, spread my work ethic—that was his motto. If the people in warring and starving countries really wanted to, if they would stop feeling sorry for their circumstances and apply themselves, they could pull their families out of poverty. Pull themselves up by the bootstraps, his father always said. Lindgren didn't speak again, though his breaths came quicker. They mirrored his thoughts as he stood before Mills, who'd made it clear there were no plans to end the toxic agenda.

But after years of systematically sabotaging the Earth, Lindgren was beginning to think it might be time to sit back and reap the fruits of their labor. To let the world recover. To begin anew. He wanted to see another alder tree before he died.

45

A TOUGH GOODBYE

Nori's emotions were a gnarled cluster of confusion. Cooper's intention to leave had struck suddenly, and she hadn't had time to fully process it. She resented him for going back on his word. She had trusted him, counted on him. But if she was honest, it was fear she felt, too, and not just for herself. She'd known he would get her to her parents safely, hadn't doubted that for a minute. But what if he ran into that mercenary again? Should she rage and insist he take her all the way to the 25th Parallel like he'd promised? Shame washed over her at the thought. No, of course not. If he had a chance to save even one person, he should do it.

But that didn't mean she had to like it. The thought of saying goodbye to Cooper made her chest tight and achy. There was a hole there, too, like she'd suffered a loss. No, she was not ready for him to leave. She was angry, and sad, and lonely already.

"Will I ever see you again?" Nori couldn't meet his gaze.

Cooper stepped in close and ran his thumb over the single tear scurrying down her cheek. When she finally looked up, his green-gold eyes pinned hers. "Never say never," he said so low that only she could hear. He slid his fingers into her thick hair, which was still wet from their swim. He leaned into her with exquisite tenderness, the flecks of gold in his eyes flaming as he searched her startled gaze.

Nori's heart pounded against her ribcage before it stopped completely. She'd never been kissed. Not ever. And God, but she wanted to be kissed by Cooper. Nori met his body with hers, some instinct filling in the holes of her inexperience. His face moved ever closer, and both her eyes and her will were open to his intentions. When she licked her bottom lip, his eyes followed the movement. A tiny smile pulled at his mouth just before he touched his lips to hers. One, two, three velvety-soft kisses before he pulled away.

Nori stood stunned, her heart stalled and brain short-circuited. And when she finally recovered her senses, it was to wave goodbye as Sam Cooper kick-started his motorcycle and sped out of her life.

"WELL, THIS SUCKS," Grant said after several hours on the road.

Nori had to agree. Without Cooper's bike, one of the three of them was left to walk. She could hardly travel ahead with Kade and leave Grant behind, and they would never leave her; she'd tried that. They took the vow to see her home safely very seriously.

"Look," Nori explained, not for the first time. "Cooper said Esperanza was just on the other side of the mountain range. The *cenote* meant we're not far, and we've gone miles

315

beyond even that." She stopped and rubbed her lower back. "You two take the bike and go. I can make it from here."

Just as before, her offer was met with disgusted looks.

"We're not leaving you, Nori," Kade said brusquely. "And that's final."

"Besides," Grant's tone was playful, but she couldn't help feeling there was an underlying sadness to it, "we've got nowhere else to go."

"Where will you go?" she asked. "After you get me to my parents, I mean. Will you stay in Esperanza?" The two men shared a sour look. A topic of contention, then.

"You think Cooper's right?" she asked to change the subject.

"He'd better be." Grant's limp suddenly became more pronounced. "Considering all the trouble he's caused us. I'm sick of walking, and my pinkie toe is blistered to the bone."

"I told you to take the bike," Kade said hotly.

"You know I can't drive that thing."

Kade clenched his teeth and looked at Nori. "What Cooper said is hard to believe, but everything he's done, everything he knows... It checks out."

"But that would mean billions of people were murdered." She simply couldn't believe it was true. "That the Earth was sabotaged, and its plants and animals...our whole world was destroyed on purpose."

"It would," Kade agreed.

No one spoke after that. There was nothing left to say.

46

REUNITED. IT SHOULD FEEL
SO GOOD

"What are we supposed to be looking for?" Grant asked again.

Nori and Grant walked ahead of Kade, who'd been stuck for most of the trek pushing the motorcycle despite his injury. He'd given up riding ahead and waiting for them to catch up, too bored and worried, he said, to make it worthwhile. Their system of trading off walking the bike had worked for a while, but Kade gave much more than his fair share, eventually taking sole responsibility.

"Graffiti, carvings, signs of any kind," Nori answered, stopping to wait for Kade. "Cooper said we'll know it when we see it, but at this point I'm wondering if he didn't make up the whole incinerated-Earth thing just to escape us."

Grant laughed, but Kade met her gaze, his face serious. "You know he didn't," he said. "I don't know what you two had, but it wasn't nothing."

Nori flushed, her virgin heart taking flight as she remembered their emotional goodbye. Just as quickly, though, it plummeted to the ground. She and Cooper might've had something, but it was gone now. He was gone. To save the world, it would seem. How selfish to want him back. How very short-sighted. And yet, she did.

"Could this be it?" Kade asked them.

The question dragged her attention back to the now. The motorcycle's headlamp had been left on so Kade and Grant could better search for the exit, but she could still make out what they saw ahead. There wasn't a sign, no watchful graffiti. The road simply made a Y, the left side going on and the right ending at a metal door.

"It must be," she whispered. Light snuck through the sides of the old metal door. She stopped farther away than was probably necessary, but the damage even those slim rays could do to her eyes or skin wasn't worth the risk.

"Is it really that bad?" Grant asked.

She nodded and blew out a breath.

"We'll wait until dark." Kade tested the rusty door knob, but didn't open it. "Then we'll go up and see about finding your parents."

Nori was quiet as Grant picked through the last of their food stores. "Kade?" she asked after a while.

"Hmm?" The big man had pushed his jeans up to his knees to massage thick calves.

"I've been thinking." She swallowed hard. "I...I think you and Grant have to go now, while it's still daylight."

He turned toward her, eyes wide. "What? No. Why would you say that?"

Nori paced the narrow space of the tunnel and ticked off on her fingers as she made her points. "We don't know how far it is to Esperanza. We don't know how much time we have under the cover of dark. We don't know where my parents are once we get there. And, God, we don't even know if they've made it there yet."

"I'm sure they're all right, Nori." Grant moved to stand beside her, but she took up pacing again.

"I mean, none of us has ever been here before. Without Cooper, there's no way to know the distance or the landscape. What if there's trouble? As much as I hate to say it, I think it's best if you two find them then come back for me."

"There's no way I'm leaving you here alone," Kade said.

"You have to. It could take days to find them. I can't be stuck on the Surface not knowing how to get back to safety. Getting caught in the sun would kill me. Kill me. And if what Cooper says is true, and there's a scorch coming, we don't have any time to waste."

"You know the kinds of people who use these tunnels, Nori. And if we're this close to the CCC headquarters, there's sure to be more of them. What if they find you?"

"They won't."

"You can't know that," he said.

"I'll take precautions. I'll hide, keep a weapon."

Kade growled and shook his head. "Dammit, Nori. No."

She jerked at his impassioned demand. She'd never seen Kade angry. Never. Silence stretched between them like melted plastic. Eventually, it went on too long and broke.

"I can't go aboveground, Kade," she finally said. "It's a bad idea."

"I know." He kicked a rock that tumbled down the tunnel. "Grant will have to stay, too."

"Whaaaa?" Grant's face was wounded.

"You two will stay here together," Kade said then turned to Nori. "I'll take the motorcycle and go in search of your parents. Alone."

"But that's too dangerous," Grant protested. "You have no idea what you're getting into up there."

"I can protect myself. You know that. I'll be fine. It's faster this way, anyway."

Grant made several more protests, but his attempts to dissuade Kade were futile. He was right. This was their best shot.

"Up you go, then." Nori said and hugged her friend one last time "I'm going back around that last corner to make sure I'm away from the light when you open the door." She wandered off, trying to give Kade and Grant what privacy she could.

Nori's chest grew tight when Kade started up the bike. Had her parents made it to Esperanza? Were they all right? Did they remember the plan about a blue padlock? Oh, God. She and Kade hadn't discussed it again. Did he remember? As the roar of the motorcycle faded in the distance, she closed her eyes and sent a silent prayer that everything would go according to plan. Then she leaned against the rock wall and slid abruptly down, laying her head on her knees.

Grant tentatively touched her shoulder then gave her two quick pats. "It'll be fine," he said. "We'll all be fine."

Nori didn't have the nerve to look up at his face, to see if he actually believed his own words. So she added his hope — false or not — to hers, and even with it, her cup was less than half-full.

"My mom always said a watched pot never boils." Nori leaned her head against the wall. "I think it must also be true that awaited time never passes."

"Tell me about it," Grant grumbled. "How long's he been gone?"

"Twelve or fourteen hours, I think."

"God, it feels like two days." Grant rose and began pacing again. "And I'm starving. I swear I'd give my right arm for a Vitabar right now."

Nori smirked. "The one you hypothetically chewed off not to have to eat another protein pellet?"

"Yes, that one," he nodded, then leaned his head to the side. "You hear that?"

"Your stomach talks almost as much as you —"

"No, I'm serious." Grant cut her off, his eyes wide and panicked. He shined his flashlight up and down the tunnel.

"Turn that off," Nori's harsh whisper echoed as he fumbled for the button.

"You think it's Kade?" he asked.

"I hope so." She threw her backpack over a shoulder.

"Should we go back to the door to meet him?"

Nori shook her head before realizing Grant couldn't see it. "I don't think so. We're hidden here. Let's wait until we're sure it's him before we move."

She could barely hear anything over the rush of blood roaring through her ears, and made an effort to calm her ragged breathing before she hyperventilated. It was a sad state of things when Grant was calmer than she was.

But she'd been imagining seeing her parents for days. She had no idea how long it had been since they parted ways back in Ralston. Weeks? A month? Nori swallowed and clasped Grant's hand in hers.

He squeezed back, but stayed silent.

"Nori?" The sound of her father's voice echoed through the tunnel, through her mind. Had she wished so hard she'd imagined it. "Nori?"

"Daddy?" Her shaking voice came out small and childlike. She said, louder, "Daddy?"

"Nor? Nori, where are you?"

"Here!" She left the alcove and ran toward her father's voice. "I'm here!"

"Oh, God, Nori." His voice broke on her name as he clutched her around the shoulders and lifted her in a bear hug. "Are you all right?" He touched her face, her hair.

"I'm fine, Daddy." A laugh of pure joy bubbled to the surface from her soul. "You?" She stopped, her face suddenly serious. "And Mom? Is Mom okay?"

"Fine," he said. "Just too hard to get down here. She's waiting up top."

"I'm sorry it took so long," Kade said. Nori hadn't noticed him standing behind her father.

She shook her head. "Doesn't matter. " She jumped and hugged Kade's neck. "You found them," she said and squeezed even harder. "You did it."

Nori's self control evaporated at the sight of her mother. She sobbed as she bent to embrace her, leaning over the arm of the wheelchair. Her body was so thin, so frail, Nori worked not to squeeze her too hard.

When she finally pulled back, her mother reached for her face and held it in bony fingers before kissing her cheek, her hair, and looking over every inch of her face. "You're all right." Her mother's breath hitched as she repeated, "You're all right. I worried every second of every day."

"No need to worry now, Mom," she said. "We did it. We found each other, even at the other end of the world."

47

HOPE IN ESPERANZA

"Did you tell them about Cooper? About the CCC?" Nori asked Kade when she finally got him out of her parents' earshot. Her father and Grant rode in the front seats of their dented and dingy van. She and Kade took the back with her mother, who'd nodded off during the bumpy ride back to Esperanza.

"No. They were already so worried, I thought I'd spare them until we found you." He swallowed and searched her face. "Your mom looks so different since I last saw her."

"I know." Nori's eyes lit on her mother's sweet but strained face as she slept. Nori had propped a pillow between her shoulder and head. "You did the right thing. One worry at a time."

"They're not fans of Cooper's right now, I'll tell you that," Kade said.

"Do they think he just abandoned us for no reason?"

"I just said we parted ways. Didn't get into it."

Nori nodded. She didn't care if they hated Cooper. She'd tell them the truth, and they'd understand. Eventually.

With a jerk, Nori remembered the CCC worker's warning. Forty-eight hours. "Kade, how long has it been since we were in that *cenote*?"

"'Bout thirty-six hours," he said.

"Have there been any news reports about another sunscorch?"

He shook his head. "Nothing."

"You're sure?" Nori scooted forward in the seat. "I thought they could predict scorches now?"

He shrugged wide shoulders. "I don't know. Maybe those guys were wrong. Maybe this whole thing's been blown out of proportion."

"No, I don't think so," Nori said and then her body went rigid when the thought struck her. She couldn't move. Couldn't breathe.

"What is it, Nor?" Kade leaned around to look at her face and flinched at what he found.

"What if Cooper didn't make it?" she breathed, her voice shaky and weak. "What if he never got word to whoever's in Chicago?" She met Kade's worried glance and knew they were both thinking the same thing. "What if no one knows the scorch is coming?"

"Yes, but we've heard nothing from the new alert system," Nori's father said. "How can you be so sure a scorch is coming?" He searched her face as they sat around a table in the basement of their new home. It wasn't that he didn't believe her, she thought, just that the thing itself was unbelievable.

She shared a look with Kade and Grant. He was her

father. Of course she should tell him. And Nate and Deanna were trusted, lifelong friends who'd gone miles out of their way to help her and her parents. But she took her promise to Cooper seriously. They all did. At length, Kade gave a stiff nod, and she sagged with relief before telling them all what they'd overheard, and what Cooper had revealed.

Her father stood up from the table so quickly his chair flew back and hit the floor with a clank. "We've got to tell the people at the Climate Research Center."

"Yes," Deanna agreed. "The media, too. And fast."

"All right." Nori's father took charge of the battle plan. "The Research Center isn't far from here." He turned to Kade. "Will you come with me and Nate? And Nori, the landline here works. The phone lines are buried, so the scorch doesn't affect them. You, Grant, and Deanna call any news outlets you can find and try to get them to report it."

"What about...me? What can I...do?" her mother's breathless voice came from the top of the steps. They'd left her resting in her bedroom after the tough ride home. They'd made it, though just barely, scrambling into the house before sunrise with only minutes to spare.

Nori's father beamed and jogged upstairs. "Hey, hon. You overhear all that?" At her nod, he said, "Can you help get the word out?"

"You just give me a phone and I'll *make* them listen."

"Dad?" Nori cornered her father as he readied to leave. "It's important you don't tell the Climate Research people about the CCC. We promised Cooper. Don't mention anything about the organization or the headquarters. Nothing. If they find out someone's on to them, it could sabotage all the work Cooper's group has put into stopping them."

"I understand." He nodded. "I know it's important to keep

his secret. I see the long-term goal." Her father rubbed his forehead. "It's going to be hard to convince the Research Center without some proof, but I'll do my best. At the very least, maybe I can encourage them to run some tests, or whatever it is they do."

Though she tried not to, with each call to a news outlet that hadn't heard of an impending sunscorch, Nori worried Cooper hadn't made it to the communications post. And if he hadn't made it, then something—or someone—had stopped him. She closed her eyes against the images ravaging her mind. Had the CCC caught him? The Sword of Yahweh's Mexican cousins? Some other unknown threat?

She rubbed her eyes and dialed another number her mother had found in an old phone book.

"What did that one say?" Grant asked as Nori slammed the handset onto the heavy receiver.

"They thought I was crazy, too." Nori stood, holding her forehead as she paced the basement floor. "Maybe I am crazy. I can't think past worrying about what's happened to Cooper."

"That's not crazy, babe." Her mother strained to push the rusting silver wheels of her chair toward Nori. Her hands were more calloused than she remembered. "It's concern. Of course you worry about your friend."

Nori gave a stiff nod and turned from her mother, who breathed a soft, "Oh." When Nori turned back, her mother's eyes were wide with sympathy. "He was more than that, wasn't he?"

Nori sniffed and cleared her throat. "I just hope he's okay, Mom. He has to be okay."

"One breath at a time, one step at a time, one day at a

time," her mother said. "We have plenty to worry about right now."

When Nori didn't answer, her mother tugged on her hand. "Right?"

Nori nodded.

"Okay. Who do we call next?"

"I HOPE Y'ALL HAD BETTER luck than we did." Nate's movements were stiff and angry when the three men returned several hours later. "Those know-it-alls at the Climate Research Center can just fry in the scorch, for all I care."

"Nate!" Deanna admonished.

"No, I mean it." He flung himself onto the basement sofa and crossed his arms. "We have information that can save people. And zero time to screw around."

"They didn't believe you?" her mother asked her father, who shook his head.

Nori looked from him to Kade. "What did they say?"

"They said..." Kade shook his head angrily. "They said they'd know if we were under threat of a scorch. That they're confident in their system and their people."

"And they said we should take our kooky butts back home." Her father plopped beside Nate and put his feet on the coffee table, but quickly pulled them back down at his wife's censorious look.

"They did not!" her mother gasped.

"They might as well have," he said. "They looked at us like a bunch of conspiracy theorists. They listened to appease us but as soon as we finished, they ushered us out the door."

"I'm so sorry." Nori shook her head. "I know you guys did your best."

"Tell me about the news stations," her father said. "Are they going to report it?"

Nori's mouth twisted with disappointment. "No one believed us, either."

"God!" Her father kicked a metal chair, making everyone in the room jump. "We're trying to save lives here. Can't they understand that? I mean, even if we're wrong, what does it hurt to issue a warning? Best case scenario, people live. Worst case, they say some lunatics got it wrong."

"I bet they get stuff like this all the time." Kade shrugged. "The whole world lives in fear. Maybe we were just three more pecans in a bowl of nuts."

Nori groaned. "Well, what now? We have, what, eight hours?"

The air in the room was stiff with tension. "I've got it!" Nori's father jumped from the sofa. "Nate, we need your ham radio."

"Are you sure this will work?" Nori asked as all seven of them crowded around a set of square boxes covered with knobs, and dials, and buttons.

"It's the only option we have at this point." Norman exhaled sharply. "Tell us again how it works, Nate."

"Hams work on radio frequencies, which are still viable despite the sunscorches." He straightened and met six attentive gazes. "Now, most hams were destroyed after the first scorch." His eyebrows lifted proudly. "But that's because they weren't in Faraday cages. And even the newer equipment that had been protected was just trash. This old boat anchor," he spread his arm to reveal his setup with a proud flourish, "is from the '60s, and has a tube transmitter."

Nori and Grant shared an okay-that's-enough-tech-talk look, but Kade and her father were still absorbed in the lesson.

"Anyway," Nate wound down, "there are only a few ham operators left with working equipment. But, we're an organized bunch with systems in place to get a message out." His face was serious, his blue gaze penetrating as he turned to Nori. "Now, what's our message?"

"CQ, CQ, CQ. This is ND5LSS… "

Nori shook her head, fascinated as Nate issued an emergency alert to his fellow ham operators. They took him seriously, and set out right away to spread the message.

When he was finished, Nate turned from the radio system, rubbing his temples. "We did it," he said, nodding at Nori. "Let's hope it's enough."

48

INITIATE COMBUSTION

Council of Concerned Citizens World Headquarters
Sierra Papagayos Mountain Range
Free and Sovereign State of Nuevo Leon, Mexico
Latitude: 25° North

"Duke, are all systems in place for combustion protocol?" Lindgren stood behind his team of scientists, some seated at their computer stations and others pacing the patch of floor behind their colleagues.

Too-white LED lights flickered overhead, their steady hum the only sound as the CCC team prepared to forge another sunscorch.

"Combustion protocol is a go, Dr. Lindgren," the man replied. "Ready on your order."

Jason Duke had been with him from the start, a brilliant young geophysicist with loads of initiative and something to prove. While his and Duke's expertise lay in science, Commander Mills and Harley Pettit had military backgrounds. Pettit was an explosives specialist who'd worked underground pipelines and oil rigs in the private sector after he left the military.

"Pettit." Lindgren speared the man with his gaze and met confidence. "Can you confirm our allies have been informed of our plans to combust?"

"I can." Pettit cleared his throat, his deep voice cracking with phlegm as years of smoking caught up with him. "Most remain underground full-time now anyway, only venturing out for missions or communique."

The heavy thud of a metal door slamming shut set the room on edge. The air was already charged with tension, a month's work culminating in one press of a button. The presence of Commander Mills sent backs rigidly straight.

The Commander's attention turned to Lindgren, as it always did. "You're certain we've told our people, Lindgren? God forbid we nuke our own kind."

Lindgren didn't look Pettit's way for confirmation. His team was trained, focused, and committed. "Yes, sir. Would you like the honors, sir?"

The calculating glint in Mills's eyes made them all the more severe. "By all means," the Commander's gaze met Lindgren's. "The privilege is yours."

Lindgren's gut twisted. He knew why Mills was declining to make the final call, why he insisted Lindgren command his team to ignite the methane mixture that barely made muster. He was being tested, his commitment to their cause confirmed.

He never looked away from the Commander. "Initiate combustion," he ordered.

49

THE END

Nori and Kade helped Deanna with dinner. It didn't take her mind off the impending scorch—or Cooper—but it did keep her busy, and that was good.

Nate and Deanna's house had been constructed as a post-scorch fallout shelter, equipped with a kitchen and all the essentials of living in the cement-reinforced basement. It was as good as being underground, and they could all stay there until the scorch passed.

Grant had challenged Nori's mom to a card game, and Nate and her father spoke in hushed tones near the door. Honestly, Nori didn't even want to know what they were so worried about.

High-pitched alert notices cut through the hushed basement atmosphere like a serrated knife to canvas. All seven of them turned toward the old box-set television to see the announcement. There wasn't a press conference like before, only a red screen with bold white letters, and a computerized voice-over repeating a script.

Warning. Find shelter immediately. The Climate Research Center has issued an immediate sunscorch warning. Residents should take cover in designated shelters immediately.

Repeating.

Warning. Find shelter immediately. The Climate Research Center has issued an immediate sunscorch warning. Residents should take cover in designated shelters immediately.

A relieved sob escaped Nori before she could contain it. Her parents, Kade and Grant, and Deanna and Nate all turned to her, and collectively they shared both sighs of relief and the satisfaction of having been right. Nori beamed at them, her team of heroes.

The swell of satisfaction filled every porous chamber of Nori's heart, and it threatened to burst from her chest. They'd done it; they'd saved lives. For the first time, she'd had a purpose, a plan, and she had made a difference.

She vowed it wouldn't be the last time.

ACKNOWLEDGMENTS

To the best readers and friends in the world: Thank you for supporting me. Thanks for your encouragement, thank you for your kind notes and generous reviews. Thank you for recommending this series to your friends. Books need readers, and I'm so glad you're mine.

Being an author can sometimes be a solitary business, but with colleagues, friends, and family like mine, it's not lonely.

To Brock for rock-solid support, for pushing me out of the house to write, for always saying "I got this."

To Bebe and Gary, Marianne, Angela, Nathan and Deanna, and to Tammie Jo for unceasing support and encouragement. To my oldest friend, Beau, for answering my many military questions.

To the critique partners and beta readers who made this a better book: Kathleen, Brooke, Brinda, Erica, Skyler, Peyton, Kristin and Rebecca- thank you from the bottom of my heart.

To Cary Smith for exceptional cover art: thank you for sticking with me! I love the finished product.

ABOUT THE AUTHOR

 Though she grew up on a working cattle ranch, it's fantasy and sci-fi that shine Jen Crane's saddle. Her newest novel, Sunscorched, received the 2017 Rosemary Award for excellence in young adult fiction.

Jen has a master's degree and solid work histories in government and nonprofit administration. But just in the nick of time she pronounced life *too real* for nonfiction. She now creates endearing characters and alternate realms filled with adventure, magic, and love. She lives in the southern US with her family and too many pets.

Sign up for sneak peeks, news, and giveaways at
  bit.ly/JenCraneNewsletter

Follow Jen on social media @JenCraneBooks

CPSIA information can be obtained
at www.ICGtesting.com
Printed in the USA
FSHW022023131218
54469FS